THE HALLOWS QUEEN

THE DARK DUET BOOK TWO
ROSIE ALICE

Editing by Mackenzie—Nice Girl, Naughty Edits
Cover Design by Rosie Alice
Formatting by Rosie Alice
Proofreading by Rebel Literary Services

CONTENTS

Playlist   7
Author note & Content Warning   9

PART ONE
SAGE BLACKMORE

Chapter 1   15
Chapter 2   23
Chapter 3   31
Chapter 4   41
Chapter 5   47
Chapter 6   55
Chapter 7   63
Chapter 8   71
Chapter 9   79
Chapter 10   89
Chapter 11   99
Chapter 12   109
Chapter 13   119
Chapter 14   125
Chapter 15   135

PART TWO
REST IN PEACE

Chapter 16   145
Chapter 17   155
Chapter 18   167
Chapter 19   173
Chapter 20   181
Chapter 21   185
Chapter 22   191
Chapter 23   199
Chapter 24   205

Chapter 25 209
Chapter 26 217
Chapter 27 225
Chapter 28 235
Chapter 29 247
Chapter 30 257
Chapter 31 263
Chapter 32 271
Chapter 33 279

PART THREE
REVENGE

Chapter 34 285
Chapter 35 289
Chapter 36 299
Chapter 37 307
Chapter 38 311
Chapter 39 319
Chapter 40 323
Chapter 41 333
Chapter 42 339
Chapter 43 353
Chapter 44 359

PART FOUR
HALLOWS EVER AFTER

Chapter 45 373
Chapter 46 381
Chapter 47 389
Chapter 48 397

Epilogue 401

Acknowledgments 419
About the Author 421
Also by Rosie Alice 423

DEDICATION

For my readers.
You waited a long time for this… I hope you're ready.

PLAYLIST

Where Are You?—Elvis Drew, Avivian
Eyes On You—SWIM
Learning to Survive—We Came As Romans
Mind of Mine—Lø Spirit
Drown Me Out—Rarity
Ascensionism—Sleep Token
For Her—Xavier Mayne, ELIO, Chase Atlantic
Vigilante Shit—Taylor Swift
Not Afraid Anymore—Halsey
Lost in the Fire—Gesaffelstein & The Weeknd
If I—Lim
The Hunted—The Rigs
Bells in Santa Fe—Halsey
Whispers—Halsey
Hurricane—Halsey
Empty Gold—Halsey

Headlights—PVRIS
Wicked—Miki Ratsula

AUTHOR NOTE & CONTENT WARNING

This book is NOT a standalone, and you must read book one—The Hallows Boys—before reading this. If you start here, you'll be incredibly confused.

The Hallows Queen is a much darker book than the first and contains much heavier content. Where book one focused mostly on the physical connection between these four characters, and the Hallows Games themselves, book two focuses on what comes after. There is significantly more plot than sex in this book. This is a poly romance book—meaning the heroine will not choose one guy at the end, and two of the guys have an emotional, loving and sexual relationship as well.

If you would like to go into this book blind, please feel free, but I will include a list of content warnings on the next page. Your mental health is important, please heed this warning if necessary.

For all intents and purposes (because this book's timeline was created years ago), it is based in the year 2020. This is only mentioned because of death/birth dates and the timeline of the Hallows Games, etc.

I pride myself on writing strong heroines that can handle their own—but with this book I really needed to remind myself that *it's okay to be weak sometimes, that does not make Sage **any** less of a character than my stronger leads.*
Sage thrives with the three guys that make her feel safe, and there is absolutely nothing wrong with that.

————

Please be advised some of these content warnings can be considered spoilers.

THIS BOOK CONTAINS THE FOLLOWING CONTENT:

High spice with a handful of different kinks and dynamics including: *degradation, praise, sharing/menage, somnophilia, slapping, spitting, choking, restraints, masks, DVP, DP, assplay/anal, blood play, knife play, MM, MMF, MMFM, MFM and MF.*

A poly relationship that ends in a HEA between 3 men and 1 woman.

The following list should be considered important and graphic plot points: *rape, sexual assault by a family member, murder, death of a loved one, suicidal ideation, insta-love, pregnancy which includes implication of loss of pregnancy, child abuse, depression, anxiety, panic attacks, obsession, kidnapping, stalking, underage drinking and smoking, high school aged characters who are all 17-18 in the state of Georgia, where the age of consent is 16.*

THIS BOOK IS NOT A GUIDELINE FOR SAFE SEXUAL OR BDSM PRACTICES. THIS IS A WORK OF FICTION AND SHOULD NOT BE USED AS A HOW-TO OR INSPIRATION FOR REAL LIFE SEX.

PART ONE

SAGE
BLACKMORE

CHAPTER 1

SAGE

"Time for us to have a little talk, Sage."

I suck oxygen into my lungs, eager to calm the panic snaking its way through my torso. Shaking my head to get Kaiden's hand off the back of my neck, I spin to look at the three Hallows Boys standing behind me. Kai's firm grip stays on my skin, though, finding its home around the column of my throat with my sudden movement.

I focus my attention on him, *The King*, my nostrils flaring as I refuse to blink before he does. But he's better at this than me, and after a minute, my eyes are stinging, making me break away from his gaze.

"I told you that you wouldn't like what you found, Sage," Vinny says, ending the silence and pulling my attention to him. He's grinning, propped against the edge of my bed like he's right at home.

"*Talk*, then," I snap, and Kaiden's hand tightens around my throat.

"Mind your fucking tone," Kai growls, making my lips tip up at the sides as I tilt my head back to look at him.

"I want to know." I swallow against his palm. "What the *fuck* happened." A sneer snakes across my face. "To Megan Gallagher."

Her name slithers through me like a bad dream, everything I've imagined about her weighing on my chest—and that's why I force myself to speak, even if each word squeezes out through the hold he has on my windpipe, voice scratchy. When I try to swallow, he loosens his grip a little, and I clear my throat before I continue. "I want to know the truth, and I want to know it *now*."

"You're getting so bossy." Beckham laughs from where he's positioned next to Vinny, his perfect face splitting into a humored smile that, even when I'm trying to stand my ground, makes me feel warm.

I cross my legs, committing to being the *bossy* version of myself that wants answers. "Well, being nice to you three has never gotten me anywhere, so maybe I should play your games after all."

"Our games?" Kaiden questions, his eyebrow kicking up in amusement.

"Yeah," I bite out. "Where you treat me like shit to get whatever you want from me, use me and lie to me."

All three of the boys before me laugh in unison, and Kaiden's hand finally drops from my skin so he can cross his arms over his chest.

"Hey." Vinny raises his hands. "I never did any of those things."

"No, you just ignore me and fuck my cheer captain." Tipping my head to the side, I look at him, expression taunting.

He grins that wicked, sexy smile that makes the dimples in his cheeks stand out. "*Oooh*, you sound jealous."

I match his grin for one of my own. "Jealous? *Nah*. Why be jealous when your friends keep my bed *so* nice and cozy."

He booms with laughter, shaking his head. "Because you miss the way my dick feels slamming against your guts."

I roll my eyes, dismissing Vinny as I turn back to Kai. "Tell me everything."

He sighs, his lips curling downward with malicious thought as he steps backwards so he can sit down. I read the expression for exactly what it is—he's concocting a story in his head, one that is laced with lies and bullshit to deceive me once more.

Beckham joins Vinny as he takes a seat, crossing his legs and watching Kai steadily breathe across the room.

Kaiden stares at me, and every few seconds his lips twitch, like he's having an internal battle with whatever shit is breezing through his twisted mind.

"*Talk!*" I shout, my frustration at its peak. So much so, I can feel my face go hot.

Kaiden sucks his teeth, glaring at me from across the room as his hands ball into fists at his sides. Part of me is aware that I'm pushing my luck with Mr. Controlling—that if I keep getting loud with him, he'll retaliate—but I don't fucking care. I want answers, and I want them *now*.

"Fine," Kaiden finally says, surprising me. But when his lips press together again, and silence washes over the room once more, I start to lose the hope he'll actually tell me anything.

As tension fills the little space of my bedroom, all the muscles in my body clench up in anticipation.

Beckham groans, rubbing a hand down his face. "*Jesus*, just tell her, Kai."

Kaiden licks his lips as he glances over at Beckham with a warning. "Careful."

I sigh, feeling desperate. "*Please*, Kaiden."

Kaiden spends another heartbeat without moving a muscle

or uttering a word, but then he sits back and crosses his arms over his chest. Then, he begins, seeming to concede, and my heart races in response.

"Your family history is long, Sage. It would take me a week to go down your family tree and explain every crevice of fuckery, so let me just skip ahead to your father." He takes a breath. "When your father created the games, it was because he was so fucking tired of the restrictions the Blackmore name had on him—him *and* your uncle. Twin brothers who wanted to sin in the darkness but couldn't because they were town *royalty*. They were observed by everyone in town, and everything they did trickled back down to their father, your grandfather."

His eyes stroke over my face like a caress, trying to gauge how I'm responding, but I keep my features neutral. Even if my insides are going haywire.

"The Hallows Games were the one night they could be reckless. They could live their darkest desires and be *free*. Benjamin was their best friend—they were close like brothers, but it was something so much deeper. Like what Vinny, Beckham and I have. Family by choice is thicker than blood that fucks you up."

"How do you know all of this?" I question, picking at my nail beds.

"They cataloged it, in journals and diaries of sorts that are locked away in the crypt. Every generation of Hallows Boys must follow that tradition as well—to write the story of their generation's Games."

"So, you wrote about me?" I snap.

Kaiden nods, answering in a nonchalant way that has my blood boiling. "Don't get touchy already. Let me continue."

My gut churns with nausea, thinking about everything we did together on Halloween being written down in some book somewhere, but I just bite down on my lip and keep my thoughts to myself.

"It didn't start with a tradition. They thought they would keep the game to themselves and let the time they had trapped in Blackmore pass by a little more freely. Even if just for one night a year. But after that first year, others had heard rumors of the boys who went into the old crypts, and rumors spread. More and more people were heading into the cemetery to party, and they realized it wasn't just them who felt leashed and trapped in this town. It was everyone. They wrote the rules, and then they started scouting for who would replace them as the Hallows Boys when they graduated, writing everything down. I think they liked the superiority it gave them, creating a tradition that would outlive them in the town that suffocated them."

"Where does my mom fit into this?" I ask, even though I'm not sure I want the answer.

"She was their first Hallows Girl," Kaiden says, looking at me for a reaction.

I just nod and wait for him to continue. I had already guessed that my mother was a Hallows Girl, so it isn't some big revelation.

"But she was more than that." Kaiden continues. "Your dad fell in love with her—they *all* did."

"*What?*" I gasp, all breath leaving my lungs. "Wait…"

I swallow down the thick saliva that's coating my mouth, and they let me process the information. After a few heartbeats, I blink and look back up at Kaiden. "She loved them all?"

"No, Sage. She didn't." He smiles. "But they loved her."

My eyebrows pull down in confusion, and then Vinny's voice pulls my attention. "There was only one for her. Your father."

All three boys stare at me, waiting for me to say something —almost like his words have a deeper meaning, like he's hinting that I am following in my mother's footsteps at picking only one Hallows Boy.

I lick my lips, returning my gaze to Kaiden. "What about Megan?"

"Megan," Kaiden says, sighing. "Megan was your mother's best friend."

"And Benjamin killed her?" I breathe, the words tasting bitter on my tongue.

"That's what it says in the newspaper," Kaiden answers, but a look crosses his face that tells me he's forgoing some information.

"Tell me more about Megan."

"Megan was the second Hallows Girl—the final Hallows Girl for the founders, since they only played two years. Your mother selected her for the games."

"My mother?"

"She played with them their final year, too—they didn't want to play without her, especially your father," he reveals, his legs kicking out so he can get comfortable. "Megan hated the Hallows Boys, and even though she was your mother's best friend, she held resentment toward her for hating the three boys she had grown to see as family."

"So, my mother chose her to what, punish her?"

"Yes and no," Kaiden answers, but I ignore his vagueness.

"And she died." I shake my head.

Kaiden sighs, then stands up abruptly and rubs his hands down his face. "I think that's enough."

I stand too, following him to my bedroom door. "*No!*"

Grabbing him by the arms, I try to hold him in place so he can't pull my bedroom door open, and he goes stiff. "I'm trying to *protect* you, Sage. You aren't ready for the truth. You'll be better off if you just let this go."

"I don't need you to protect me! I'm not some fragile little girl," I snip, though I feel like I'm pleading more than anything. "I can handle it."

"It's her family, Kai," Beckham says, holding an arm toward me, his brows furrowed. Despite myself, my heart warms.

Kaiden's head snaps to the side so he can look at Beckham, but he doesn't speak, just stares at his friends sitting on my bed before he shakes my hands off and returns to his seat at the vanity. I stay by the door, scared he'll bolt again, and wait for someone to say something.

Silence ghosts along my skin like it's about to swallow me up, but then Kaiden finally speaks quietly, his voice grating against his throat like he's protesting the words. "Tell her the rest."

My lungs quickly fill and empty, and I glance between Beckham and Vinny just as they look at me, gazes searching mine.

"Sit down, Sage," Vinny says, waving toward my desk.

CHAPTER 2

KAIDEN

My skin fucking crawls—everything inside of me protesting, urging me that we're making a mistake in telling the story we were sworn to never tell. She can't handle this—I can barely stomach carrying around the weight of it, and Sage is fucking emotional. She's bound to fly off the handle and do something stupid.

I keep my mouth pressed closed, though, putting my trust in my brothers, hoping they know what the fuck they're doing.

Once Sage has returned to the seat at her desk, Vinny sighs. "The records of the second year of games are documented, but I can't tell you that everything written is the God's honest truth, or the entire story, I can only tell you the way that I know it."

Sage's face is red, pupils dilated, her chest rising and falling quickly as anxiety floods her bloodstream. The twisted part of me loves seeing her flushed and scared.

"The Hallows Games weren't always like the one you

played, Sage," Vinny starts, but stops and looks at me for a moment. I breathe out through my nostrils, then nod at him.

"When they started, the founders just wanted one safe place to live out their deepest desires. It's not completely clear their separate intentions, but we know that Benjamin and your uncle had a relationship—one they couldn't be public about in Blackmore." Vinny glances at Beckham, who grins back.

When I look at Sage, she shakes her head a little. "But my uncle is married... to a woman."

My eyebrow quirks, but my mouth stays shut, letting her piece it together for herself.

Beckham laughs, though, his loud boom cutting through the room as he waves a hand between himself and Vinny. "I know you're familiar with the concept of bisexuality, Savage."

Vinny chuckles, and Sage clicks her tongue. "My brain is just trying to catch up, *asshole*."

My lips tip up in a grin at her attitude, and when Beckham laughs again, I shake my head, a small laugh escaping my lips.

"Benjamin and your Uncle Aaron loved each other." Vinny continues, the room falling silent again. "But they couldn't be together—the Blackmores were very old fashioned, especially your grandfather, so they kept their romance a secret. When your dad presented the idea of the games to them, they saw it as an opportunity to be together, even if it was just for that one night. But your dad, he had other ideas. He was rooted in darkness and violence—he wanted a place where he could unleash his demons, let them run free, and then lock them back up at the end of the night until the next year came."

When Vinny pauses, no one says anything, even Sage who looks like she's going to spill the contents of her stomach onto the carpet.

"He was the one who decided to bring a girl into it—your mother, Christine. He wanted to *hurt* her; he wanted to spend the night marring her skin with his hands and teeth and belt. He didn't expect to fall in love with her. I don't even think he expected to fuck her."

Sage swallows hard, and when Vinny meets her gaze for reassurance to continue, she dips her head in a nod so small I almost miss it.

"She was just as dark as him—twisted and morphed into this person she didn't want to be." Vinny chuckles. "She played right alongside him, even in that first year. She loved the pain, the joy, the freedom he gave her, and she became the Hallows fucking *Girl*."

"Skip forward," Sage blurts, looking sick. "To Megan."

Vinny nods minutely. "Christine was the only person besides Andrew who knew about Aaron and Benjamin's relationship, and she fit into their formed family so flawlessly that they fell in love with her right alongside each other. She liked the... *attention*, and Andrew liked knowing he was in complete control of all three of them."

Sage's lip curls up in disgust at that, and I smirk at how uncomfortable she is.

"Your mother confided in her best friend, Megan, about her relationship with the Hallows Boys and the things they liked to do, but Megan shamed her. After a decade of friendship, growing up together, learning together, Megan shoved her aside with repulsion and malice, all because she liked to get kinky and bloody with three boys in the cemetery." Vinny scoffs, then keeps going. "Your mother was hurt beyond words, broken and betrayed by the person she had called her best friend, so when Megan started telling the whole town that the Hallows Boys were *freaks*, your mother brought up the idea of playing the game with her, showing her how fun it can be, immersing her in their world so she would understand."

"But Andrew was *angry*—all the boys were. Their secrets in

the dark were exposed to the town, and they needed to teach Megan a lesson." Vinny sighs. "I don't know who knew what—I don't know if your mother was in on whatever was planned, or if she really just wanted to try to convince her closest friend that she wasn't a freak. I don't know if she knew the *power* and *control* Andrew had grown to love, so when Halloween night came, she could have been caught off guard over what really happened in the crypt, but we'll never know for sure."

The room falls silent, nearly suffocating, and when I catch Vincent's eye across the space that separates us, I know he can't go on with the rest of the story. I clear my throat, sitting up straighter in my seat.

"They went *too* far, Sage." I meet Sage's gaze, and her eyes glisten with moisture. "And they *liked* it."

"No," Sage breathes, shaking her head as tears slip from her eyes and trail down her cheeks. "You're lying! My parents would never fucking hurt someone!"

"I'm not lying, Sage," I say, placing my hands in my lap. "We don't know if it was on purpose—if they meant to kill her —but they did. Your dad *did*."

"But Benjamin—" Sage says, her mind busy. "They arrested him for it."

My brows raise. "A one-in-three chance of whose DNA they found, I guess."

Sage stands abruptly, pointing at the door. "Get out—all of you. Get out of my house."

Beckham stands too, stepping toward her, already trying to soothe her. "Sage."

"No!" she yells, pushing her hands out to stop him from touching her. "You don't get to sit here and tell me my parents are *murderers*, and then act fucking *chill* about it, like it's some schoolyard gossip! They couldn't kill someone—not the parents I knew!"

I stand, my lip curling. "You asked for the fucking truth, Sage—and that's what you got. Stop acting like a baby and listen to the rest of the story." Her eyes narrow, gaze searing.

"I don't need the rest of the story. I already know it! They fled, letting their friend take the fall, then they had me, pretended to be people they weren't, and then they died." Sage laughs without humor, stepping in my direction. "And here I am, in Blackmore, playing the same fucked-up game with you three when you *know* it's rooted in death and darkness—when you've been lying to me since the moment we fucking met!"

I shake my head. "We aren't playing the same *fucked-up game* with you Sage. The game has changed."

She takes another step, rolling her eyes. "Oh, so you *aren't* going to murder me?"

My jaw clenches. "The game isn't about fucking violence—"

"Oh, it's not?!" she interrupts me, sending my blood rushing through my veins. "Do you want to see the bruises all over me? Maybe the fucking scabs on my back?!"

I throw my head back and laugh, letting her stalk right up to me and push against my chest with her weak little hands. When I meet her eyes again, her face is red, and she's heaving for air. "Don't pretend your *tight little cunt* didn't love every second of it, Sage, I remember you asking for *more*."

"Fuck you!" she shouts as she starts punching my chest with her tiny fists that couldn't hurt a fly.

"Go on. Get it all out." I chuckle, rearing my head back so she doesn't hit my face.

She continues with a growl, screaming at me. "I fucking *hate* you!"

My eyebrow kicks up, and I grab her wrists to stop her from hitting me. "Do you now?"

With my cock rock hard, it's a task in itself not to rip her pants down and slide into her, but instead I just stare at her while I hold her in place in front of me, waiting for her to calm down.

"Yes!" she yells, sobbing now. "I wish I never met you—I wish I never let you touch me!"

I roll my eyes, looking over her head to glance at Beckham and Vincent. "A little help here? I think she's having a fucking breakdown."

Beckham sighs, walking up behind Sage and wrapping his arms around her chest. "Enough, Sage. Sit back down, please."

I don't know what it is, maybe his touch or his gentle tone, but she goes limp in my grasp and falls forward onto my chest. She wails, crying so hard that her entire body shakes, so I do the first thing that comes to mind—I wrap my arms around her and hold her.

CHAPTER 3

SAGE

"So, what happens to Benjamin?" I ask, sitting back in my desk chair and facing my bed where the three Hallows Boys are lined up. My face is burning hot, and my eyes are sore from crying, but I feel a little better now that a meltdown is out of the way.

"What do you mean? He's in jail," Kaiden says, appearing bored.

"But he's innocent," I press, looking at him like he's insane.

"Not entirely," he responds. "Besides, what do you care?"

I look at Beckham for help, but when he shrugs, I growl and turn my attention to Vincent. He gives me a pitiful look, like I'm a wounded baby bird or something, so I just roll my eyes and cross my arms over my chest in defeat.

"So, what? Megan's real story just dies with my parents?"

Kaiden shrugs. "I guess so, I mean, we'll tell the story to the next generation, and I'm sure one day it'll come out of someone somewhere. Hopefully, we'll all be long gone by then."

"It doesn't seem fair…" I say, turning around to close all the tabs on my laptop before I drop the screen. "Everyone deserves the truth in the end."

"The truth is overrated," Vinny says, making me turn around again to look at him. "Look at what it just did to you."

I stand up with a huff. "I'm going to bed. You guys can see yourselves out."

Kaiden stands to meet me, getting too close for comfort. "You know what happens if you tell someone, right?"

I roll my eyes, a retort sitting on my tongue, but he grabs my jaw in his hand and squeezes it. "Don't roll your fucking eyes at me again."

My stomach swells, and I lick my lips, grinning. "Or what?"

He clicks his tongue, shaking his head as a maniacal smile pulls up his lips, then the hold he has on my jaw tightens. "Sage, it isn't the time nor place to give me attitude. Your grandmother will be home soon."

I lean forward, putting my face an inch from his before I speak slowly. "I won't tell anyone. Now get out of my house."

His mouth twists into a bigger smile. "*God*, I want to paint your skin red."

I shake my head until his hand falls from my jaw, then take a step backwards, pushing him away. "You know where the front door is."

Kaiden hums between his lips, narrowing his eyes for a breath, but turns around to head for my bedroom door to leave. Beckham and Vinny stand up, meeting my gaze.

"Goodnight, Savage," Beckham says, a small smile touching his lips. I don't say anything in response, just watch as all three of them step past the threshold of my bedroom, and then listen for them to go out the front door.

———

I SLEEP LIKE SHIT—NIGHTMARES HAUNT ME, WAKING ME UP every hour with soaking sheets from sweat and tears. When I drag myself downstairs for my morning coffee, Gran is sitting at the table as usual.

"Mornin', sweetie!" she greets me, and I groan.

"Rough morning?" Chuckling, she shakes out the newspaper in front of her. "I got some good news that might cheer ya up."

I reach for the coffeepot, exhaustion and an attitude coating my tone. "Oh yeah, what's that, Gran?"

"Lawyer called. Your inheritance came through," she says casually, her attention still on the newspaper.

I spin around to face her. "Really?!"

"Honest to God."

I sigh, my head tipping back in gratitude. "Thank God."

"Got a lotta shoppin' to do?" Gran laughs.

Turning around to continue making my coffee, I chuckle. "I need some new clothes, for one. Plus, it wouldn't hurt to have a coffeemaker that wasn't purchased at the corner store. I miss lattes."

"Ya sound spoiled rotten, Sage Grace." Gran clicks her tongue.

I go to the table with coffee in hand and sit down. "I *have* been spoiled my whole life, Gran."

After all the bullshit I've been put through since my parents died, learning how to adapt in a new environment and existing completely different than I've ever had to, it'll be nice to feel some sort of normalcy again. In L.A., my go-to mental health treatment was to go shopping, and after the bombs that were dropped on me yesterday, I need some retail therapy. If that makes me spoiled, then so be it.

"So, where's the money?" I ask, quirking my eyebrow playfully.

"In your account, darlin'. Let's go get ya a car after school so I can have mine back."

"Sounds good, Gran." I stand, pushing my chair out behind me and rounding the table to kiss her on top of the head. "See you after cheer practice."

"Have a good day, Sage," she quips, putting her attention back on the newspaper as I head for the door.

I grab my backpack from where I left it at the foot of the stairs, throw it over my shoulder, then slip the keys off the hook by the door. Pushing out into the morning, I shiver when the crisp air hits me. It's a colder day, so I'm glad I put on a hoodie.

Slipping into the driver's seat of my grandmother's Toyota, I crank the engine, not worrying about putting my seatbelt on since the drive is so short. When I've backed out into the street and shifted into drive, I flex my fingers on the steering wheel as I travel down the road.

Every day in Blackmore seems like a new disaster, and I'm hoping today can just be normal. I *need* normal. I need a carefree day where nothing jumps out from the shadows and mentally dropkicks me.

My phone buzzes in the center console, so when I pull up to the stop sign at the end of Main, I grab it and read the message. It's from a number I don't have saved, but luckily the sender has signed it with his name.

UNSAVED NUMBER:

Meet me for breakfast? -Becks

I roll my eyes, even as the butterflies in my stomach start flapping their wings, but don't bother responding. Dropping my phone in between my legs, I press the gas, flexing my fingers a few more times on the steering wheel to get my blood pumping.

I don't think I want to see the Hallows Boys today—not after yesterday.

I laugh to myself at the thought because it's a lie. I'd want to see them even if they were the ones who murdered Megan themselves. They have their hooks in me—I'm just a fish hanging on their line, waiting to be reeled in for consumption.

I need fucking help.

They've proven to me, time and time again, that they'll do nothing but ruin me, so why does the sick part of me want to let them? Take any crumb or morsel they let fall my way and consume it entirely and without hesitation?

What *is* it about them? All three of them so different—dark angels with devil horns and wicked forked tongues to match, they make me crazy and sane at the same time. It's like they're seeing my soul, grasping it and protecting it in their dangerous hands, then when I bat my eyelashes, they crush it. But they're quick to pick up the pieces and tape it back together again, returning me only a little scarred.

They make me feel worshiped and wanted; rejected and hated; hopeless and hopeful. They make my head pound, my heart ache, my mind melt. They ruin me—and fix me.

The parking lot at school is filling up when I pull in, but I find a good spot and park before all the ones up front are gone. I put the car in park, then flip down the visor to look in the mirror.

Dark eyes look back at me, causing a shiver to run through my body, my own reflection making me feel a little intimidated. I'm still the same girl, blonde hair, and deep brown eyes, but with the dark makeup circling my features and two French braids running down my scalp, I look *different*.

I feel different too—stronger this morning than I have for a while.

I throw my hood up, pulling my braids out so they're trailing down to my breasts, then open the door, grab my backpack, and get out.

The sound of music playing from different cars in the parking lot is loud but welcomed, making my lips twist into a smile when I recognize the hip-hop song I pick out of the noise. *It's going to be a good day,* I say to myself internally, willing it to happen as I slam the car door shut and head for the cafeteria.

Beckham is sitting alone at a table in the center of the cafeteria, surprising me, so I head for him and drop my bag on the bench in greeting. He looks up at me from his food, a smile touching his lips.

"You started eating without me?" I muse, sitting next to my bag.

"I didn't think you were coming," he says, setting down the biscuit in his hand and brushing his fingers off. "You want me to get you something?"

"No." I laugh. "I'm not hungry."

His blue eyes fill with humor. "So, why'd you come?"

I mash my lips together as I smile, thinking over his question, but decide not to answer and instead reroute the conversation. "Where's the rest of the boy band?"

He chuckles. "Vinny is on the football field, and Kai is in the courtyard. I wanted to be with you alone."

"Why?" I ask, twisting my lips.

He sighs, hanging his arms at his sides. "I wanted to make sure you were okay after yesterday."

I chuckle mindlessly. *"Okay?* Am I *okay?* No, Beckham, I'm not okay."

His expression turns solemn. "I'm sorry."

Shaking my head, I tap my fingernails on the table. "You have nothing to apologize for. I would have found out sooner or later; I just feel like everything I've learned since moving here is rising above my chin, about to fucking drown me."

"What can I do to help you, Sage? How can I make it

better?" The words are a whisper from his lips, his eyes filled with sincerity that makes a stone fall to my gut. Sitting here, looking at the guilt in Beckham's eyes, I want to scream and cry and bang my fists against the table.

"You can't do anything," I finally answer, breathing through my mouth as I blink back the moisture in my eyes. "I just need to fucking process everything."

"Okay." He reaches across the table and takes my hand, but I pull it away and thread my fingers together in my lap.

"And I think I need to process *alone.*"

He nods, laying his hands flat on the table. "I get it, Sage, I do. But just know that you don't *have* to be alone with this, okay?"

The side of my lips twitch. "How'd you become a Hallows Boy when you're so sweet?"

Beckham's face breaks into a devious smirk that holds all our secrets within it. "I think you know."

———

Juliet is out sick again, so I spend most of my day not speaking to anyone. That is, until I'm walking into the gym after school to join the rest of the cheer squad for practice.

"Look who was brave enough to show her face today." Rachel's face morphs with a hateful smile as she brings her leg up and holds it in a high stretch.

Shaking my head, I ignore her and walk across the gym to the locker room. It's fairly empty, a few girls occupying the small space while they get ready for whatever after-school activity has brought them here. Throwing my bag into the locker I've claimed as my own, I kick off my shoes and start to change.

"Ignore Rachel." A voice pulls my attention to the left, and I find one of the other cheerleaders standing at a locker about ten feet away. "She's projecting her nasty attitude because Vinny didn't show up to practice yesterday."

I study the girl's tanned, freckled face. "So what?"

She laughs, flipping her head over to gather her hair in between her hands so she can put it up in a messy bun. "So, Vinny's never missed a day of practice before—except on Halloween—and she put two-and-two together when you were *both* no-shows."

"She thinks we were together?" I tug up my shorts and slip my feet into my sneakers.

The girl snorts, standing up straight and pulling tendrils of her dark hair around her face. "I mean, *weren't you?*"

Smiling, I bite down on my lip and turn back to my locker without answering.

"Exactly." She laughs.

Turning back to her, I lean over the bench and hold my hand out. "I'm Sage."

She slams her locker shut, ignoring my outstretched hand. "Madison."

Dropping my arm, I turn back to my locker and close it, then sit down and start tying my sneakers. As Madison passes me, she pats me on the shoulder. "Hang in there, Hallows Girl. It gets easier."

My face turns hot at her nickname for me, so I focus on tying my shoes. After she's walked through the door back out into the gym, I grab my phone and scroll through my messages until I find my thread with Juliet.

ME:

Going shopping tonight. You feeling well enough to join? Lots to tell you.

She responds almost immediately.

JULIET:

Sure, I'll meet you at your house after practice.

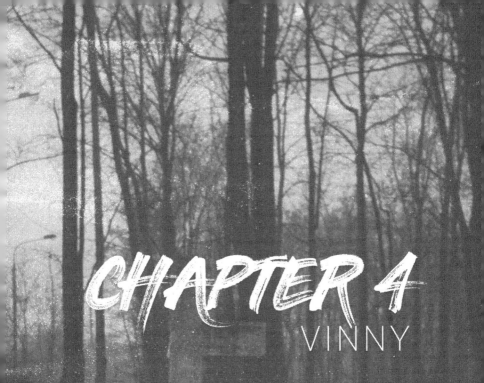

CHAPTER 4

VINNY

Even though Becks told us earlier that Sage wants to be left alone, I head for football practice with the intention of getting some alone time with her.

The cheerleaders usually practice on the edge of the field while we have football practice, so I don't bother going into the gym to look for her, knowing she'll show up eventually.

Coach lets me lead, claiming he has games to study in his office, when really, he has a bottle of Jack waiting for him in there. It's nothing new. He lets me run shit pretty much every day, and I can't say I mind. We're one of the best teams in the county, all because I know how to run a practice and lead the team.

As the quarterback, it gives me more to do, though. Not only am I worrying about the offensive lineup, but I'm also leading defense. I'm captain, coach, defensive *and* offensive QB.

It's exhausting, but the less time I have to be home, the better.

We split into offense and defense, then start running our drills. I throw the ball as soon as I have eyes on a wide receiver about halfway to the endzone, and watch it spiral through the air almost in slow motion.

It isn't until he's caught it, dodged two defensive linemen, and ran to the endzone for a touchdown that I notice the cheerleaders have joined us on the field.

Rachel's the first to start yelling, then all the other girls follow, cheering and celebrating our touchdown, including Sage.

My lips pull into a smile as my eyes find her across the field, and part of me thinks she can see under my helmet, because she smiles right back, making my stomach flip.

It's enough for now, so I run the team back, get into position, and start over again with practice, feeling Sage's eyes on me the entire time.

———

I'M DRIPPING SWEAT AND MY DARK HAIR IS SLICKED BACK UNDER a headband by the time the team is huddling up to celebrate the end of practice. Everyone is getting better and better, and it's perfect timing for us to head for the playoffs.

I pull my shirt off to get some fresh air on my sweaty skin, removing my pads while I address the team, including our coach, who has rejoined us to listen.

"Alright, guys." I wipe my balled-up shirt over my chest to dry off. "That was an amazing practice. We're going to *destroy* Douglas High on Friday. Get to the showers, get some rest, and I'll see you at the game. No bullshit!"

They all answer me the way they always do: *"Yes, captain."* And we all clap hands and turn to head off the field.

The cheerleaders are still going, climbing into a pyramid that looks like a pile of limbs, and I step to the side to watch them, hoping maybe they'll fall and I'll have to run in to make Sage feel better.

"Five, six, seven, eight!" Rachel yells, clapping her hands from the very tip top of the pyramid, then the girls all move in unison, clapping or grabbing their ankles in some impossible stretch that makes me clench.

They all hold their positions for a few seconds, then Coach Steele claps. "Great job, girls! See you tomorrow."

They carefully disassemble their human pyramid, and I catch Sage's eye as she's standing up from her spot at the very bottom. Walking toward her, I run my hand through my sweaty hair. "Hi."

Her eyes snake down my bare torso, then back up. "Hi, yourself."

"Wanna get some dinner?" I ask, stepping closer. "My treat."

Shaking her head, she gives me a sad look. "Sorry, I have plans tonight."

"Sage," I say, taking another step, not caring that there's still a handful of girls within earshot. "C'mon, you can't be serious about this whole *being alone* thing."

She laughs. "Wow, Beckham works fast."

I hum between my lips, looking down her bare legs and back up. "I'll make it worth your while."

Shaking her head, Sage sighs and it feels loaded. "I just need time to get my mind back together. You guys have trauma dumped so much information on me at once, and I want to feel a sense of normalcy again."

"Alright." Moving closer to her so she brushes against my sweaty chest, I lean in and whisper into her ear, "Just don't forget who you belong to, Sage."

She puts a hand on my chest for a breath, tapping her fingers silently, then she kisses me on the cheek before she strides away. I don't bother grabbing her and pulling her back, even though I want to. I just watch as she crosses the field and heads through the back doors to the gym.

I take a minute to stand in silence, letting my mind fill with images of Sage—deep wonder and longing filling me like an empty glass, threatening to spill over. Part of me knows why I'm so drawn to her. She's the missing piece we've needed—the one *I've* needed. She feels like home, like the way Beckham feels whenever we're together. I can act tough and careless all I want, but at the end of the day... I want her. I crave her. I need her. We all do. All three of us in different ways.

"Hey." Rachel's voice rips me from the memories of Sage, that are playing in my head like a movie, and I jump a little. I hadn't even noticed anyone was still out here with me.

I find Rachel a few feet from me, her hands on her hips. Tipping my head in greeting, I slide my hands into the pockets of my shorts. "Rach."

Walking to the bench where I left my water bottle, I bend over to pick it up and drink some of the liquid inside. When I turn back around, Rachel has followed me. A smile is snaking across her face, and I want to smack it off.

"Shower?" she asks, brushing her hair over her shoulder. "Everyone else will be clearing out soon."

It's a usual thing, hooking up with Rachel, but there's no chance it's going to happen anymore, not now that Sage is present in my life. Shaking my head, I meet Rachel's eye. "No, thanks."

"What?" She spins around as I pass by her, following me with her gaze. I keep walking and hear her choke on a laugh. "Vinny, what the fuck?"

I stop, facing her again. "What?"

Rachel's brow pulls down. "Um, since when aren't you interested in showering with me after practice?"

For a moment, I chew on the side of my mouth, just blinking in thought, then I cross my arms over my chest and lick my lips before I speak. "Since you punched Sage in the face the other day."

Huffing, her face goes a little pink, but she doesn't let her insecurity shine through any other way. She just gives me a confused look. "I'm not supposed to defend what's mine? She's trying to get with you."

I take a small step toward her, careful not to get too close so I don't wring her neck. "When have I ever given you the impression that I'm *yours*?"

"We've been hooking up for like a year," she answers simply, chuckling.

"And?" I smirk, looking at her with a blank expression. "Do you know how many holes I've filled in the last year? Yours aren't special."

She falls silent, so I take another step, letting her feel my body heat. "And let me make one thing very clear, Rachel. If you even so much as look at Sage wrong again, you'll find yourself in the cemetery for a whole different reason than gargling my cock. Do you understand?"

Blinking, her mouth falls open on a breath, but she doesn't speak.

"*I said*"—I grab her jaw softly, angling her face so she's looking right at me—"*do you understand?*"

"All of this," she whispers, voice shaky, "for some girl that just moved here? You'll just end things with that quick? *Why?*"

"Because you mean nothing," I answer, letting go of her jaw so I can take a step away from her. "And she means everything."

CHAPTER 5
SAGE

Even though everyone goes into Friday's game with confidence, we end up losing to Douglas High by one touchdown, ending our season and my high school cheer career in Blackmore before it has barely begun.

While the mass of the Douglas High student body floods their field and celebrates a victory, Blackmore is in a state of catatonia—either fallen to the ground or sitting silently in the stands, waiting for what the fuck we do next.

The girls around me drop their pompoms, holding them at their thighs, and I do the same, feeling defeated and like I missed my opportunity to follow our team to a championship.

My eyes trail out to the sidelines of the field, where the Blackmore High football team is heading, and I watch as they all embrace or clap hands, congratulating each other on their season.

Vinny is in the center of it, leading his teammates through

their loss in a gracious and positive way. It makes my heart warm. His face is sad, but his body language is inspiring. The way he claps each player on the back as he gives them their moment of congratulations, it's kind of amazing. I decide to take a page out of his book and turn to the girl to my right.

"Well, it was a great season." I smile.

The blonde rolls her eyes at me. "You weren't even here."

Pressing my lips together, I decide to nip that plan in the bud and start heading toward the bench to find better company. With my pompoms in hand, I skip over to the football players, the cold wind blowing through my hair and causing a shiver down my spine.

Vinny turns, like he knows I'm coming up behind him through a sixth sense, and he smiles at me when our gazes connect.

I don't know why I do it, but I launch myself at him, wrapping my arms around his neck once I'm on the tips of my toes, but then I freeze in place, about eight inches from his face. His brows pull down in confusion, like he doesn't know why I've stopped, and then his eyes slowly lower to my lips.

His large hand slides up my back slowly, and the blood rushes through my ears. Everything around us drops away, then his hand is threading into the hair on the back of my head, and he's bringing my mouth to his.

I suck in a small gasp before our lips touch, holding on to my pompoms as tight as I can while Vinny assaults my mouth with his tongue.

We're the perfect picture, I can imagine—football player and cheerleader.

A small moan escapes me as we kiss, and his hand tightens in my hair, making the moment turn hotter and more tense and deliciously painful all at once.

I pull away before I get too turned on to trust myself. Vinny grins against my mouth, a chuckle blowing across my wet lips. "What was that for?"

Clearing my throat, I step back, dropping my arms to my sides and swinging my pompoms. "I don't know."

"I thought you needed *time alone*." His lips twist to the side, the taunt making me laugh. "Miss me already?"

Nodding minutely, I smile at him for a heartbeat before I walk backwards, away from him. "Great game, Vinny."

He runs a hand over his jaw, a smile spreading across his face. "Thanks, Sage."

With a flock of butterflies playing in my stomach, I make my way back to where my squad is still standing. A small worry that Rachel might claw my face off runs through me, but I'm pleasantly surprised when she doesn't even look at me, just continues talking to a few of her friends.

I bend over, retying my sneaker to keep my sweaty hands busy, and then Coach Steele is walking up and clapping her hands.

"Great game, girls. Let's hit the locker room and head home."

Douglas is still celebrating, the whole stadium in a disarray of yelling and jumping and screaming, so I barely hear Coach Steele when she approaches me and starts talking.

"Sorry you didn't get to cheer as much as you wanted, Sage."

I smile at her. "One game was enough. I just appreciate you giving me the opportunity."

"The dance team performs at the Basketball games, if you're interested," she suggests with a shrug.

Laughing, I shake my head. "I'm okay for now. Maybe I should take this as a sign and focus on my schoolwork."

She nods, smiling as she puts her hand on my shoulder. "Glad we had you on the squad, even for a short while."

"Thanks, Coach." I smile back, then watch her walk away.

With my pompoms in hand, I head for the locker room slowly, savoring the way the cold air makes goosebumps prickle on my exposed skin. I'm still buzzing and burning from my kiss with Vinny, and I hate how happy it made me feel in such a small moment. In the last few days, I've tried my hardest to shut all three of the boys out, convincing myself that I need to concentrate on healing from everything they told me in private. But maybe the missing piece is *them.*

———

I spend the weekend constantly thinking about Kaiden, Vincent, and Beckham. They haunt my dreams, always save me in my nightmares, and plague my mind all day long.

By Sunday afternoon, I find the courage to ask my grandmother some questions.

I knock on the wall before walking into the living room, and her head perks up. A smile spreads across her face and she puts down the crossword puzzle book in her hand. "Yes, darlin'?"

"Do you have a minute to talk, Gran?" As I step into the room, she sits up straighter, patting the couch next to her.

"For you, I got a lifetime. What's goin' on in that head, Sage Grace?"

I sigh as I sit down, pulling my legs up and wrapping my arms around my knees. "My parents. This town. *The truth.*"

"I told you everything I know, baby. What else is there?"

I feel tears licking at the backs of my eyes, and I blink them away before I start talking. "I don't know. Do you know someone named Megan?"

Gran's face pales a little. "Where'd you hear that name?"

"I found a picture of her and mom in your closet," I confess.

Gran clicks her tongue playfully, laughter in her tone. "Goin' through my stuff when I'm not here, just like your mama used to."

I giggle. "Sorry."

She shakes her head, putting her hand on my arm. "Anything in this house is yours to see, Sage—just gotta ask. As for Megan, she was your mama's best friend since birth. She lived down the road her whole life."

"And she died," I add, looking up at Gran through my lashes.

She presses her lips together, sighing through her nose and nodding. "She died when they were in high school. Horrible. Your mama had a hard time with it."

"Who killed her?" I ask, swallowing hard.

"Sage." Gran sighs again, shaking her head. "Why're you askin' me this when it seems like you already know the answers?"

Clearing my throat, I shrug. "Online it says my dad's best friend, Benjamin, killed her. Did you know him?"

"Never met the boy," Gran says, disgust passing over her features. "But to do what he did... you gotta be a soulless monster."

My chest feels lighter at the realization that she really does believe that Benjamin did it. Maybe the Hallows Boys were wrong about my father after all, but part of me knows I'm just hoping for the best... hoping they're innocent in all of this, when there're red flags everywhere backing up the story they told me.

My parents wouldn't have run, changed their names, hidden their real life if they were innocent. They wouldn't have lied to me about where I was born, who I am, what my name is.

I let silence wash over me and my grandmother for a

moment, then I take a breath. "Gran… do you think it would be okay if I officially changed my last name to Blackmore?"

She gives me a smile. "If you want to, darlin', I don't see why not."

CHAPTER 6
SAGE

"What's your deal?" Juliet asks me as we pull into the student parking lot on Monday morning. "Had a shitty weekend?"

My SUV still has that *new car* smell, and it's starting to make my head hurt. Even after spilling a coffee in the passenger seat and dousing the carpet with Lysol last week.

I look at Juliet from the corner of my eye. "It was fine. The usual. Whatever."

Laughing, she puts her elbow on the center console to hold her head up. "Wow, aren't you a treat today. Are you still all bent out of shape about everything you told me?"

Pulling into the school parking lot, I chuckle. "Oh, you mean my parents being murderers? Yeah, I'm still *bent out of shape*."

Juliet unbuckles her seatbelt before I stop the car, then turns to look at me. "Maybe you should consider lifting the Hallows Boys ban…"

I get my car into a parking spot at the front of the lot, put it in park, and twist to the side. "Pass."

"So, are we just pretending you didn't make out with Vinny in front of the whole school on Friday?" she asks, amusement sneaking into her tone.

Ignoring her question, I reroute the conversation back to the point. "I still haven't dealt with any of the shit with my parents, or my uncle, or this town, or *myself.* I'm not ready to get even more tangled in something dark and messy right now."

"Except, they are the ones with all the information. They could help you comb through this shit and deal with it the way you need to," she suggests, a sad smile touching her lips. "I just hate knowing you're struggling and there's nothing I can do to help you. Maybe you can get some more clarity from them. Plus, you like them, and don't you deserve something to be happy about?"

I shake my head. "Can we just have a normal high school day without worrying about my parents being murderers, or me falling for three dudes at once?"

She snorts. "What a fucking life you have."

Swinging my door open, I get out, then go to the backseat and get my bag. A boulder of anxiety sits in my gut, though, and it feels like it might roll straight out my ass the second I see the Hallows Boys.

"Ready?" Juliet asks, circling my SUV.

I close the door, throwing my bag over my shoulder with a sigh. "Ready."

Threading her arm through mine, Juliet leans her head on my shoulder as we walk toward the front of school, the cold November air kissing my face and making me shiver. California got cold—but never *this* cold. It's freezing, my breath a cloud of fog in front of my face every time I exhale.

"10 o'clock," Juliet mutters under her breath, and my brows pull down.

"10 o'clock?" I ask, confused. "It's like seven right now."

"You dumbass." Juliet laughs, using her head to direct my eyes. *"Ten. O. Clock."*

I follow her line of sight as we approach the quad, finding that she's directing my attention to the three boys sitting under the big oak tree at the edge of the building. Cigarettes hang in between their lips while they stare out into the day and talk quietly.

What I would give to kiss those three sets of lips again.

"Oh…" I breathe out, admiring them from afar before I get too close that I have to look away.

Right before I make the decision to turn away, Beckham lifts his eyes and connects with mine. My stomach burns with nerves and need and fear, but I can't get my gaze to let go of his— we're like two magnets, fighting that natural pull keeping us together.

When he smiles, I smile back, feeling the caress of his gaze from across the quad, and another shiver runs down my spine. Not from the cold this time.

The other two Hallows Boys don't look up from what they're doing, Kaiden on his phone and Vinny scribbling something in a notebook, and Beckham doesn't bring their attention to me, giving us the intimate connection we both need after not speaking for almost a week.

I finally rip my eyes away from him when I reach the doors for the cafeteria, and follow Juliet inside to get some breakfast, feeling more alone and more hungry for them than I've been since the first moment I first saw them.

———

I arrive to History before anyone else. The teacher is the only person in the room, and I'm thankful since this is my class with Beckham. I haven't *fully* decided I miss the boys enough to let them back in yet, even though I feel them in my skin like scars too deep to heal.

Juliet walks in just as I'm finding my seat, following behind me and sitting down at the desk at my right, then the classroom slowly fills with students, setting me on edge.

Biting down painfully on my cheek, I twist my fingers together and focus on them.

"What's wrong?" Juliet asks, and I glance at her out the corner of my eye.

"Anxiety," I mumble through my teeth, looking over at her.

She leans down and slips her hand into her backpack, pulling out her flask and holding it out to me. But I shake her off, not wanting to make myself even more vulnerable. As she drops the flask back in her bag, the bell rings overhead, signaling the beginning of class.

Beckham still hasn't arrived as the teacher steps up to the board and welcomes us. My mind grows busy with disappointment and serenity all at once as my anxiety calms, except there's a part of me that wanted to see him, to smell him, to talk to him.

Just as the teacher is starting a lesson, and I'm digging around in my bag for a notebook and pen, the classroom door bangs open, and Beckham appears.

"Sorry we're late," he says, a grin pulling his plump lips up. I find his gaze across the room at the same time he finds mine, and a burning pit opens up in my gut, and then the other two Hallows Boys are walking through the door into the classroom as well.

"Find your seats, please," the teacher says with a sigh, and I barely register the words as the three boys who haunt my mind walk across the room, right toward me.

Kaiden leads the other two up the aisle close to where I'm sitting, then he taps his knuckles on the top of the desk in front of mine, signaling for the guy sitting there to get up. Beckham and Vinny do the same, removing the students from the desks next to me and behind me, and sitting in their places.

Once they're surrounding me, each seated, I expect them to say something, but they don't. They just face forward and listen as the teacher begins talking again.

Turning my head, I look over at Juliet, who is pressing her lips together to keep herself from laughing, and it makes me snort.

A few seconds go by, then I feel Vinny lean into my hair and whisper against my ear, "Something funny?"

Chills travel down my back, and I shake my head in response, making him lean away from me again.

I swallow over my dry throat, and when the teacher turns around to write something on the white board, I lean forward into Kaiden's nape and breathe him in. He stiffens, and I find the confidence to speak. "What are you guys doing here?"

He turns his head slightly, and I pull away to look at him better.

"Sit down and pay attention to the lesson, Sage," he says quietly, then he picks up his pen to start making notes in his notebook. I feel breathless and dizzy from their proximity as I sit straight back down and glance at Beckham, who is staring at me from my left.

His mouth curves into a smile as our gazes meet like long-lost lovers, and it makes my lips twitch into a happy expression as well.

He looks down at the paper on his desk, scribbling

something with his pen. After a moment, he turns the paper upwards so I can read what it says.

I miss you.

I smile wider and look down at my desk, where my fingers are still twisting together from painful anxiousness. I don't want to be that cliché bullshit girl who relies on a guy—or three—to cope with her shit, and maybe that's the reason I pushed them away in the first place—or maybe it's because loss is so prominent in my life, and I can't risk getting attached to them.

It's too late, though. I'm attached. They consume my mind like pieces of me that were always missing.

CHAPTER 7
KAIDEN

S AGE JUMPS FROM HER SEAT THE MOMENT THE BELL RINGS, AND A laugh vibrates in my chest. Her friend Juliet follows behind her quickly, and once they've both disappeared from the room, I swing my legs around and stand up.

"Well, she couldn't get away from us faster, huh?" Becks says, sadness in his tone.

"Relax," I answer, as carelessly as possible, even though deep down I'm hating that we're all so equally affected by the loss of her presence in our lives. But out of the three of us, I need to be the one to keep her farthest away. I need to be the one who thinks with a level head instead of a longing heart and a hard dick.

"*Relax?!*" Vinny spits from behind me, and I turn around to catch his face twisting in anger. "Who knows what she's been doing. She could be fucking someone else by now!"

His hands curl into fists the second the words leave his mouth, and I shake my head. "It's been a week, dude. She isn't."

"You don't know that." Lifting his backpack, he throws it over his shoulder. When he moves to walk away, I grab him by the shoulder and yank him back.

"We aren't done with this conversation, Vincent," I growl, my veins filling with fire when he rolls his eyes at me. Becks clicks his tongue, stepping up next to Vinny before I continue speaking. "She kissed you three days ago. She wants us just as much as we want her. Keep your fucking shit together."

"Like you have *your* shit together?" Becks asks, accusation and attitude dripping from his tone. "Did you sneak in her window again last night?"

I go hot with anger that he's invading my privacy, "Fucking watch it."

They both shake their heads, and I can see in their faces that they're hurting—even though they have each other, parts of them are yearning for what Sage gives them—*us*. I hate to admit I'm feeling exactly the fucking same.

———

IT'S FREEZING COLD WHEN I LEAVE MY HOUSE AFTER NIGHTFALL, my hoodie doing nothing to protect me from the aching frost climbing underneath my skin and wrapping itself around me as I walk.

I don't shiver, though, I hold my muscles tight, moving one foot in front of the other as I head to my destination.

Sage.

My blood is pumping so fierce and fast; I can barely feel the cold hitting my skin anyway.

Stuffing my hands into the front pocket of my hoodie, I twist my fingers together and try to get the feeling back in them. My eyes water as I pick up pace, the cold wind kissing my eyelashes and making me blink a few times.

My entire body is aching for her, every inch of me dying to touch her. When I get into her neighborhood, I walk directly in the center of the empty road, not worrying about anyone being out this late. When I spot her house, my hands fist, and I move my legs faster, pushing harder to get to her.

It's easy enough climbing up the tree next to her house, then walking across the roof to her bedroom window on the second floor, since I've done it a handful of times now. Not that she knows how much I slide through her window and watch her sleep.

Over the last week, while Sage has needed time away from us to sort out her personal bullshit, I've felt so out of control that I needed a tiny piece of comfort. I needed to know she was *okay*. That she wasn't plotting or self-destructing or trying to hurt us alongside herself.

I don't know.

Maybe I just wanted to see her.

Sliding her window up slowly, a smile pulls at my lips as I step through and onto her carpet, the smell of her — vanilla and caramel and something so delectably feminine that I've grown addicted to it — engulfing my senses and making me ravenous.

When I'm in the darkness of her room, I silently close the window behind me, then I turn to look out across her room. My heart stops when I find Sage sitting up in bed, her face bored and her shoulders stiff.

"*Please*, come on in." She waves her hand out, sarcasm dripping from her lips like poison, and it makes my dick throb in my jeans.

Instead of speaking, I slowly creep across the room, my gaze never moving from hers.

When I reach the end of her bed, I kick my shoes off, then

climb onto the mattress. She quickly pulls her knees up to her chest. "What are you doing here, Kaiden?"

I lick my lips, crawling up her bed in silence, then I grab her ankles and yank her legs, straightening them out and dragging her down into a lying position. She squeaks but doesn't say anything else as I slide up her body, angling my own on hers.

Sage's chest rises and falls quicker, her heart racing under her chest so hard that I feel it shake through my own when I lie myself down on top of her.

"Kaiden," she says, but it's more like a question, rolling her hips without meaning to, making me fall between her open thighs as she spreads her legs.

Dragging my nose up her jaw, I breathe her in, the sensation of being near her making my entire body quake with a groan. Her hips roll once more, and I know she's feeling the same thing I am. After a week of torturing ourselves with distance, finally coming together and touching again is the purest form of pleasure.

When my mouth angles over hers, she moans, low and deep.

I drag my tongue over her lips, then swirl it around her mouth, wanting to eat her whole and consume her. When she grinds against my cock, it almost bursts through the zipper on my pants.

"*Kai,*" she breathes, her voice pleading.

I kiss down her throat, her chest, her stomach, then I rip her t-shirt over her head so I can feed on her tits.

"*Kai.*" My name slipping from her lips is a desperate and pathetic prayer as I suck on her nipples one by one.

Sitting back, I look down at her through the darkness, studying how she wiggles her hips as hunger and desire eat her alive. I reach over my head and yank my hoodie off, rolling it up and placing it over her eyes.

"*Kaiden,*" she begs, and my mouth twists into a smile, loving the way my name constantly drips from her mouth like it's her favorite word. Her hands grab at the hoodie, and I smack them away, lifting her wrists to the top of her headboard and holding them there.

"Don't move." I speak for the first time, my voice grating.

With two of her senses taken away, she moans and writhes against the bed before me, aching from the inside out for release, and it makes my head swim.

If I didn't need to feel her right now, I'd get enough pleasure from simply watching her writhe and whimper with lust.

I use both hands to yank her shorts and panties down her legs, leaving her completely naked for the taking. My mouth waters, so I press my hands to her swollen lips and spread her cunt, giving myself a beautiful view of her tiny clit and soaked entrance.

She moans loud, even though I've barely touched her, and it makes precum leak into my boxers.

Releasing her pussy, I quickly and silently rip my jeans and boxers down, then I slam my cock inside her without warning, relishing how she screams and jolts her hips against me.

"Oh, *God*," she moans, her head rolling back on the bed hard enough that the makeshift blindfold I made from my hoodie ends up covering her whole face.

I smile, leaning down and grabbing both sides of the fabric and pushing it tight against her face to cut off her oxygen and silence her all at once.

She says something under the thick fleece, but it's unrecognizable, and I start to fuck into her hard and fast to make her shout unintelligibly again.

Her pussy throbs and quivers around my cock as I thrust into her over and over, chasing my orgasm so desperately that I don't bother letting go of the hoodie, and it isn't until her body falls completely lax that I realize I've been suffocating her the whole time I've been fucking her.

Ripping the fleece from her face, I grin when I see she's passed out.

Her chest rises and falls quickly, so to wake her up I lean back, push my cock all the way inside her, then I press her clit with my fingers.

She doesn't stir, so I rub her clit hard and fast.

I feel her coming around my dick before she wakes, and then her eyes fly open and her body convulses with a shout.

"Fuck! Kaiden!" Looking up at me for a moment, her back curls and she loses control completely.

"*Jesus Christ,* Sage," I breathe, my hand cramping from how hard I'm massaging her clit, then my spine burns as my orgasm builds. Grinding my hips, I thrust into her hard and fast, even as her cunt holds on to my cock for dear life. Then I'm coming, spurting inside of her and moaning into the darkness of her bedroom.

She screams, her orgasm having subsided, but I continue to assault her clit with three fingers, pressing into her while rolling them around in circles.

"Take my fucking cum, my perfect little slut," I groan, my climax making me desperate. "Give me another orgasm. I need to feel your pussy squeeze around me again."

She twitches and writhes against the bed, but my vision goes dark, my need for another orgasm from her taking over and blurring everything else. "Sage—*now.* Come again for me."

My orgasm slows, but I don't pull out.

Spitting between us onto her clit to give my fingers more lubrication, I milk another release from her. "C'mon, I know you want to. You live to give me what I fucking want, baby."

She screams so loudly her voice cracks, her fingers threading into the messy blonde hair on her head, then her cunt is swallowing my cock as she comes again.

My hand slams into her windpipe to silence her, then her pussy is gushing, flooding my crotch and the bed with cum as her body quakes and rolls underneath me.

My gaze finds hers, and as her face turns red as oxygen is taken away from her again, my cock starts to fill with blood and harden inside her.

When her orgasm has fizzled out, I let go of her throat and fall on top of her, rolling my hips between her legs and slowly thrusting into her as the sounds of our mixed releases fills the room.

With a moan, her hands find my back, clawing into me, just as her mouth finds mine.

We fuck slowly this time, like we've spent all our energy, but still can't help ourselves from giving each other more pleasure. When her fingers dig into the skin at my lower back, I know she's close again, so I kiss her hard, then pull back to look into her eyes.

"I miss you," she whispers, and I slide my hands into her hair.

"Me too," I whisper back, hating the vulnerability of the words, but loving how she reacts to them.

Her mouth twists into a smile, then her body is trembling as she's taken under another orgasm, her pussy suffocating my cock until I'm coming alongside her, filling her until her cunt is overflowing with my seed.

CHAPTER 8

SAGE

Kaiden and I lie together for about thirty minutes before either one of us has the courage to say another word.

To my surprise, he speaks first.

"Are you okay?" he asks, his voice almost a whisper.

I smile at him through the darkness. "I'm fine."

"We dropped a lot of information on you, then you pushed us away. It would be okay if you weren't okay." His kindness feels wrong—out of character.

"I'm fine, Kaiden," I manage to get out without my voice shaking. "I'm tough."

He chuckles, curling his hands around my waist and down to my ass. "I know you are, Sage."

Silence washes over us again, and after a few minutes, I wrap my legs around his bare waist and shuffle my hips closer to him.

"How often do you sneak into my bedroom?"

He shakes with a laugh, his fingers digging into my ass as he pulls my pussy flush against his growing cock. "Every night for the last week."

"That sounds exhausting," I say breathlessly, getting distracted by the feeling of his smooth shaft sliding through my center. "Why do you do it?"

He rolls his hips, putting pressure on my clit. His voice rumbles when he answers me. "Because I can."

Moaning, I press my eyes closed and focus on the feeling of him rubbing against my wetness. "But why, Kai?"

Pushing his weight against mine, he lays me on my back and fits himself between my legs. I find his dark eyes and stare into them while I wait for his answer.

"I had to make sure no one was enjoying what's mine." He kisses down my throat, his hands squeezing my tits.

"*Yours,*" I repeat, arching my back and wrapping my legs around his waist.

"Again," he growls, reaching between us to grab his hardening dick and positioning it at my entrance.

I moan as he slides into me, my hands grabbing his arms. "I'm yours, and you are *mine.*"

Hips pulling back slowly, he thrusts again and again, moans escaping his lips that make my pussy throb with pleasure. "Kaiden. Say it... tell me that you'll be mine too."

His hand slides up the side of my face, and I admire the sparkle in his dark eyes as he fucks me slowly and threads his fingers through my hair. "No."

I grow hot with anger, but his hips speed up between my legs and his cock hits my G-spot over and over. I don't miss the cocky smile that pulls at his lips as I moan out my pleasure. Pushing his chest in protest, I try to get him off me, hating that he won't give me what I want. But he only chuckles softly and pins my arms down on the bed.

Leaning his face into my neck, he licks at my skin. "Stop it, Sage. Let me fuck what's mine."

I can feel my orgasm burning deep in my belly, and I squeeze every muscle tight to postpone it. I know he feels what I'm doing, because he sits back on his knees and quirks a brow at me before spitting between my legs.

"Don't fight me, Sage." He grins, his abs flexing as he continues to move inside me. His fingers seek out my clit, and pleasure spreads from my head to my toes. "I can make you come whether you want to or not."

Shaking my head, I squeeze around him. "It isn't fair—you can't have me if I can't have you."

Pounding his hips and lifting me by the waist, he strokes the head of his cock against my G-spot at the same time his fingers rub and press against my clit painfully, then my climax is taking over my body.

"Fuck you!" I shout, shaking and writhing against the bed as my release wrecks me. A malicious smile spreads across his face, one that sends anger coursing through my veins, and when his own climax begins, he fucks me hard and fast into the bed.

Falling on top of me, his mouth finds mine. "I'll be yours, Sage, but don't forget that you have no control over me."

I dig my fingernails into his back until he hisses in pain, and his face presses into my chest as his orgasm peaks, shouting out his pleasure. "Fuck!"

"Yes, I fucking do," I moan, rolling my hips and curling my back up. "I control your fucking pleasure, Kaiden Thorne, and don't forget it."

His teeth scrape across my neck, and he bites down on my flesh until I'm screaming again, my legs shaking in exhaustion at his sides. When we're both spent, he collapses on top of me, our chests heaving.

With his cock still inside me, he rolls us to the side and

brings my face to his. When I try to pull my hips away, he grabs me and holds me in place. "Stop. I want to stay inside you."

I sigh in pleasure, humming, "I like you."

Chuckling, he brushes his nose against mine. "No, you don't. That's your orgasms talking."

I smile, pressing my eyes closed. "You're a mean, heartless dick, but you're *my* mean, heartless dick."

"You should write greeting cards," he whispers, laughing softly against my lips before he kisses me.

My whole body turns to bubbles, and I feel like I may float away, because there's nothing better than the feeling Kaiden gives me when he's intimate. He's a different person in the darkness and privacy of my bedroom, after we've spent all our energy on each other's bodies. He's almost *soft*.

———

KAIDEN IS GONE WHEN I WAKE UP THE NEXT MORNING, HIS CUM dried between my legs and on my sheets. Groaning, I stand up and wrap my blanket around my naked body to head for the shower.

The thought of washing away the evidence that last night was real makes me feel sad, but I know I have to. I know I can't go to school with his essence between my legs or his scent on my skin.

It's the thought of seeing all three boys that has me showering in a hurry. Last night felt like a turning point for all four of us—even if it was just me and Kai. I've finally accepted that I belong to them, and they belong to me. And I'm ready to figure out what this life in Blackmore looks like with them.

I get ready for school in the next half hour, then I'm skipping downstairs.

"Morning, Gran," I sing as I head for the coffeemaker.

She looks up at me over her newspaper. "Good mornin', darlin'."

I pour some coffee into a mug, take a big sip, then lean against the counter to look at my grandmother. "Any big plans for today, Gran?"

"Goin' down to city hall and filin' those papers to change your name, then I have a meetin' at the church before bingo." She smiles.

"Always so busy, Little Miss Popular," I tease, and she laughs.

"Your uncle called again for you. Are you goin' to speak to him soon?" she asks, her voice suddenly serious.

My stomach has turned, though, thinking about the fact that my uncle stood by while my parents killed their friend, and then let them pin it on someone else. Not to mention, he's been complicit in lying to me for my entire life.

"I don't know," I say, because I don't. It isn't just that he's been lying to me, it's that I thought we were genuinely close before my parents died, and he just let me get shipped off, away from my life, when he could have taken me in. "It's just too much, Gran. I don't want to deal with it."

She holds a hand out for me, and I take it so she can run her fingers over my knuckles. "I won't live forever, darlin'. You need family."

I shake my head and laugh. "Don't get dark on me now."

She squeezes my hand. "Tell me you'll think about it, Sage. Family is important."

Nodding, I smile, trying to reassure her. "I promise I'll think about it. Now… can I go to school?"

She stands, wrapping her arms around me. "I love you, Sage Grace. I'm glad you came to Blackmore."

My eyes tingle with moisture, so I blink back the tears. "Me, too, Gran."

———

The first half of my day goes by in a blur—midterms are next week, so every class consists of cramming information into my brain and making sure I'm ready to ace my tests.

After English, I find Juliet by her locker, her hood up and her face in a book.

"Boo!" I sneak up behind her, but I don't manage to frighten her. She just lifts her head slowly and raises an eyebrow at me.

"Was that supposed to scare me?"

I roll my eyes and lean against the lockers. "Yes."

She shakes her head, but she doesn't laugh. "You'd have to actually be threatening to scare me."

I hold my hands up in mock surrender. "Okay, Captain Grumpy. What crawled up your ass?"

She sighs, tossing her books into her locker and slamming it shut. "Just a bad day. A bad *life.*"

My brows furrow. "What's going on?"

"Don't worry about it. You would never understand." She throws her backpack over her shoulder before she turns the other way. "I'm gonna skip. See you later."

"Wait!" I grab her shoulder and pull her back, this whole interaction not feeling right or normal for us. "Jules, what's going on? Talk to me."

Shaking me off, she steps just far enough away that I can't grab her again. "Believe me, *Blackmore*, you're the last person I want to talk to about this."

My soul feels sad at how she's treating me, and my face burns with confusion. "Juliet, what the fuck? Did I do something?"

She stares at me for a moment, then she shakes her head and turns away, heading for the exit. I decide to let her this time, not wanting to push her too much, and even though I'm confused beyond belief, I can understand being in a bad mood and taking it out on my friends.

I've done it so many times over the last few months. Maybe Juliet is just having one of those days... maybe I just need to give her the space she's obviously showing me she needs.

I can't help feeling rejected and upset, though, as I turn to walk to class, wondering why my one and only friend has turned on me out of nowhere.

CHAPTER 9

BECKHAM

I LEAN AGAINST THE LOCKERS, STARING AT VINNY WHILE HE talks about some football shit, pretending I'm listening but actually daydreaming about putting him on his knees.

"I mean, I know we had a great defense; we just weren't solid enough to protect ourselves against Douglas. They *are* the best team in the state, but I just thought we had a shot this year," Vinny is saying, all the while I'm growing hard in my pants while I picture his wide mouth and thick lips dripping with a mixture of saliva and cum.

"I'll never get a football scholarship now. It was a long shot to begin with, and who wants to recruit someone from Blackmore anyway? The college scouts spend all their time in Atlanta."

I wonder if he would be down to skip class, go to my house, and fuck all day until we both can't hold ourselves up anymore.

"Becks? Are you listening to me?" he asks, and I realize he's staring right at me, his green eyes curious.

"What?" I stand up straight. "Of course I am, V. Go on."

His brows lower, and he puts the back of his hand against my cheek. "Your face is all flushed. Are you feeling okay?"

I grin, taking this as my opening. "Maybe we should go home."

"What?" He chuckles, turning and closing his locker. "What's wrong with you?"

I grab onto his arm, squeezing the soft flesh between my fingers. "I want to nut so bad."

He chokes out a laugh, running his hand through his hair. "B, keep it together."

"I can't," I grit between my teeth, stepping closer to him. "I checked Kai's location this morning around five—he was still at Sage's. Do you think that means he's done playing games and she's finally ours? Or do you think he was using her? I can't get it off my mind, and no matter how I twist it, I get so fucking turned on I want to explode."

"Okay," Vinny says, dropping his voice and looking at me through hooded eyes. "Just try to get through today, and tonight we can get it all out of your system."

I sigh softly, closing my eyes and digging my fingers into his arm. "Okay."

I hear Kai walk up behind us then, so I let go of Vinny and take a step back while making eye contact with him.

"What're you guys doing?" Kai asks, holding on to the straps of his backpack, dropping a shoulder against the lockers.

"Where were you this morning?" Vinny asks him, his brows rising. "Did you see Sage last night?"

"Yeah," he answers ominously, his dark eyes filled with secrets.

"Well, what happened?" I ask, desperate for dirty details that will turn me on even more, push me even further into the madness that is my libido since Halloween. I chew on my lip. "Did you fuck her?"

"Becks," Kai grunts. "Get ahold of yourself, please. Your fucking dick is hard."

I look down at the front of my pants, then a laugh bursts from my chest. My whole body shakes as I laugh at myself, and my own laughter sets off Vinny's and Kai's as well.

When the bell rings overhead, signaling we're late for second period, Kai shakes his head and stands up straighter. "C'mon, let's find somewhere to skip."

Vinny looks at me curiously, but grabs onto my arm and pulls me after him as he follows Kai down the hall. We make our way through the main academic building, outside and into the arts building, then into the empty theater.

Kai leads us to the back of the stage, through the wings and into a large room they use to store props and sets, then he throws his bag down onto the floor and drops onto his ass.

Slamming the door behind me, I eye my friends. "What're we doing? This is our class period with Sage."

"I know," Kai says, pulling a bottle of water from his backpack and taking the cap off. "I want to keep her on her toes a little."

"What does that mean?" Vinny asks, tossing his bag down on the floor. "Didn't you fix shit with her last night?"

"I mean…" Kai drinks some water, replaces the cap, then gives us a shit-eating smile. "We fucked, sure, but that doesn't mean the bitch is my girlfriend. I want her to remember how unimportant she is."

My hand curls into a fist. "Are you *serious*?"

Vinny scoffs, shaking his head and sitting down. "You're something fucking else, Kaiden."

"Watch it," Kai sneers. "Don't forget who the fuck is in charge here."

I finally rip my backpack off and throw it to the ground. "*Fuck you, Kai!* You said you would fucking get her back into our lives, and you're still doing this alpha-macho-asshole-douchebag *shit* when you know deep down you fucking love her just like we do!"

Kai's eyes narrow, and he bends his knees so he can rest his arm on them. "*Love?!* Don't be a fucking idiot, Beckham."

Frustration barrels through me. "*Stop fucking lying!* You can feel it too, I know you can. I know you want her in our lives!"

Vinny puts a hand on my shoulder when Kai jumps up and stalks toward me, his face a mask of anger. "*Watch. It.*"

"No!" I shake Vinny off, stepping into Kai's face and pushing his chest with both hands. But I don't have a chance to say anything else, because he moves closer and punches me clean across the face, knocking my head to the side.

Blood drips down the side of my mouth, and I slowly turn to look back at Kaiden, anger simmering in my veins so hot that I can barely breathe. I spit blood onto the floor, then chuckle as I shove his chest with both hands. "*Admit it.* You want her."

He punches me again, making me grunt.

"Shut the fuck up, Beckham. You don't know what the fuck you're talking about," Kai growls, cracking his knuckles.

Laughing, I look at his pretty, tanned face across the five feet that separate us, shaking my head and licking my bloody lip. "I know you better than anyone, Kai. You've been my brother since we were in fucking Pre-K. I know when someone has gotten under your skin."

Kai steps up to me again, pulling his arm back to drive another punch into me, but Vinny pulls me back by the shoulders and steps between us, making him freeze.

"Enough," Vinny breathes. "*Please.*"

"You two can do whatever you want," Kaiden says softly. "I'm not talking about this anymore."

I start to protest, but Vinny turns around and gives me a look—one that says *back off for now*, and it makes me bite my tongue. Because maybe I need to, maybe I'm so caught up in craving Sage that I'm ruining the most important relationship in my life—the one with my brother, the person who has been there for me longer than anyone else.

"Okay," I concede, meeting Kai's eye over Vinny's shoulder.

Kai steps backwards, a cocky grin gracing his face now because he *won*, and my chest tightens. Instead of fighting again, though, I just keep my mouth shut and shake off Vinny's hold, walking across the room and sitting down on the floor.

———

BY THE TIME WE'RE HEADING TO LUNCH, I'M STILL A BALL OF pent-up sexual tension mixed with anger and resentment. I skip the line for food, and just sit down at our usual table, putting my head on the surface. Vinny and Kai sit on either side of me in the next few minutes, food in hand, and start up a meaningless conversation while they eat.

"You okay, B?" Vinny asks after a moment, running a hand down my forearm under the table.

Lifting my head, I nod and sigh through my mouth, "Fine."

"Still angry at me?" Kai asks, his eyebrow lifting in question at the same time his lips curl into a grin.

Before I can answer him, I spot Sage walk into the cafeteria behind his head, and my stomach sours. Vinny sees her too, looking over at the doors, and that makes Kai turn around to see what we're staring at. He sighs when he sees her, then turns back to look at us.

She's alone—so it seems that Juliet is out sick again, and I silently hope that she finds the confidence to come over and sit with us. But she doesn't glance in our direction, just stands in the line for food and gets lost in her phone while she waits.

"Don't say a goddamn word," Kai says softly, eyeing me as he puts his food down and stands up.

"What're you doing?" Vinny asks, but Kai ignores him and starts walking across the cafeteria.

He reaches a crowded table, then leans down into the ear of his previous hook-up and says something. Stephanie laughs, slapping him away, then he grabs her hand as he stands up straight again.

Before I can comprehend what he's doing, she stands up and walks across the room with him.

When Kai reaches our table, he sits back down in his vacant seat, then he pulls Stephanie down onto his lap and curls his hands around her waist.

"What are you doing?" I growl, knowing he's going to push Sage's buttons.

"Making a point," Kai answers, dipping his head into Stephanie's neck as he pushes her hair over her shoulder.

Stephanie is gorgeous, and she's used to Kai's shit. Besides her dark hair and tan skin, she is the opposite to everything Kai is—she's bright and flourishes, shining with positivity from every edge. But for some reason, she's tangled herself in Kai's twisted web, maybe for the thrill of it. I think maybe she just does it to piss off her boyfriend, who's always around the corner, watching the king of the Hallows Boys with his hands on his girl.

Whatever gets them going, who am I to judge?

"This isn't a good fucking idea, Kai." I lean forward, glaring at him and hoping he stops this shit before Sage notices.

"*Don't*," he bites out, looking at me for a second before he leans back into Stephanie's neck.

"Oh boy," Vinny says from my side, a small laugh catching in his throat. "Here we go."

I glance up in time to notice Sage looking over at us from the cashier at the end of the line, her face morphed into jealousy and something that looks a lot like humor.

"Oh, Jesus Christ." I shake with a laugh, even though I want to fly across the table and knock Kai out.

Sage strides across the room, and it seems like she's been switched into slow motion. Her steps are calm and calculated, like a vicious lioness stalking her prey, but instead of pouncing when she reaches Kai, she just drops her food down on the table and sits down next to him.

He doesn't look up from his spot in Stephanie's neck, instead he slides his hands up her thighs and squeezes. Becks and I sit in silence, watching as Sage's mouth twists into a malicious smile, and she reaches over, tapping Kai on the shoulder.

"Excuse me." She clears her throat, and Kai looks up at her through hooded eyes. "Did I not make things clear enough last night?"

Kai lifts his face, mock confusion glistening in his eyes. "What?"

Sage grins, and she leans forward to spit her next words in Kai's face. "You're done with *this*. You're *mine*."

Laughing, Kai threads his hands through Stephanie's hair and twists her head to the side, then he kisses her neck.

Vin groans, sliding his hand to mine under the table and squeezing.

Sage stands, steps behind Kai, and places her hand on top of his in Stephanie's hair. "I'm going to give you three seconds, girl. If you aren't off his lap by then, I'm ripping this pretty hair from your head."

Stephanie looks up at Sage, not taking her seriously. "Are you joking? He clearly doesn't want me to."

Sage laughs, and Kai shakes with laughter too, like it's one big joke that they're in on.

"One," Sage says, smiling.

Stephanie doesn't move, and Kai's hand tightens in her hair. "Two."

"Okay, okay!" Stephanie says, shaking her head until Kai lets go of her. "This isn't fucking worth it."

"*What?*" Kai snaps. "Don't you dare get up."

"Dude." Stephanie laughs, standing up. "The sex is good and all, but I'm not tryna get my ass beat over you. It's not like you're my boyfriend."

As Stephanie walks back to her table, Kai shoots up from his seat and spins around, coming face to face with a satisfied Sage.

"What the *fuck* do you think you're doing?" he breathes, careful not to raise his voice.

Sage steps around him, ignoring his silent rage, sitting down again and opening her salad. I catch her eye across the table, and I smile. She grins at me and Vinny, asking sweetly, "How's your day going?"

We both laugh, but don't dare answer.

Kai is still standing, his chest rising and falling so quickly that he could be having a heart attack. Hands snapping out, he grabs Sage by the arm and yanks her up. "Get up and let's go."

CHAPTER 10

SAGE

I GROAN FROM THE PINCH OF PAIN IN MY ARM AS KAI YANKS ME from my seat.

"Get up and let's go."

Chuckling, I twist around and press my nose against his, speaking between my gritted teeth. "Let go of me so I can eat my lunch. I'm fucking hungry."

He grins. "I'll throw you over my shoulder and carry you out of here, if you want."

I don't know where I found the confidence to act on my jealousy today, but when I saw that girl on Kaiden's lap, I just saw red. It feels as if the last few weeks have been a year long—from Halloween to now, it's all blended together and stretched out at once. I've shed skin and grown into someone else, someone my parents wouldn't recognize, someone who feels brand fucking new and like coming home all at once.

And the Hallows Boys feel like part of my real identity. If I need to piss all over them like a fucking dog to mark my territory, *I will.*

Licking my lips, I smile at Kaiden as I turn and start walking across the cafeteria, his hand squeezing my bicep as he follows. I let him lead me from behind, and he guides me through the hall and into one of the classrooms that's dark and empty.

After he slams the door shut behind us, he lets go of my arm, and I spin around to face him.

His expression is a wash of anger, from his brows to his lip, where his teeth are digging into the flesh. Before he says anything, he looks to his left for a moment before he grabs a chair, securing it under the door handle so no one can come in.

When he looks back at me, my stomach fills with nerves.

We stare at each other for a moment before he stalks closer, his eyes molten and sharp jaw ticking. I step backwards, feeling scared and excited and nervous, heart racing and skin flushing.

"Do you think you're funny, Sage?" Kaiden asks, cocking his head to the side as he continues to walk me across the room.

"Not particularly," I answer with a twist to my lips, backing up until my ass hits the wall.

Clicking his tongue, he steps into my space, and the smell of him engulfs my senses, making me feel dizzy. He breathes slowly for a heartbeat, then he slides his hand to the top of my head and pushes. "On your knees."

"What?" I spit, standing strong.

"Get on your fucking knees," he grits out between his teeth. "Don't make me say it again."

Reluctantly, I drop to my knees and look up at him through my lashes. "What are you doing?"

He grips onto my hair tighter with one hand, then uses the other to undo his pants. "Take my dick out."

"What?" I ask again, and he yanks on my hair.

"You want to make some big display in the cafeteria to stake your fucking claim over me?" He wraps a hand around my neck, his gaze clashing with mine. "Then you'll take care of me like I'm fucking *yours*."

I swallow hard, staring up at him, but I don't move. Too nervous and hesitant that maybe he's fucking with me, trying to prove a point that he doesn't belong to me, and the thought makes me burn with anger.

Sliding my hand inside his pants, I find his dick hard and hot. I maintain eye contact while I pull him free from his pants, then I wrap my hand around his length, pumping my fist a few times. "What do you want, Kaiden?"

He smirks at me from above. "Sit up straight and open your mouth."

My gut tightens with need as I do as I'm told, putting my back flat against the wall and dropping my mouth open. Kaiden slides his hand around my jaw, using his thumb to pull my mouth open farther.

"Hands behind your back," he grunts, his cock slipping from my hold as I do as he says. Looking up at him through my lashes, I blink a few times and wait for my next instruction. His thumb grazes over my bottom lip as he smiles. "Good girl. Tongue out and widen your jaw."

Sliding my tongue out, I widen my mouth and wait.

Kaiden drops down to a crouch, then spits between my open lips, the wad of saliva finding its new home on my tongue, then he stands up abruptly and slides his cock into my mouth.

I start to pull back when the head of his dick hits the back of my throat, but his hand slides into my hair. "Don't fucking move."

Freezing, I flick my eyes up and find him staring at me from above, his dark eyes angry and hot, making my panties dampen.

His hips pull back, giving me relief from my gag reflex, but it's short-lived. He quickly slides back down into my throat, a small groan shaking through his chest. I don't move, just watch the best I can while Kaiden fucks my face, desperately happy that pleasure is spreading through his body because of me.

His legs tense as a groan falls from his lips on his next thrust, and he pushes even farther down my throat this time, making me shiver as I gag.

I try to pull away, but he holds me in place, pushing his pelvis against my face hard enough that the wall digs into the back of my head.

"Don't. Fucking. Move," He grunts, yanking on my hair. "Choke on my dick. Fucking choke."

I gag over and over, desperate for oxygen as his thick cock fills my mouth and throat. Tears stream from my eyes, mascara making them burn and blur. Audibly choking, I try to swallow around his thick length to relieve some of the pressure, but he's too deep in my throat, and I end up gargling on saliva and pushing oxygen farther from reach.

Kaiden's fingers squeeze through the strands of my hair as he pulls his hips back, giving me access to oxygen. I heave, coughing and swallowing roughly before he pushes back down my throat.

"You're so fucking beautiful," he groans, pulling my hair so hard that I worry it may rip from my scalp. When he pulls his hips back again, I look up at him through tear-filled eyes and gasp around the head of his cock. "You like my big fat cock in your throat, baby?"

Nodding, I slide back down his length, suctioning around him and pulling him back into my sore throat.

"Ah, fuck," he groans, getting lost in the sensation of my tongue swirling around his shaft. His head goes back, and I find the confidence to smooth my hands up his thighs to feel his muscles tense.

A moan vibrates through my throat, and Kaiden moans

loud and long from above me, so the next time I do it, I also slide my hand between his legs to grip his balls. When he grunts and groans, I feel a smile tugging at my spread lips.

He pushes down my throat in time for his orgasm to rock through him, and the back of my head slams against the wall painfully. He spurts so much cum into my throat that, even as I try to swallow it all, it pools and spills from the side of my lips and down my chin.

His hand is tight in my hair, holding me in place as he shakes through his climax, and I revel in the feeling of him at the most vulnerable he can be—at my mercy and relying on me for the pure, delicious release he craves.

"*Fucking hell,*" he moans, his legs stiff as his cock softens in my mouth. When he pulls out, he drops down and looks deep into my eyes before he wipes his thumb around the outside of my lips. "My dirty fucking slut."

My nipples are rocks beneath my bra, and my panties are slick with need, so I quickly suction around his thumb before he can pull it away, savoring the taste of his skin coated in the cum I let slip from my lips. I find his eyes, dark and wild and bloodshot, as I suck around his thumb, then I press my teeth into his flesh and moan.

When he pulls his thumb from my lips, I grab his hand before he can stand up. "Kaiden, *touch me.*"

He grins as he circles my jaw with his palm. "My pathetic little slut needs me to fuck her?"

Nodding, I drop my eyes closed as he leans into my neck and licks a line up to my ear. I moan when he pulls the lobe in between his teeth and sucks on it.

"Dirty fucking sluts who stake their claim in the middle of the cafeteria don't get orgasms. They get used for a nut and left on the ground where they belong," he growls softly, then he stands up to walk away.

My eyes fly open, and I rise to my feet, desperation simmering in my veins. "I'll have one of your friends take care of me then. They'll have no problem doing it."

Kaiden turns slowly to look at me, and I know I've struck a nerve when he rubs his palms together, and then he starts cracking his knuckles one by one. He laughs, but the noise carries no humor. "You think I care?"

"Yes," I answer without thinking, knowing I'm pushing my luck with the manic sociopath in front of me. "I think it drives you mad that your friends get to touch me and fuck me too."

He smiles from ear to ear, and a chill runs down my spine. "Oh, Sage. I know it's my cock you think about in the darkness of your bedroom when you spread your pussy open and impale yourself on your fingers. You think I'm some insecure little boy? It doesn't make a difference to me if you fuck every man in town; it'll still be me on your mind at the end of the day."

I smirk, taking a small step toward him. "Actually, it's Beckham and Vinny, both of them together, like on Halloween. One in my pussy and one in my ass. You've never made me come like that."

He grits his teeth, making his jaw sharp and more pronounced, and we stand in silence, staring at one another for a painfully slow half-minute.

When I start to think I've gone too far, he grabs me by the shoulders, slamming me up against the wall hard. "Don't. Fuck. With. Me. Sage."

I moan, grinning as my head rolls against the wall. "What's wrong, Kaiden? I thought you didn't ca—"

His hand grips my throat, pressing against my windpipe painfully, cutting my sentence short. Face rippling with anger and possession, he uses his hand and arm like a leash to pull me across the room, then he releases me and pushes me face down onto a desk.

In the next second, he's ripping my pants and underwear down my legs and slapping his palm down on my ass cheek.

I yell, lifting upwards, but he presses against the back of my head to hold me down. When he slaps my bare ass again, a scream rips through my throat.

"Someone's going to hear you screaming," he says, spanking me again. "They'll come in here and see your pussy dripping all over the floor for me."

I squeeze my lips together when he spanks the same spot on my ass again and again, and a powerful moan ripples through my body. "*Kaiden!*"

He chuckles, pushing his hand against my ass and spreading me the best he can with one hand. "What's wrong, Sage? I thought you wanted me to touch you."

I whimper, feeling dizzy and overstimulated and under stimulated all at once. "Kai, please. *Please.*"

He slides a finger through my ass, downwards until he's pressing into my pussy. "So fucking wet, my desperate fucking girl. Tell me what you want."

I cry out, pressing back against his finger, but it isn't enough, just a small thrum of pleasure pulsing through my core. "You, Kaiden. *More. Please.*"

He pulls back, and I hear how wet I am when he pushes two fingers into me this time. Moaning, I grind my ass back against his hand.

As he rubs his fingers against my G-spot, I cry out. "You still want more?"

I nod against the surface of the desk, breathing hard and gripping the edge with one hand. "*Yes.*"

He pulls his fingers free, and a second later, I feel the head of his cock pressing against my entrance. "How about my dick? Is that what you want?"

I push back against him again, trying to get him to slip

inside me, and he laughs before he slaps my ass. "So obsessed with my big fucking dick, my little play toy."

"Stand up and turn around. I want to see you."

I do as he says, spinning and placing my ass against the edge of the desk and meeting his gaze with my own.

"Look at you." He rubs his thumb over my cheek. "So fucking *desperate*."

"*Kaiden*," I moan, reaching down to push my pants and underwear over my ankles before I sit down. Spreading my legs wide, I lift them and wrap them around him, using my hands to grab at his shirt and pull him into me. "Fuck me."

He groans, stroking his cock before he leans forward and impales me. I release a loud moan, and his mouth comes down on mine to silence me, kissing me harshly as his hips start thrusting hard and fast.

While his cock tortures my center, his tongue swirls around my mouth, and his hands slide up into my hair so I can't pull away from him. I'm completely at his mercy, desperate and hungry for my orgasm. Part of me hates how weak and small that makes me compared to him right now, but fuck it. *I don't think I care.*

Where Kaiden is the king of my pleasure, I'm the queen of his, and together we ride each other through our passion and need for control, meeting each other at the finish line.

I scream as my climax rocks through me, turning me to a twitching, solid mass of muscle, then his cock is swelling and pulsing inside me.

Pulling away from my mouth to whisper filthy words against my lips, he's right back to kissing me, feeding on my moans.

My hands find his back, and I yank him closer, tightening my legs around his waist, wanting to secure him against every part of me while we both ride out our orgasms together.

He breathes into me and moans my name, his hands

squeezing into my hair, making me gasp from the sting. "My perfect fucking girl, always giving me exactly what I need."

His praise has me coming harder, my skin moistening with sweat as pleasure shoots through my center and makes me feel lighter than the clouds in heaven. "I'll always do whatever you need, Kai. I just need *you* in return."

A loud moan ricochets from his chest, then he's kissing me hard enough that my teeth shake and my jaw aches.

His hand cups my face, and he pulls his mouth from mine as our climaxes both dissipate. "Again."

My chest heaves. "What?"

"Say you need me again," he growls, and I find his eyes wild and manic.

Swallowing, I kiss his mouth softly and tighten my arms around his body. "You know that I need you, Kaiden. You're my miserable, hateful, terrifying dick, and you complete me."

His grip moves from my cheek to the back of my hair, and his mouth comes crashing down on mine once more, his cock growing hard and throbbing inside of me again. I have a feeling no one has ever told Kaiden that they need him before, especially when he thrusts inside of me slowly and his thumb finds my clit, pulling euphoria from my body in a way only he can—telling me he needs me back in the only way he knows how.

CHAPTER 11

VINNY

Kai doesn't return to lunch, and neither does Sage.

Neither of them show their faces in school for the rest of the day, so by the time the final bell rings, Becks is a ball of sexual tension and jealousy.

"C'mon." I grab his shoulder and slide my hand down his arm. "We can go to my house. My dad will be at the bar."

Nodding, his gaze finds mine, and I get sucked into the dark blue abyss of his eyes. I can see he's on the brink of losing it. I grab his hand and lead him along the hallway, not caring that there's people around, and when we finally make it outside, I hear him take a deep breath in.

"You okay?" I ask, walking through the quad at his side.

"I'm just pissed off, V." He sighs, rubbing his hand down his face. "He treats Sage like shit, and then drags her away and spends the day with her? It isn't okay. He's driving me fucking crazy."

I sigh, looking out into the cold afternoon. "You know how

he is, B, and you need to remember that not everyone is as comfortable with their feelings as you."

"What's that supposed to mean?" he growls.

Shaking my head, I chuckle. "You're loving, soft. But Kai isn't. He's hard, and he's never loved anyone before."

"I've never loved anyone either. It's not like we've ever looked outside our circle before." He huffs. "But I can still be nice to the person I'm fucking."

We've reached the road, and it's mostly empty, so I grab his arm and pull him toward me, lifting an accusatory brow. "You've never loved anyone?"

He laughs, small dimples popping into his cheeks as he looks at me through his lashes. "You know what I mean."

I hold him close. "You and me, B, we've always had each other, but Kai has never had someone. Let him learn how to accept Sage into his heart, and then everything will fall into place, I promise. Be patient."

Beckham takes a breath, then pushes my hair back with his fingers. "Okay."

Smiling, I lean forward and kiss his mouth quickly before pulling away and walking down the road again. "We can have a movie night to distract you. I'll even let you pick the pizza toppings."

He grabs my hand, slipping his fingers through mine to hold as we walk the rest of the way. The air is crisp, even under the sun, which is still hanging high in the sky. Thanksgiving is right around the corner, and I'm dreading it, just like every year. My dad usually spends the holiday break drowning in whiskey with a side of beer and angry punching. Instead of risking spending the days inside the house with him, I've always gone between Kai's and Becks' houses.

Except on the actual holiday, since that day is reserved for the cemetery.

The cold graveyard is more than home on those days—days where family is supposed to be at the forefront and happiness is supposed to warm my bones through the winter chill. I've had a handful of *good* holidays over the years, only ones where Beckham and Kaiden made it special for me.

By the time we reach the beginning of my neighborhood, Beckham lets go of my hand and gives me a sweet smile, knowing I was about to release his hand myself, just in case my father or anyone we know is around.

Where I have no shame when it comes to my sexuality, or my feelings for Becks, it's just easier to keep my private life *private* while I'm under the same roof as a psychopath with anger issues and a conservative viewpoint.

I'm thankful that my father's truck isn't in the driveway when we reach my house, and I lead Becks inside without bothering to put my mental guards up for once.

There's a layer of safety I feel when Beckham is here, like maybe even if my father came home at any moment, everything would still be okay because he's here with me.

Becks follows me to my bedroom and kicks his shoes off while I close the door behind us. He groans, tossing his backpack down on the floor. "I want to take a nap."

Dropping down onto my bed, he curls under the blankets and looks over at me, heat lining his eyes. His voice goes soft as he asks, "Want to sleep with me, baby?"

Nodding, I drop my backpack and kick off my shoes before I go to the window to draw the blinds to make the room darker. Pulling my shirt over my head, I throw it to the floor, then climb under the blankets.

"Scoot over," I say, pushing against Beckham to gain more space on the bed.

"No." He grins, lifting his leg and putting it over my hip so he can wiggle closer.

"I thought you wanted to sleep." I chuckle, pushing him until he rolls onto his back and I land on top of him between his thighs. Pressing my mouth against his, I breathe hard and grind my hips, letting him feel my cock, which has grown heavy in the front of my pants. "What do you want, B?"

He moans, his hands sliding into my short hair while his tongue slips between my lips. My stomach burns with hunger, and my dick fills with blood as I kiss him back.

After a moment, we pull apart, our chests heaving.

"I want you," Beckham breathes against my mouth, his hand lowering between us to grip my dick roughly.

Beckham and I have such an intense connection, that it's like the whole world moves in a blurry light, speeding all around us when we're in heated moments together. We're both pieces of one soul, moving together in a way that's messy and chaotic and flawless all at once.

I flex my hips, letting him feel how hard I am under the confines of my pants. "You want me to fuck you, B? Make you come so hard that you can't fucking see straight?"

Groaning, he pops the button on my pants and slides the zipper down so he can reach under the fabric and wrap his fingers around my length. "Yeah, baby. I want you to fuck me so hard I feel you for a week."

I leak precum against his hand, my hips rolling into him to gain friction. "Get up. Put me in your mouth."

He's quick to wriggle from underneath me, pushing on my chest so I sit back on my knees, then rips my pants under my ass so my dick is free.

Sliding down onto his forearms in front of me, he suctions around the head of my cock, pulling a moan from my lips. I look down at him, sliding my hand into the curly black hair that's grown wild on top of his head. "Fuck, Becks."

He moans around me, then slides his mouth farther until

he's choking on my length. My eyes roll back at the sensation, and my fingers pull his hair so tight that his hand squeezes my thigh for a second.

After bobbing his head a few times, he pops off and sits up to kiss me. His dick is rock solid in the front of his pants, and I take the opportunity to unfasten them and yank them down.

Beckham leans back, rips his shirt over his head, then sits up and pulls his pants and boxers off, throwing them to the floor.

"How do you want me, baby?" he asks, wrapping a hand around his own cock and pumping a few times, his muscular stomach flexing.

Licking my lips, I trace every inch of him with my gaze, memorizing how he looks when he's at my mercy, then I pull the rest of my clothes off and toss them onto the floor.

"On your back, spread open for me," I groan, watching as he moves into the position I've asked for, then I lean forward and suck his cock down in one swift movement.

"Jesus, V," Beckham breathes, his head falling back against the headboard.

When I pull off his cock, I grab him by the knees and spread him up and open so I can lick down to his asshole, using my tongue to flick against the puckered hole until he's a whimpering mess underneath me. When his back arches, and his hand threads into my hair desperately, I slide a finger through the wetness my mouth has created and press into his ass.

A moan ripples through him, and his ass clamps down on my finger.

"Relax, babe," I say, spitting onto his ass as I pull out and plunge two inside this time. Thrusting my fingers, I stretch his ass out enough to fit another finger, then he's whimpering and grinding against me again.

"*V...*" he moans, his voice breathy and needy. "Fuck me."

I slowly remove my fingers from inside him, then I spit onto his asshole before I sit up on my knees in front of him. "I don't have any lube here, so my spit will have to do."

His hand is moving wildly on his cock, and I grin down at him as I push his legs farther up until his feet are hovering in the air and I can slide my dick through his crack.

"Take a breath for me, B," I say, pressing against his asshole with the head of my cock.

"Spit again," he says, then he takes a breath as I slowly release a trail of saliva from my mouth to the head of my cock.

Before he can say anything else, I slip through the ring of muscle until my dick is engulfed in him.

We both moan loudly, and my hands grip onto his thighs as I slowly push deeper and deeper.

"*Vinny,*" Beckham whimpers. "Harder."

Thrusting my hips with more force, I find Beckham's deep blue eyes, so filled with desire and pleasure and love, and my cock throbs inside him, loving every second I get to spend with the soft, sexy, amazing guy beneath me.

"I love you," I moan, using a hand to pull his face to mine so I can kiss him.

"Me, too, baby," he moans after we've pulled our mouths apart. "You mean fucking everything to me."

Pleasure spreads from my head to my toes as I fuck him, my cock thrusting in and out of him so beautifully that I can't help but move faster, harder, more passionately. Then I'm using my hand to grip his cock and pump the same way my hips are moving, bringing him closer to his climax so we can come together.

Heat spreads down my spine, my balls pull up, and then I'm shouting out my orgasm, pounding my hips against his ass as lust takes over my vision at the same time my hand pumps his orgasm from him, his hot cum shooting up and onto me from below.

"Fuck, fuck, fuck, fuck," I chant, kissing him hard.

"Vinny, *baby*," he moans, his fingers threading into my hair as we both gasp through our releases, then we're both falling into a pile of lifeless limbs and heaving chests.

"What the fuck is going on here?!"

My father's voice cracks through the room like splintering thunder, making adrenaline burst through my system at a speed that almost kills me. I lunge to the side of Beckham, using my comforter to cover both of our naked bodies from his view.

When I connect with his hateful gaze in my doorframe, I'm met with green eyes that match my own, except they're bloodshot and filled with so much malice they could paralyze someone.

"Dad! What are you doing here?" I yell, scrambling for words through my pounding heartbeat.

His voice crashes through the room again, every other word a slur. *"What am I doing here?* I fucking live here, you worthless piece of shit. Get the fuck up, Vincent! Get your fucking ass up *now!"*

I leap from the bed, grabbing my boxers and pulling them up my legs. "Dad, listen, I can explain."

"Explain?!" He huffs, walking deeper into my room on wobbly legs. "I'll fucking kill you. I will not have a son who's a fa—"

I cut him off before he can spit the word, not because I'm shocked, but because I'm embarrassed. "Dad!"

Putting myself in front of Becks as a shield, I bend down to pick up his boxers and toss them to him.

"Dad, just—" I start to scramble, but my words are taken from me by his fist, which swings out and knocks me across the face three times in a row, sending a cracking noise from my jaw through my ears. I grunt, blood shooting from my mouth and landing on the floor.

"What the fuck!" Beckham shouts from behind me, then he's shoving me back onto the bed and jumping on my dad, screaming at the top of his lungs while his fists fly, slamming against my father's face over and over until they're both falling to the floor in a pile.

"Becks!" I scream, out of breath, leaping forward and grabbing him by the shoulders to rip him away from my dad.

He spins around, his fists dripping with my father's blood and his face manic as red covers his vision and anger simmers right on the surface. I swallow hard, then he pushes me away and turns to face my dad again, who's now lying helpless on the ground.

Beckham spits down onto my father, then moves again, using his powerful legs to kick his torso until my father is gargling on blood.

"Don't you ever fucking touch him again!" he shouts, then kicks my father in the ribs.

"He isn't yours to fucking hurt!" He kicks him in the chest.

"*You're* a worthless piece of shit!" His foot connects with my father's throat.

Then Becks is straddling him again, throwing his fists against his face as he continues to scream. "You'll never fucking hurt him again! You can't fucking hurt him anymore! He isn't yours to fucking hurt!"

I jump up, grab him by the shoulders, and pull him off my dad, making both of us fall back to the floor. "Beckham, Beckham, Beckham! *Stop.*"

He has tears coating his cheeks, and he's shaking violently as he gasps for air. "He can't fucking hurt you anymore. He can't hurt you. He can't hurt you anymore."

"Becks," I whisper, pulling him to my chest and covering his broken, bloody knuckles with my palms. "It's okay."

CHAPTER 12

KAIDEN

I'M NINE INCHES DEEP INTO SAGE'S PUSSY WHEN MY PHONE rings, vibrating across the table I have her bent over. I pull back, then push back inside her while I reach over and grab it, seeing Vinny's name on the screen.

"You better not answer that," Sage warns, and my hand slides into her hair as I silence the call. Pulling her head back, I pound into her from behind.

"Don't worry, Little Rabbit. Nothing could pull me away from this delicious cunt."

She's a mess of moans underneath me, and I can feel my orgasm pulling my balls up simply from the depth of this position.

We've been doing nothing but fucking for the last few hours, and we're both a mess of sweat, cum, and scratch marks. Sage has come so many times already that I'm surprised she's still able to hold herself upright.

"Kaiden, fuck, don't stop."

I smack her ass, then spit into her crack. Using my thumb, I spread my saliva around her asshole, then I slip the digit through the ring of muscle. "Come for me, you little fucking slut, I want to fuck this tight ass."

My phone goes off again, and as I buck against Sage from behind, I grab it and spot Vinny's name on the screen again. I silence it once more, then Sage's climax takes over her body, her cunt squeezing around me and making it nearly impossible to keep moving inside her.

"Jesus. Christ," I grunt out, trying to move my hips as hard as possible while Sage shakes against the table. My phone goes off again, ringing loudly.

"Kaiden! Turn it the fuck off!" Sage screams, banging her hands on the table while she rides out the rest of her climax.

Laughing at her, I grab my phone and see Vinny's name across the screen once more.

I slam my cock deep into Sage and accept the call.

"What?!"

Sage shouts from the force, her back bending up and her head craning so she can bite my neck. "You've got to be kidding."

I'm more focused on the noises I'm hearing through the phone, though. Sniffling, crying, heavy breathing. Then Vinny's voice breaks through, my name scratching up his throat. "*Kaiden?*"

"What is it?" I go still, holding my phone tighter, and Sage seems to read in my body language that something is wrong, because she pushes me back a step so I'm no longer inside her and she can turn around to face me.

"You gotta get over here, Kai," Vinny says, almost inaudibly.

"What happened? What's going on?" I meet Sage's worried gaze, my heart picking up speed as anxiety hits my bloodstream.

"Please," Vinny says, and I hear crying in the background. "You just need to get over here, Kai. Right now."

"I'm on my way."

———

THANKFULLY, SAGE HAS HER CAR WITH HER, SO WE'RE ABLE TO get to Vinny's house in two minutes. I spot his father's truck in the driveway, and I'm instantly sick to my stomach, thinking that his dickhead sperm donor has spent the afternoon beating the piss out of Vincent before passing out.

I push through the front door without knocking, Sage hot on my heels, and head for the only light on in the house, which is coming from Vinny's bedroom.

I'm taken back by the scene I walk into, and I hear Sage gasp behind me as she grabs onto the back of my shirt when I stop in the doorway.

Vinny and Beckham are sitting on the floor, just at the edge of Vinny's bed, both in nothing but their boxers—and they're both wrapped around each other like they need the protection. They both have slack faces, Vinny's red and purple with blood and bruises, but both have tears on their cheeks.

At the center of Vinny's bedroom, though, is his father—in a bloody pile—*dead*.

A silent minute passes, then I walk through the room and crouch down next to my brothers.

"What happened?"

Beckham closes his eyes, shaking his head slowly, then Vinny speaks quietly, almost to no one. "He's dead."

"Yes," I say, sighing and rubbing my palms together. It's clear they're both in some trauma trance, so I give myself a moment to piece together the scene.

After I've had enough time to figure it out, I speak again.

"He attacked you, and you snapped," I say to Vinny, putting a hand on his shoulder. "It's okay. We can figure this out. He's been abusing you your whole life… It was self-defense. We can prove it. We need to call the police."

"No," he rushes out, looking up at me, his dark green eyes filled with moisture. "It wasn't me… *it was Beckham.*"

My brows raise. "What?"

Beckham is still shaking his head, his eyes pressed closed. Glancing at his bloody hands, I hiss between my teeth when I see more than one broken knuckle dripping with blood.

I jump when a hand gently wraps around my shoulder, and I turn in time to see Sage sit down to my right. She's shaking, tears dripping down her face, and her lips quivering. I wipe my palm across her cheek. "Go sit in the living room."

Shaking her head, she rubs her hands over her cheeks and sniffles. "No. I'm here, I'm okay."

I don't question her, and she crawls over the carpet to wrap her arms around Beckham's neck, who still hasn't opened his eyes. He's trembling, and she squeezes him tighter when he starts to cry, pulling his face into her neck.

Looking at Vinny and running my hand through my messy hair, I speak again. "Tell me exactly what happened."

With his fingers thread through Beckham's, he finally looks back at me and sighs. "He came in and saw us together. He attacked me, then Becks went after him."

"And fucking killed him?!" I snap, not meaning to.

"He didn't mean to…" Vinny says softly, shaking his head.

"Yes, I did." Beckham finally speaks, lifting his head out of Sage's nape and looking at Vinny with bloodshot eyes. "I meant to fucking kill the bastard. Now he can never hurt you again."

Vinny sucks down a breath, and a small laugh rolls through me. "Jesus."

Sage runs her hands over Becks' face. "Beckham…"

"Now he can never fucking hurt you again," Becks whispers again, his eyes moving between everyone.

Sighing, I stand up and walk over to the dead body in the middle of the room, then take a silent moment to study it. I've never seen a dead body before—not a real one, and parts of my stomach I didn't know existed curl as I stare at Vincent Donahue Sr.'s solid body before me. His face is drenched in blood, his own and Beckham's, but that isn't what has my mouth sweating. It's his wide-open eyes, so filled with darkness, like there's no soul left behind them—if there ever was one to begin with.

There isn't a man who deserved death more than this one, so overtaken with grief and anger that he spent the last eighteen years taking it out on his only son. I say a silent prayer for him, though, hoping Satan or God or whoever he's with now is punishing him just as viciously as he used to *punish* Vinny.

I spend one more minute staring at him, thinking over what we should do, then I spin and walk back to where my friends are still sitting on the floor.

"Sage." She snaps her chocolate brown eyes to mine. "You're going to take Beckham, get in your car, and drive until you hit Alabama. Take him to the first emergency room you find and get those hands taken care of. Say he got into a fight at school, make something up, just get him taken care of then come home."

Spinning, I look at Vinny. "You're going to come outside with me and beat the shit out of the back of the house. Fuck up your knuckles, then we're going to call the police. He attacked you, okay? It was self-defense. You have enough hospital records that no one will even question it. You're eighteen, you'll get the house, the state will pay to cremate the fucker, then we'll never think about him again. Got it?"

Vinny is nodding, but Beckham shouts before we can even

think about moving into action. "No! What if they fucking arrest him?! He didn't do this—*I did*. I won't let him go down for it."

I shoot my gaze to Beckham, who is gritting his jaw. "They aren't going to arrest him."

"Why are we going to Alabama?" Sage asks, her brows furrowing.

"Because we don't want anyone to know that Becks beat the life out of this piece of shit," I answer coolly. "*If* they decide to do some sort of investigation, there will be no trace of your injuries in the state of Georgia. They won't look any farther, if at all."

"No, we *aren't fucking doing this!*" Beckham shouts, and I see red.

"It isn't up to you," I snap. "You're *clearly* far too fucking emotional and unhinged to make rational decisions right now."

Vinny turns to face Becks, then he leans in and puts a hand on his cheek. "This is a good plan, B. Please, do this for me. I don't want to lose you."

"Can't we just bury him in the woods somewhere?" Becks asks, and I halfway hope he's joking.

A laugh rumbles through me. "*Bury him in the woods?* Do you think we're goddamn career criminals? Members of the mob? And how would Vincent explain where his father has disappeared to?"

Beckham growls, and Vinny runs his thumb over his cheekbone. "Go with Sage. Get your hand fixed, and I'll see you tonight. You were never here, okay?"

Silence falls over the room, and I search Sage's eyes as Vinny and Beckham have their moment. Like a magnetic pull, her gaze lifts to mine and a string pulls up the side of my mouth to smirk at her. Her lips twitch like she wants to smile, but she holds it back—probably too uncomfortable with the fact we're in an active crime scene, with a body that's going cold.

After a minute, Beckham sighs, and I look at him in time to see him lean forward and kiss Vincent on the mouth for a half second before he pulls away. "Alright."

I clap my hands once. "Alright."

———

BECKHAM AND SAGE HEAD FOR THE STATE LINE, AND I TAKE Vinny out behind his house to smash his knuckles into the concrete.

"I don't know if I'll be able to do this more than once," he says, eyeing me under the setting sun.

"Want me to say a bunch of stuff that will piss you off?" I ask, grinning.

He laughs, approaching the concrete. "No, thanks."

I watch as he licks his lips, takes a breath, then pulls his arm back and freezes. Blowing out a breath, then sucking another one down, he sends his fist barreling into the house. He doesn't shout as his knuckles crack against the concrete, just bites onto his lip and continues, sending his fists flying at the house until there's blood covering the dirty white concrete.

"Fuck!" he yells as he stills his arms, looking up into the sky and hissing between his teeth. "Jesus fucking Christ."

I grab his wrist carefully, examining his knuckles one by one, then I do the same to the other hand. "Pretty sure a bunch of your fingers are broken."

A sarcastic expression stares back at me. "You think so, Kaiden?"

I laugh, then smack his right hand with my palm. "Don't be a pussy."

Vinny grunts in pain, and I chuckle, turning to head inside so we can make sure there's no hint of Beckham in the house.

After changing the sheets on the bed, I toss the dirty ones in the washer and grab some paper towels before I walk back to Vinny's room, finding him sitting on the floor next to his father's lifeless body.

Clearing my throat, I step next to him. "We need to get Beckham's blood off his face."

Vinny nods as he looks up at me, then he holds a hand out for the paper towels.

"I can do it, Vin," I say softly, reading the grief on his blank face.

He snatches the paper towels from me. "Don't treat me like a little bitch who can't handle this. I hated the fucker."

Breathing through my nose, I keep my thoughts to myself as I watch Vinny wipe the blood from his father's broken face, then he tosses the paper towels to the side before he rubs his own bloody knuckles on his dad's skin.

When Vinny is done, he grabs the paper towels again, standing up and looking at me. "You need to leave before I call the cops."

"No," I say, with no room for argument. "I'm not going anywhere. I'm not leaving you."

"The story doesn't make sense with you here," Vinny argues, his green eyes so bloodshot that it brings sadness to my chest.

"You called me, and I came over right after it happened." I put my hand on his shoulder for support. "Now call the cops."

CHAPTER 13

VINNY

"911, WHAT IS YOUR EMERGENCY?"

I swallow hard, seeking out Kai's gaze for strength before I speak. "My dad attacked me, and I fought back. He's not moving. You need to send someone now. Please, hurry."

Kai nods, and the 911 operator speaks again. "Can you tell me what he looks like? Is he breathing?"

"No, he's not breathing." I say, feeling my mouth go dry as my limbs shake from the inside out.

"Okay, do you know CPR?" the operator asks. "I've tracked your location, police and EMS are on the way. Stay on the phone with me, okay? What's your name?"

"Vincent Donahue." I feel a tear fall down my cheek, and Kai brushes it aside. "I... I think he's dead."

"Okay, Vincent, can you check if he has a pulse for me?" I fall to the floor at my father's side, like the lies I'm spewing are the God's honest truth. Reaching for his neck, I search for a pulse.

"He doesn't have a pulse. He's not breathing."

"They're two minutes away, Vincent. Is anyone else there with you?" the operator asks.

"I called my friend. He's here. I didn't know what to do." More tears spill over my eyelids, and I stare at my father's body, feeling relief and grief both at once.

"Vincent, the police are pulling up. Can you ask your friend to open the door?" I repeat the instruction to Kai, but he's already on it, listening in on the call.

"My dad is dead," I whisper, my lungs squeezing so tight that oxygen becomes nonexistent.

————

"VIN? CAN YOU HEAR ME?" LIGHT SPREADS INTO MY VISION, and I look around. I'm on the floor, my dad's dead body to my right.

"What happened?" I ask, sitting up too quickly and making my head spin. Kai catches me by the shoulders before I fall back again, and I look up at him.

"I think you passed out," he says, and from the look on his face, I'm brought back to reality before he even tells me, "The police are here, Vin."

Nodding, I bend my legs to test their strength. When I'm confident I can stand up without falling, I hold my hand out for Kai to help me.

When I'm on my feet, I notice the four people standing inside my bedroom—cops and paramedics. The cops approach us as the paramedics head for my father. "Vincent?"

"Yeah," I croak, nodding.

"Let's get you to the ambulance, then you can tell us what happened." He points a thumb behind himself. "My guys are going to check the scene and get some photos while we talk, okay?"

"Okay," I say, looking at Kai. "Can my friend stay with me?"

Typically, I wouldn't show on the surface how much I rely on Kaiden for support, but right now, I'm not bothered. If I start going foggy or veering too far off the storyline, I need him there to make sure it all goes smoothly.

"Sure, son," the cop says, turning and holding an arm toward the door. "Can you walk, or do you need some help?"

I look behind me in time for the cop checking my father's pulse to stand up again, his head shaking at whoever he's silently communicating with, officially declaring my father deceased. Turning back, I grab onto Kai. "I'm fine, let's go."

———

WHILE THE PARAMEDIC LOOKS OVER THE CUTS AND BRUISES ON my face, another takes care of my hands as the cops question me.

"What were you doing when your father came home?" one asks, holding a little notebook up.

"Just taking a nap," I say, my heart pounding.

"So why did he attack you?" another police officer asks.

"Because that's what he likes to do for fun," I say, hissing as some alcohol is rubbed across the cut in the corner of my mouth.

"Have you ever reported that to the police before?" the first cop asks, his eyebrows pulling down.

"No, I've always just taken it. Hoped one day he would stop. I was waiting until graduation, then I was going to leave and never look back. Leave him to rot in his pathetic life by himself."

"You sound angry," one of the officers says, tilting his head a little. "Do you often fight back?"

"I never have before," I answer, trying to leash the burning anger raging inside my veins.

"So, the first time you fight your father off, he ends up dead."

Kai snaps before I do. "Is there a question, or are you going to accuse him of something without being fucking ominous?"

"*Kai*," I whisper, gritting my teeth, worried he's going to make it worse. "Don't."

The police officer opens his mouth to speak, but Kai is faster. "Not only is my friend going to live with the memory of his father's dead body on the ground for the rest of his life, but now you're, what, accusing him of murdering his own dad for kicks? A few months before moving out? Wouldn't he have done it sooner if he was going to? Avoided all the pain and trauma of getting his ass beat for eighteen years?"

"You need to calm down," one of the cops says. "We're just doing our jobs. We have to ask these questions, son. It's clear that this was self-defense, okay? Just let us get through this."

"What else do you need from me?" I ask the cops before Kai can open his fat mouth again.

"What did he do when he got home?" one of them asks, writing something down in his notepad.

I clear my throat. "I was in bed, trying to fall asleep, and he came banging through the house like he always does—*drunk*—and started yelling about something, the house being a mess, maybe, and when I got up, he lunged for me."

I don't know how the lies slip off my tongue so easily, but my story starts to feel completely natural. "He punched me in the face a few times, and I hit him back. We kept punching each other, then he finally fell down and when he tried to get back up,

I kicked him. I just wanted it to stop. I just wanted to stop getting used as his punching bag."

I make a point to add in the kick for when the autopsy shows all the damage Beckham made with his powerful legs. "I'm a football player. I work out a lot… I guess I didn't know how much strength I really had or something. I didn't mean to kill him."

The cops are all nodding when I stop talking, and my chest feels lighter.

"We need to get him to the hospital," one of the paramedics interrupts. "You can question him more there if you need to."

"I think we're done," the first cop I spoke with says, leaning forward to put a hand on my shoulder. He drops his voice a bit lower, maybe to make me feel safe. "I'm really sorry you had to go through this, son. But at least he can't hurt you anymore."

Nodding, I thank him, and then watch as the police all exit the ambulance, leaving me and Kai with the paramedics.

CHAPTER 14

SAGE

We manage to get into Alabama, find a hospital, and get Beckham's hands taken care of within four hours total. He has a fracture to his pinky and had to get a dozen stitches, but he's okay.

We head back to Georgia around 9 o'clock, riding in silence for half an hour before Beckham finally speaks.

"Thank you, Sage."

I look at him out of the corner of my eye, a smile touching my lips. "Of course."

He leans forward, putting his head against the dashboard. "I really fucked up, huh?"

Reaching over, I put my hand on his back. "You were protecting Vinny."

"I just couldn't sit back and let that bastard keep hurting him." He looks up at me, and there are tears in his eyes. "But now I just feel so fucking hollow inside, like I gave away my soul in exchange."

"You didn't, Beckham. You saved Vinny, and that makes you a fucking hero, if you ask me."

"Do you think he'll forgive me?" Beckham whispers, and my heart cracks wide open for him.

"I can guarantee he already has," I answer, trying to assure him with the look in my eyes as I look over at him again. "We all have."

He stares at me, even after I've looked back at the road, and after a few minutes have passed, when I'm starting to get used to the silence, he speaks again. "Are you with Kai now? Or will you belong to all of us?"

My stomach spins, and I keep my gaze forward. Swallowing down my nerves, I respond with my own question. "Do you want me to belong to all of you?"

"I think you always have, Sage."

A small smile kicks up the corners of my mouth, even as butterflies attack my insides. "Yeah, I think so, too."

———

When we get back to Blackmore, I drive to Kaiden's and park just outside the little freestanding garage behind his house.

It feels like days ago that I was here with Kai, spread out and taking him inside me for hours on end, when really it was a little over six hours ago. A lifetime of events has happened since then, and my head is growing heavy on my shoulders as the weight of the day pulls it down.

Beckham and I push through the door, finding Kaiden and Vinny sitting on the couches, watching TV. When they notice us, they both jump up.

Vinny has a thick bandage on one hand almost identical to the one Beckham has, a few of the fingers on his other hand wrapped in tape and his face a shade of purple I've never seen on someone's skin, making my heart hurt as I stare at him.

Beckham kisses him, then wraps his arms around him tightly while I stand beside them and watch. Kaiden lets them have the moment, sitting back down and waiting. When Vinny pulls back, he seeks me out and pulls me against his chest, wrapping his arms around me so tight I lose my breath.

"Are you okay?" I whisper, breathing in his amber and smoke scent.

Nodding, he kisses the top of my head.

"Are you sure?" Pulling back, I find his green eyes.

He puts a hand on my jaw, his thumb stroking over my cheek. "I'm okay."

I lift onto my toes and kiss him, careful to avoid the cut at the corner of his mouth, and he slides his hands around my waist. After a moment, he pulls away.

"Let's sit down," Beckham says, looking at Vinny. "I want to hear what happened with the cops."

"Nothing happened," Kai says coolly as we all find seats on the two couches. "They asked him what happened, then we went to the hospital."

"That's it?" I question, tucking my feet under myself and cuddling on the couch next to Vinny.

"That's it," Vinny says, putting a hand on my leg. "Now come sit on my lap, princess. I missed you."

Chuckling, I eye Kai—not for permission, but to see if he thinks it's a good idea, after everything Vinny's been through today, and he nods. Moving over Vinny, I straddle his lap and wrap my arms around his neck, letting my face fall against his so I can share his breath.

"Should we talk about what all this means?" Beckham asks from the other couch, and I feel Vinny's hands slide down to my lower back.

"It doesn't mean anything. The cops have no idea you were even there, Vinny will stop getting his ass beat every day, and no one outside of the four of us will ever know what happened today," Kai says, shrugging. "Relax, I told you everything would be fine."

"I'm not talking about that." Beckham clicks his tongue. "I'm talking about *this. Us.*"

I feel the hairs on the back of my neck rise when Vinny's hands move under the hem of my t-shirt and his fingers start making small circles against my skin.

Dropping my face into his neck, I savor the scent of his clean skin. He must have showered before coming over here, because he smells like soap and deodorant and that specific smokiness that his skin always carries.

"What about us?" Vinny asks, the words vibrating through his chest and throat.

"Now isn't the time, Becks," Kaiden says, standing up and walking to the small cooler by the door to pull out a soda. "Let's process the last twenty-four hours before you start complicating things even more."

"*Me?!*" Beckham laughs. "I'm not the one who snuck off and spent the day between Sage's legs."

My face goes hot, and Vinny's body stiffens a little before he squeezes my waist and speaks to Beckham. "Don't start, B."

"I'm not starting anything; I'm trying to finish it," Beckham answers, "I want to know where we all stand."

I lift my face from Vinny's neck and look to Beckham. "I already told you. If I'm Kai's, then I'm yours too." I look back at Vinny. "All of yours."

Vinny's lips twitch, and his hands glide down my torso to my ass, squeezing me there before kissing me hard. After a minute, he pulls back, and I realize I've been grinding my hips on his lap, making him grow hard under the fabric of his pants.

"Up," Vinny says, patting my ass with his hand.

Standing, I look down at him and try to read the thoughts swirling around in his wicked mind. As he bites down on his lip, he reaches forward and undoes the button on my pants.

"You're sure you want to do this now?" I say, my voice a whisper. "It's been a rough day."

Pulling my zipper down slowly, he looks up at me, heat in his emerald eyes. "That's why I *need* to do this, baby. I need you to make it all better."

I nod and let him slide his hands under my bottoms and pull them down my legs. After I step out of my jeans and panties, he tosses them to the side and reaches for the hem of my shirt. "Arms up."

After I've raised my arms in the air, he strips me of my shirt and bra, leaving me completely naked.

"Now turn around. Show my brothers what belongs to us," Vinny says, and moisture pools between my legs.

Turning around slowly, I face Kaiden and Beckham, who are sitting on the couch opposite us, and I study their heated gazes with burning flames running through my own veins.

Vinny's hands smooth up the sides of my thighs, then he pulls me down on top of him, so my back is against his front. "Spread those legs, princess. Show them your perfect little pink pussy. Show them the heaven between your thighs that we get to enjoy whenever we want."

My heart is racing as I spread my thighs and lift my feet up onto the couch, giving Kaiden and Beckham the perfect view of my pussy.

I feel Vinny's hard cock underneath his pants as I put all my weight down on his lap, and more moisture collects between the lips of my cunt, making me shift in place as desire consumes me.

Kaiden and Beckham don't say anything, just watch from across the room as Vinny skates his bandaged hand over my skin, walking his fingers between my thighs slowly until he's spreading my pussy farther, his head craning over my shoulder. "Look how wet our girl already is for us. Which one of you wants to take her first?"

My chest heaves, and when Vinny slides a finger through my center to rub my clit, I roll my head back on his shoulder.

Kaiden answers him, his voice thick with need. "I want her."

Vinny's finger speeds up on my clit, and I whimper against his throat. When he wraps a hand into my hair and pulls my face up against his, I cry out and find his lust-filled gaze.

"Should I let Kaiden have you first? Do you want to make a mess all over his cock before I feed you mine?" Vinny asks me, and I whimper again.

"Yes," I moan, feeling electroshocks of pleasure tingling my core as Vinny's fingers still play between my legs.

Vinny smirks, kissing me hard and fast before letting me go. "Get on your hands and knees and crawl to him, then."

I slide down to the ground, my knees hitting the concrete, and start to crawl across the room to Kaiden. Before I reach him, he undoes his pants and shuffles them down, his hand gripping the base of his cock and stroking.

When I'm at his feet, I take a moment to look to his left and give Beckham my attention. He's seated calmly, his arms thrown over the back of the couch, watching what's happening before him like it's his favorite movie. When he meets my gaze, he grins at me for a moment before he nods to Kaiden, rerouting my attention.

I lift off my palms, sliding my hands up Kai's thighs as I lean forward with the intention of putting him in my mouth, but he quickly sits forward and lifts me onto his lap.

"I need to be inside you."

Kaiden grunts, gripping himself and sliding inside me until I can feel him in my gut. My head throws back, and I shuffle myself so my legs are better aligned on either side of his hips and my clit can brush against his pelvic bone every time I grind.

Kaiden's powerful thrusts have me on the crest of my orgasm in only a few minutes, and his hand secures around my windpipe when I start to shout and moan.

"Fuck, you feel good. Always so fucking wet and ready for me," Kai says, and I feel my chest burn with satisfaction. "You're going to make me blow inside this tight cunt already."

I hum against the hold he has on my throat, nodding and biting down on my lip.

He thrusts faster. "You want it, don't you? Dirty, desperate fucking slut. So greedy for my cum in your perfect pussy."

My orgasm explodes into a million stars, and black dots blur the edges of my vision as my mind and body beg for oxygen. My fingers dig into Kaiden's shoulders, and his chiseled face spreads into a satisfied smirk as I ride out the rest of my climax.

Once I've stopped shaking, he lifts me, spins me around, and then sits me down on top of his lap again, my legs falling apart as I eye Vinny from across the room. Like a doll, boneless and moveable, Kaiden lifts my legs and spreads them wider as he slips his cock back inside me, making me moan as I capture Vinny's gaze with mine.

I lift my arm, holding my hand out to him, even though he's too far to reach, and beckon him to me.

"Vinny," I breathe, rolling my hips against Kaiden from above so Vinny has a clear view of me being impaled on his cock. "Please, come here. I need you."

His face has grown dark, and the veins on his muscular arms are standing at attention as he clenches his fists tight at his sides. When he stands up, he starts to undo his pants as he stalks across the room.

"Where do you want me, princess?" he asks as he approaches me, thumb playing with my lip. "Your mouth?"

I shake my head, and he grins.

"Your ass?" He slides his hand down my throat, over my breastbone and down my stomach until he reaches the apex of my thighs. His fingers pinch my clit, and I cry out. "Or your pussy?"

"Kiss me," I whimper, and Kaiden slams up into me, making me moan.

Vinny's hands wrap around my jaw, and his mouth finds mine, his tongue seeking mine out. I moan as our lips move fluidly, with passion that makes it hard to breathe, then I feel fingers spreading my pussy and probing into my entrance, where Kaiden is still thrusting slowly.

Pulling back, I go to speak, but Vinny slams his mouth back onto mine, sliding two fingers into my pussy right against Kaiden's thick cock, stretching me full.

When Vinny adds a third finger, I feel a scream rippling against my windpipe, begging to be released. I pull away from Vinny's mouth once more, looking up into his darkened gaze as he thrusts his strong fingers deeper just as Kaiden is thrusting his hips, and a loud moan pours out of me.

"Vinny," I whimper, rolling my hips as his other hand finds my clit.

"Yes, princess?" he asks, looking between my legs, his teeth pressing into his lip.

My fingers dig into his forearms, and my words come out as a breathy moan that I don't recognize. "Give me your dick."

I realize then that I haven't done anything close to sex with Vinny since Halloween, and a small part of me wonders if our reconnection should be something more intimate—maybe between just the two of us, but as Beckham comes up behind him and looks between my legs, and Vinny's cock pushes against Kaiden's to fit into my pussy, I know this is exactly the way we were supposed to reunite.

All four of us.

Together.

CHAPTER 15

BECKHAM

I watch over Vinny's shoulder as he drips saliva from his lips down onto his shaft, then he uses his fingers to spread it as he pushes farther inside Sage's cunt with Kaiden. She screams, her hands gripping his forearms as her eyes find mine. I'm burning, so fucking hot that two swipes of my hand will probably set off my climax, so I don't release my aching cock from my pants just yet.

I'm eager to watch Kai and Vinny stretch Sage's pussy around their shafts.

I'm halfway surprised Kaiden is letting Vinny do this, but he's probably letting it happen for the same reason I am—Vinny needs to get out all the negative feelings stuck inside his mind. He needs this. He needs to feel what he gets from being with us, all three of us, needs to work through what happened today in the only way he knows how.

"*Christ*," Vinny hisses, his hands securing around Sage's jaw. "You like that, baby? You like feeling both of us inside you?"

"*Yeah,*" Sage moans, her head rolling back on Kaiden's shoulder, and I look at his face for the first time, seeing pleasure and restraint in his molten gaze.

Sage's deep chocolate eyes are pressed shut, her legs shaking as she tries to hold them up on the edge of the couch. Leaning forward, I kiss Vinny's neck, and he reaches back to put a bandaged hand around my head.

"Becks…" he moans, flexing his hips hard and fast, pulling a scream from Sage's lips.

I breathe in everything Vinny as I kiss his skin, whispering under my breath, "I love you, I love you, I love you."

"Touch our girl. Show her how much she means to us, baby," Vinny breathes, grabbing my hair and pulling my mouth to his. "Make our princess come, and I'll let you take my ass while I fuck her."

Pleasure surges through my cock, and I study Vinny's face for a second. His skin is purple and black around his jaw and mouth, and his features are tired, but there's happiness and love in his eyes, making me kiss him once more before I move around him to get to Sage.

"Hi, Little Rabbit," I coo, kissing her sweaty neck and jaw. "You good?"

"*Beckham,*" she moans, her head rolling back again as her hands seek me out, her fingers getting tangled in the fabric of my shirt.

Groaning as her hand slides down to where my dick is hard and swollen under my jeans, I lick up her neck to her mouth and kiss her hard.

Kaiden and Vinny are an orchestra of moans and groans as they both thrust inside her, and when I press two fingers to Sage's swollen clit, they both let out a string of curses.

I pull back, staring into Sage's eyes as I press down hard,

rubbing her clit in circles that have her screaming and digging her fingernails into my arm.

Her eyes squeeze shut, and I slap my hand down on her cheek lightly. "Keep your eyes on me, Savage. I want to watch you fall apart."

Vinny and Kaiden move faster, groaning and grunting as Sage's hips grind and her legs twitch, my fingers massaging her clit until she's screaming out her release, liquid squirting from her cunt like a water fountain.

"*Jesus fucking Christ,*" Kaiden shouts, then his hand is curling around Sage's throat as his climax rushes through him, his release mixing with hers and leaking around where him and Vinny are still moving inside her.

When Sage's orgasm has fizzled out, she sags back onto Kai, her chest heaving and her legs shaking violently as she still tries to hold them up.

"*Oh… My… God,*" Sage breathes, and I slide my fingers down around Vinny's cock to gather some of the mixture of cum dripping from all three of them. When my fingers are soaked, I lift them up and shove them into Sage's mouth.

"Taste good?" I smirk, and she suctions around my fingers.

Even through exhaustion, Sage nods, her eyes flaring with heat, so I push farther down her throat until she's gagging around my fingers.

Vinny pulls out quickly, and Sage's eyes go wide as she releases my fingers. "Fuck, Vinny."

"C'mon," he says, holding a hand out for her. "Up."

She stands on wobbly legs, and then Vinny turns her and puts her down on the couch next to Kai. "Spread those legs, princess. Let me see you."

Kai has tucked himself back into his pants, but he leans over to kiss Sage once she's lifted her legs up, one of them sideways across his lap. When he pulls back, he slides three fingers into her pussy, thrusting a few times before he smirks at her. "Look at you, filled with my cum just how you like. My perfect little slut."

As Sage's lips turn up into a smile, mine do too.

She likes it when Kaiden calls her names and treats her like she's existing simply to please him. The thought makes me wonder if she would like it if anyone else did it, or if it's exclusive to Kai.

We all have such different relationships with this girl, and it's beautiful how she molds perfectly to all three of us.

Vinny slaps Kai's palm, and Sage quakes from the pressure on her clit. "Fingers out, I need our girl to finish me off."

Kaiden chuckles, wrapping a hand into Sage's hair as he removes his fingers from her pussy. "Spread those legs farther, baby. My brother needs to come inside your tight cunt."

Sage is breathless, nodding and panting as she stretches out on the couch, then Vinny is pushing inside her and holding a hand out for me.

As Sage moans, Vinny stuffs two fingers into her pussy with his cock to gather the mixed releases, then uses them to slicken his asshole before he pushes the digits deep inside himself.

"*Jesus*," I hiss, watching as Vinny fingers his own ass with two fingers for a moment, then he pulls his hand free and grips my shirt.

"Take your fucking pants off, Beckham," he groans, thrusting into Sage hard and fast.

I don't waste a moment, unbuttoning and pushing my pants down quickly before I position myself behind Vinny.

"Spit," Vinny moans, feeling the head of my cock pushing against his asshole.

Grinning, I reach my hand out to Sage. "You heard him, Savage, *spit*."

She moans as Vinny bucks his hips, but she spits onto my palm as her gaze clashes with mine.

"Good girl." I smile, and she bites down on her lip.

I wrap my hand around my cock, spreading Sage's saliva onto it, then I position myself back at Vinny's hole. "Good, baby?"

He pushes into Sage until she's screaming. "Fuck me."

Without restraint, I push past the ring of muscle in Vinny's ass, stretching him wide around my dick. He pants, "Fuck, fuck, fuck."

I spread his ass cheeks apart, watching my cock disappear inside of him as I thrust my hips back and forth, not worrying about going slow. I can read Vinny better than anyone, and right now, if I were to act like he was breakable, he would get pissed off.

He's a different shade of red, pounding into Sage without abandon while I try to keep up pace behind him, his hands tangling in Sage's hair and pulling her face to his. As Sage screams out her pleasure, Vinny does the same, swallowing her sounds with his lips and tongue.

"I'm gonna fucking come," Vinny groans, gripping Sage's hair tighter and putting his mouth to hers. "Tell me you want it. Beg for my fucking cum, princess."

My cock and balls are pulsing with pleasure at his words, and when Sage starts to scream out her response, my eyes roll back.

"Please, Vinny!" Sage cries, her fingers gripping tightly around his biceps as he continues to thrust between her legs. "Please, please, please—*give it to me.*"

Vinny growls, and I feel when his orgasm barrels through him, his ass clenching around me almost painfully and triggering my own.

My eyes slam shut as euphoria takes over my senses, and when I feel a hand wrap around my arm, I open them again to find Sage grabbing me—connecting with me through our shared releases that made my head spin.

"I love you," I say, and I don't know if I'm saying it to Vinny or Sage, because in this moment, it's confirmed that I feel it for them both.

PART TWO
REST IN PEACE

CHAPTER 16

SAGE

By Christmas break, we've all found a new *'normal'* that makes sense to each of us.

Beckham and I take turns staying with Vinny in his empty house. Sometimes Kai will join, and sometimes it'll be all four of us jammed into Vinny's queen-sized bed at once.

It's always comfortable, though.

Some nights I spend screaming and crying in pleasure, and other nights we simply exist in the same place together and enjoy the contentment we've seemed to find within each other.

Gran doesn't question when I spend nights out, even when I know she's caught on to the fact I'm lying about being with girlfriends. I think she's just happy I've found a slice of happiness in this town after all, especially after everything I've gone through.

The first Monday of break, I'm in line at the DMV, officially changing my driver's license from California to Georgia, as well as updating my last name to Blackmore.

I've been spending more time outside since the grass turned crispy and crunchy with frost. I've even been going to the cemetery and sitting at the edge of some of the old Blackmore graves, talking out loud to my ancestors.

I don't know why.

Maybe it makes me feel a bit closer to them and this town and the name I'm now carrying around like a badge of honor.

Sage Blackmore has a nice ring to it, and the more I say it out loud to the graveyard filled with the ghosts of my family, the more it sounds fucking *right.* The more I realize that deep down, I've been a Blackmore all along, even when I was in California, living out some teenage dream as the perfect girl from the perfect family. I've always had this piece of me; I just needed to come here, to Blackmore, to set her free.

Once I've finished up at the DMV, I get into my car and drive the five minutes across town to Kaiden's, where the guys are all waiting for me.

I collide with Kaiden first, and he wraps his arms around me, pulling me against his body.

I'll never get completely used to Kaiden showing affection—he'll always be the mean one, the dark one, the *devil*—but *my God*, when his arms embrace me, and my senses are filled with that familiar smokey, manly smell of him, I feel so complete it's crazy.

"My girl," he groans into my neck, quiet enough that no one else hears him, and my lips tip up in a smile.

Pulling back, I look into those dark night eyes and smile up at him. "My king."

He kisses me hard, his fingers digging into my back as he pulls me against his body. When he takes his lips from mine, he grins with mischief. "I want to swallow you fucking whole."

I lift an eyebrow. "Oh?"

He hums between his lips, his chiseled jaw growing tight. "Tonight, you're all mine. Got it?"

I feel the words climbing my throat, but Beckham comes up behind me and speaks before I can. "Sorry, she has plans."

Kaiden's hands tighten in my shirt, and he grits his teeth.

He hasn't conquered his jealousy, and I'm not sure I want him to. It gives me butterflies the size of monsters, and his possessive hands make it all worth it in the darkness of my bedroom when he's pulling the words *I'm yours* from my mouth like he has me under a spell.

Beckham pulls me from Kai, kisses my mouth, then smiles at me. "Let me see it, then."

I can feel Kai watching me still, even as I take my wallet from my purse and show Beckham my new ID—the one with my Blackmore address and name on it. I know all three boys were anxious to see me *officially* become a Blackmore resident, even when I really don't have any interest in going back to California at this point anyway.

Beckham grins at me. "Sage Grace Blackmore of Blackmore, Georgia. Do we get special treatment since we're dating the town princess?"

I roll my eyes, putting my ID back in my wallet and smacking Beckham's hands away from my body. "Ha-*ha*."

"So… what are you doing tonight?" Kaiden asks, turning the conversation backwards, making me giggle. His face is a mask of boredom, when I know it's killing him that he can't have me for himself tonight, even as he bangs on his chest and yells like a caveman.

"Movie night at Vinny's, you wanna come?" I say, twisting some hair around a finger playfully.

"*No*," he growls under his breath, and I laugh.

"Yes, you do." I smile, lifting on my tiptoes and kissing his cheek before I breeze through the garage to sit down with Vinny.

————

KAIDEN IS THE FIRST ONE TO FALL ASLEEP AT VINNY'S LATER that night, curled around a pillow in bed while the rest of us stay up, eating junk food and watching some Christmas movie.

It's *easy* with the Hallows Boys. They've felt like family since the moment we started this, and I feel comfortable with them. It just cements the fact that I'm supposed to be here. I was meant to come to Blackmore, find them, and discover my real self. A girl who carries her head high and doesn't care what anyone else thinks, someone who thrives under the shadows and moonlight.

It feels like years ago I was the girl who was chasing extracurriculars, straight As, and perfection. The Sage I am here doesn't *need* to be perfect—she just needs to be *real*.

And with Kaiden, Vinny, and Beckham, I am the realest and purest form of myself I've ever been.

I can't say I don't still struggle; I will always have skeletons in my closet that keep me up some nights, and I still feel the loss of my parents and the life I once lived, but it's all a little bit easier with the Hallows Boys on my side.

I still have days when I want to hunt down more answers about my parents, uncle, and what happened when they lived in Blackmore, but maybe I'm better off not knowing. Maybe the stories I was so desperate to hear aren't worth the nightmares they'll give me. Maybe I'm not *meant* to know what happened all those years ago, and part of me has accepted that.

Beckham and Vinny fall asleep within minutes of the movie ending, and I'm left to cuddle up and breathe them in until I can finally let myself get taken under sleep as well.

I hold my eyes open a little longer, listening to the three of them breathing around me, my fingers tracing down the soft skin of Kai's chest in the darkness. When he starts to stir, I roll over and do the same thing to Beckham, letting my fingers brush his bare chest. His face is illuminated by the moon through the window, and I can see the light freckles on his pale face as he breathes softly through sleep. A smile touches my lips, and that's the image I fall asleep to—my soft Hallows boy, taken under sleep, safe away from the things that haunt him when he's awake.

———

A SHOUT PULLS ME FROM SLEEP, AND I GASP AS I SIT UP IN THE darkness.

Beckham is digging his fingers into my side, his face morphed into agony as small shouts slip from between his lips. Wrapping my hands around his neck, I kiss his mouth three times before I whisper against his skin, soft enough that I won't wake up Kaiden and Vinny.

"Beckham, Beckham, Beckham. Wake up, baby. It's okay."

I wish this was the first time I've had to pull Beckham from his nightmares, but it's almost a nightly occurrence these days. He's tortured by demons inside his dreams, and it breaks my fucking heart every time.

I don't know if Kaiden and Vinny know. If they do, they haven't said anything about it. I haven't said anything either, keeping Beckham's secrets just between us.

"Beckham, wake up." I grip his jaw with my fingers, and finally he opens his eyes.

He sighs, wrapping his arms around my waist to pull me against his body. "Hey, Savage. I was having a nightmare."

I nod into his chest. "I could tell."

Sighing again, he rubs his nose against my shoulder before he pulls from my grip. "I'm gonna have a smoke, you coming?"

"Yeah," I whisper again, kissing his mouth before we silently crawl from under the blankets, careful not to disturb Vinny and Kaiden.

It's freezing outside, so we both grab a blanket from the couch as we pass, then we step out onto the porch and sit down on the floor against the wall, not bothering to turn on the light.

Beckham lights two cigarettes, handing me one, and then sucking on the filter of his.

I don't regularly smoke, only in the middle of the night with Beckham when he's had a nightmare. It's become our ritual.

After a minute and a quarter of our cigarettes, I lift my leg and put it over Beckham's. "Tell me about your nightmare, B."

Beckham runs his hand through his curly hair, taking a big hit off his cigarette before he starts talking.

"I was running through the cemetery, and I could hear Vinny screaming, but I couldn't find where his voice was coming from. I just kept running and running and running, searching for him." Beckham takes a puff from his cigarette, blowing out the smoke as he shuffles a little closer to me. "When I finally found him, he was in the Hallows Crypt, except it wasn't him screaming anymore, it was you, and him and Kai and I were hurting you, like it was the Hallows Games again, except it wasn't like what really happened. We were trying to kill you."

I take a breath, waiting for him to continue as silence falls over us. When he finally speaks again, he looks into my eyes.

"Then Vinny's dad came in, and I had to kill him, or Kai said he would kill *you*." Beckham's hand tightens into a fist, and he sucks on his cigarette for longer this time. When he blows the smoke out, he continues, the pain in his voice making my chest ache. "I had to kill him again and again and again, and then I had to kill you anyway."

"Beckham…" I breathe, scooting so close to him that I can feel his body shaking in fear. "I'm right here. I know you would never hurt me."

He stubs out his cigarette, then he slides both hands into his hair. "I feel like I'm going fucking crazy, Sage. I can't live with this shit anymore."

"You didn't do anything wrong, Beckham," I tell him gently, putting my face against his. "You saved Vinny, and if that's wrong, then I don't want to be right."

Silence washes over us, and I can hear birds and bugs in the distant winter night. When Beckham's hands wrap around me, I sigh in relief.

"How do you live with it, Sage?" he asks, and I look at him with confusion in my gaze. "The knowledge we sprung on you about your family, your parents, the games. How are you okay with being with us when we represent everything bad in your life?"

I shake my head slowly, looking at him through the darkness.

For a moment, I just think over his words, then I press a kiss to his lips before I answer.

"Do I wish that the Hallows Games didn't exist? Yeah, sure. But without them, I probably wouldn't have been born, and I certainly wouldn't be here with you right now. I found my home with you three, and even though I had to go through so much to get here, I'm glad this is where I found my salvation. With you, and Vinny, and Kaiden."

Beckham looks at me for a moment, then he gives me a sad smile. "Kai told us we need to start scouting for the next generation. We should have already chosen them by now."

A cold shiver runs through my spine, and I blow out a breath. "Oh."

"Yeah," he says, trying to read how I feel as he searches my eyes. I decide not to leave him guessing, and just open my mind.

I sigh. "I don't want there to be another generation. I want the games to end. I want my family's tradition to die with *us*. It makes me sick to think about this continuing in the name of Blackmore."

"Can I tell you the truth, Savage?" Beckham says, making small circles on my skin with his fingers. "I want to end the games with us too. I don't want to keep risking the darkness and destruction the games bring with them. What if the next generation is like your father and uncle? What if someone else gets hurt? I wouldn't be able to live with myself."

"So end it," I breathe. "Once and for all."

CHAPTER 17

KAIDEN

CHRISTMAS MORNING, I DRAG MYSELF HOME FROM VINNY'S to check on my dad. I've been so completely trapped within the world we've built with Sage that I've started to give up the things that used to occupy my time.

I don't remember the last time I showed up for basketball.

I couldn't tell you the last volunteer program I was involved in.

Halloween came, took over, and then the whole world spiraled around this girl and our shared attachment to her. Lust, love, obsession, whatever it may be. Every moment is her—*Sage.*

She feels like coming home and being reborn and seeing color for the first time all at once.

She's lighting up parts of me I've shoved far away and become a stranger to. But as well as that, she's letting me claw at parts of her she has trapped behind barriers and walls. Parts of her that are dark and sick and twisted like me, parts that she's never unleashed.

She's coming out of her shell, and mine is growing big enough to bring her inside.

Sage is someone I never saw myself being different with. She's everything I've avoided for so long, someone so bright and cheerful, but also possessive and full of fire. She's impossible to control, but the challenge turns parts of me on that I've shoved deep down for so long.

She's addiction and passion and obsession.

Everything I have with Sage—and everything she has with Vinny and Beckham—has me questioning every plan I've ever had. My wants and needs and dreams are different now, because now I have her, and there isn't one single part of me that's going to let her go.

Pushing through the front door of my house, my lips twist to the side as I think about Sage. It's Christmas, and I want to be with her. I want to celebrate with her, tangle my hands in her hair and bring her to the edge of insanity before I finally let her fall over the edge.

She's the best Christmas gift I could have ever dreamed of.

My dad is sitting at the kitchen table as I walk through the house, so I pull out a chair and sit down opposite him.

"Merry Christmas," I say by way of greeting, and he brings his tired gaze to mine.

"Merry Christmas," he echoes. "You're home early."

I look at the clock behind his head, seeing it's only seven, and shrug as I look back at my dad. "Wanted to see you. It's Christmas."

"You've been staying out so much, I figured you'd be off somewhere with whoever's occupying your time." My dad's lips twitch, and a small smile pulls across his face.

I chuckle, running my hand over my jaw. "Yeah, *well*."

Words fizzle out in my mind, and my father laughs at me. "As long as you're still focused on school, Kaiden."

"I am," I say, almost too quickly, then I take a breath. "I've been thinking about next year, where I want to go to school. I think I want to stay in Blackmore for a little longer, maybe take some online classes."

"No," my dad says, bringing his coffee mug to his lips. "We've talked about this, Kai. You're going to Georgia State, you're getting out of here. You'll get a good education and become someone who's bigger than this town."

"Dad –" I start, but he cuts me off.

"What is it you want, Kai?" he questions, shaking his head. "To be like me? Stuck in Blackmore forever, working at one of the factories on the edge of town? Your mother wanted more for you, a bright and amazing future, and dammit, I promised her you would get it."

My stomach churns at the mention of my mom.

Even after five years, the memory of her in her hospital bed, her body and mind taken from cancer, burns so bad that I have to blink back tears.

I don't blame my dad for wanting my life to be different from his. He's so scarred and torn from the lonely last five years, that he wants me to get as far away from here as possible. What he doesn't realize, though, is that Blackmore is more my home than anywhere else ever will be. I'm made of darkness and smoke, and Blackmore is the place I feel most myself. I've grown around this town, become one with the cemetery, the main street, the broken trees along the side of the roads, the cracks in our foundation. This is where I belong.

"I just want to be happy, Dad," I say, smiling at my father.

He nods. "That's all I want for you too, son."

———

AFTER WE'VE ALL DONE OUR FAMILY STUFF, BECKHAM, SAGE, AND I decide to meet up at Vinny's house to make sure he's okay.

I grab the small gift I got for Sage before I head out, then I make the short walk down the street to Vinny's. The ground is covered in a thin layer of frost, since the temperature dropped last night, but the sun is doing a good job at turning it slippery.

Pulling my hood up over my head, I slide my hands into my front pocket and walk slowly, savoring the smell of the winter day and admiring the bare trees and brown grass at the edge of the road.

The houses in Vinny's neighborhood are littered with Christmas decorations, all except for his. It makes me feel sad deep in my gut as I open the front door and walk through the warm house.

Vinny's home had no Christmas tree—I don't think in the last eighteen years it *ever* has, but this year, Sage went out and bought one for him, setting it up in the middle of the living room and decorating it with white and blue lights.

She's trying to give him a piece of the holiday we all know he's never tasted—something to be happy about this time of year.

If only she realized that even just her presence was enough for Vinny.

He's fallen, head over heels and back again.

No one has ever gotten this close, no one except me and Becks. Vinny has never been like this with someone, and no matter how cool and collected he wants to act, I can see through his tough exterior. He fucking loves this girl.

Maybe it's a trauma bond, the fact that she was here when everything happened with his dad, and the fact she picked up Beckham's pieces, then gave her body and heart over to Vinny when he really needed it. Maybe I'll never understand, and maybe all three of us will always have different bonds with Sage.

I find Vinny sitting at the edge of his bed, watching football on the small TV he has on his dresser, and his head turns when he hears me come in.

"Hey," he says, looking back at the tv.

"Merry Christmas," I say, sitting on the opposite end of the bed.

Becks walks in then, skipping across the room until he reaches the bed, then he launches himself down on the mattress. When it stops bouncing, he curls up and smiles. "Merry Christmas, boyfriend-in-laws."

"Boyfriend-in-laws?" I laugh. "Don't call us that."

He laughs, his shoulders shaking before he wraps his arms around Vinny's waist from behind and looks at me. "I guess you're my only boyfriend-in-law, anyway, huh? Since Vin is more than that." He gives me a fake pout, like he feels bad for me.

I roll my eyes. "You're lucky I let you near Sage at all. Please, don't test me."

He laughs. "Yeah, yeah. You couldn't keep me away from her."

I hum between my lips, narrowing my gaze at him, because we both know that I could if I wanted to. Sage is very lucky it's Vinny and Becks she's also involved with. Anyone else, and I would remove their eyes from their head just for looking at her.

"Let's not forget who makes her scream the loudest," I say, feeling a possessive and arrogant wave run through me, and Beckham just laughs as he sits up and holds a hand out to me.

"Wanna bet?"

"Please don't make bets about my orgasms. It's weird." Sage's voice pulls us from the petty conversation we're having, and my eyes find her standing by the open bedroom door with her arms crossed over her chest.

Vinny finally pulls his attention from the TV, and he stands up to walk across the room. When he reaches Sage, he bends down and puts his arms around her waist before he lifts her up and kisses her. She squeals as he spins her around, then carries her to the bed.

Laying her down between me and Beckham, Vinny keeps his mouth on hers and positions himself on top of her. After a minute, he pulls back and smiles. "Merry Christmas."

She's breathy as he runs her hands up his arms. "Merry Christmas."

They smile at each other for a moment, and it's like time has stopped all around us as they stare into each other's eyes. I can feel the tension radiating from them, and Becks and I are both frozen as well until a minute later when Sage pats her hand on Vinny's back and speaks.

"Get up so I can say hello to your *boyfriend-in-laws*." She laughs, eyes crinkling at the sides and her chest shaking.

Becks, Vinny, and I all laugh too, and Beckham is first to grab her when Vinny lifts off of her.

"Quit spying on us, Savage." He chuckles, kissing her jaw and grabbing her sides.

Still giggling, she pulls his hair and brings his mouth to hers. "Merry Christmas, Beckham."

He hums against her lips for a moment, then they start kissing harder. Sage's hips rolling from instinct alone, searching for someone to rub against. Clearing my throat, I pull their attention. "*Come here*, Sage."

My blood turns to a near boil as she crawls down the bed slowly, then she finds her seat on my lap, putting her legs on either side of my hips. My fingers tangle in her golden hair, and I pull her head back so I can kiss her throat. "Merry Christmas, Little Rabbit."

She moans, "Merry Christmas, King."

Her center grinds on my cock, and I hiss between my teeth before I pull her mouth to mine. Her tongue seeks mine out, sending a lightning bolt of pleasure shooting through my chest, and my fingers dig into her scalp.

As she moans, I flex my hips and press my thickening cock against her clit, making her nails dig into my chest. "Kai…"

I smirk, running my hands down her body, settling on her thighs. "I got you a present."

Pulling back, she grins. "You got me a present?"

Humming, I nod. "You want it?"

Her brows wiggle, her hand sliding between us to my dick. "Is this it?"

"Oh, you'll get that later, desperate girl," I growl, feeling blood rushing through me as I reach across to the bedside table, grabbing the small, wrapped box I brought with me from home. Holding it out for Sage, I find her chocolate eyes and smile. "Merry Christmas."

I don't mind that Beckham and Vinny are both sitting at the opposite end of the bed watching, even as Sage's face blooms with a blush and she starts to unwrap the box. "Kai, you didn't have to get me anything."

She throws the paper to the side, then opens the small jewelry box, exposing the necklace inside. It's all silver, the chain holding a large pendant of the letter K in the center. She looks up at me, her eyes burning with lust. "Kaiden Thorne, you got me a necklace with your initial on it?"

I grin. "It's not enough that I'm scarred on your back. I need everyone to know you fucking belong to me."

"A month ago, I couldn't get you to admit you enjoyed my company, and now look at you…" She twists her lips to the side playfully. "Marking me for everyone to see."

I grunt, sliding a hand up her throat. "I just don't want

anyone touching what's mine. I don't even want them *thinking* about it."

"*Ours*," Vinny corrects, pulling me from the little bubble I've managed to create around me and Sage. I glance at him, finding anger in his eyes, and I smirk before I look at Sage again.

"Let me put it on you." As I take the necklace from the box, she lifts her hair, then I fasten it around her neck. When she drops her hair back down, I grin at her. "Looks perfect."

"Thank you," she breathes, kissing me softly once before pulling away. "I love it."

Sage stands up then. "I got you guys presents, too."

"Sage, you didn't have to," Beckham says, swinging his legs over the side of the bed and standing.

"I know," she says, disappearing out into the hallway for a second before she comes back in the room with three gifts in her hands. "I wanted to."

She passes them out, one for each of us, then stands before us to watch us open them. Vinny goes first, ripping the silver paper off his gift and tossing it to the floor. He looks down at a small leather-bound journal, then flips it open and reads what Sage has written on the first page out loud.

"For when your mind is too loud, and you need to get the words out." He smiles at her, standing up and embracing her. "Thank you, princess. I love it."

She wraps her arms around him. "Merry Christmas, Vinny."

When Vinny has returned to his seat, Beckham tears the paper from his gift, revealing a medium-sized cardboard box. Inside, a polaroid camera sits, a few cartridges of film and a small photobook. He plucks the small handwritten note from the box and reads it aloud. "So we never forget the good things."

I start to get nervous for my own gift as Beckham walks to her and embraces her, thanking her for the gift. I go through what could possibly be in the small, wrapped box in my lap, and I come up empty. Vinny and Beckham's gifts were so thoughtful, tailored to their own struggles, so I wonder what Sage could have gotten me.

She smiles at me once Beckham sits back down next to Vinny again, a mischievous sparkle to her eye. Tearing the paper from my gift, I flip open the lid to a small jewelry box.

"I think we kind of had the same idea," Sage says as I lift a necklace from the box. There's a tiny pendant on the thick chain resembling a vial, except it's completely made of silver so you can't see what's inside. It's maybe the size of a dime, not very large at all, and I flip it over in my hand to inspect it and try to figure out what it is. There are small designs on the vial— thorns and tiny leaves.

I look at Sage, and she grins, holding up her finger to show me the band aid wrapped around it. "It has some of my blood in it."

Chuckling, I turn the vial over in my hand once more, studying the designs. "Thorns and leaves?"

"Thorns—for Kaiden *Thorne*. And sage leaves, for, well, *me*." She presses her lips together. "It isn't my fault sage isn't very special looking."

"Fuck." I grip the necklace in my hand, standing up to rush to her. I grab her face with my free hand, pulling her lips to mine. Holding my waist, she tugs me closer as we get lost in each other's kiss.

When we finally pull apart, I breathe against her wet mouth. "I fucking love it, crazy girl. Thank you."

"Merry Christmas." She smiles up at me, and I feel something I've never felt before. Something so bright and so full and *fucking scary* that my lungs become too small and too big all at once. I look at Sage, realizing that she's my home and my hope and the answer to any prayers I could ever have. Beckham and Vinny had been right—she's the missing piece we've always needed.

CHAPTER 18

SAGE

THE CEMETERY IS COLD AND MISTY AS I WALK THROUGH, THE sun almost completely set in the west and creating shadows around all the headstones.

I don't know why I'm here—searching for answers I know aren't going to be found, maybe, but I've grown to feel at home in this place. I'm not sure when it happened, when the cemetery stopped being creepy and spooky and became comforting.

I don't think Beckham has realized that I snuck the key for the crypts out of his wallet yet. If he has, he hasn't said anything about it. I haven't used it before today, only letting the idea burn inside me until I finally grew so restless that my legs took me out here by themselves.

A bird caws in the distance, pulling my gaze out toward the far end of the graveyard—back where the Hallows Boys took me that first night we were together—and the memory warms my chest. Who knew, back then, when I was a girl filled with sunshine who got taken into the dark, that I would eventually be falling in love with the three boys who dragged me there.

I stop by one of the headstones I've grown to recognize—an old Blackmore ancestor who's been buried here since the late 1940s. Brushing the leaves from the top of the stone, I sit down in the cold grass and pull my knees to my chest as I take a breath.

There are so many Blackmore headstones here, most of them so old that you can barely read the names and dates carved into the stone.

I stare at the earth around me, almost as if I'm waiting for the dead to rise and speak to me, give me the information I'm itching for, tell me about my ancestors' pasts—my grandparents, my parents.

After a few silent minutes, I stand back up and continue walking through the cemetery, heading for the crypts.

I haven't spoken to the Hallows Boys about what's on my mind. Part of me is worried that I'll ruin the happy little bubble we've secured ourselves into, I guess, but there's still so many questions I have about my parents. I even went as far as to lie to them about where I am tonight, making an excuse that I was spending the evening with Gran, then staying home to have breakfast with her in the morning.

Even though they explained the games to me, I'm still dying to learn more.

Kaiden said every generation has written about their time as the Hallows Boys, and that's what I'm hunting for today, the notebooks with the tradition's secrets within them.

Maybe I'll spend all night here, maybe I'll read every single word ever written by a Hallows Boy—every word except for *this* generation. I'm not sure I could stomach reading about their previous games with other girls or the one with my name in it.

Pulling the key from my pocket, I twist it in my hand as I

approach the first crypt—the one with all the writing on the wall, with the portraits of the founders hanging on the concrete.

I take a glance around the cemetery, even though I know I'm alone, simply because part of this place will always remind me of being snuck up on, then I slide the key into the lock and turn it, the metal creaking.

Pushing inside, I pull out my phone and turn on the flashlight, then I close the door behind me, securing myself inside the Hallows Crypt.

I open drawers to the large dressers that line the wall until I find a lighter, then I take my time lighting all the candles around the room so I can see what I'm doing. My eyes catch on the portraits hanging in the center of the wall, my father's young face making my stomach churn.

My uncle and Benjamin both sit parallel to my father, all three of them handsome and full of secrets.

Next to the portraits, in a perfectly straight line, the names of all the Hallows Boys are carved into the wall, starting with *Andrew Blackmore, Aaron Blackmore, and Benjamin Gilmore,* then ending with *Kaiden Thorne, Vincent Donahue, and Beckham Bentley.*

My chest burns with anxiety, sadness, and anger.

How can three boys cause so much pain? How can the three boys who created this game, three murderers, sit in the same place as the three boys I've fallen for? What makes them different? Am I in way too far over my head, blinded by lust and affection and sex, that I can't even see the similarities anymore? How can I hate the founders so much and love the current generation?

None of it makes fucking sense.

When I start to feel crazy, I turn to look around for the journals.

Since this place is locked up, they aren't hidden. There's a small bookcase at the edge of the room, leather-bound journals lining the shelves, all in chronological order, starting with the founders and ending with last year.

I pull off the first book, marked *2000* on the spine, then sit down against the wall and open the first page.

The Hallows Games—year one, October 31, 2000.
Members—Andrew Blackmore, Aaron Blackmore, and Benjamin Gilmore.
Female selection—Christine Spencer
Details of entire night to follow.

I flip through the notebook quickly, not wanting to read any intimate details about my parents' first Hallows Games and stop at the last page.

In conclusion, we will be continuing the tradition every Halloween thus forth, as well as creating a game that we can pass down to future generations in Blackmore. Welcome to the Hallows Games. This is only the beginning.
Signed, The Founders—Andrew, Aaron, and Benjamin.

Shaking my head, I slam the book shut as nausea creeps through my gut. If only they had just dealt with their issues like regular fucking people, none of this would have happened. Megan would be alive, my parents too, probably, and I would have grown up in Blackmore. I wouldn't have been lied to, deceived by everyone in my life until the moment I was abandoned.

I wonder if my parents are happy with the fact I'm in Blackmore, learning about their past and all the secrets they worked so hard to keep from me. Were they ever going to tell me about this place, our history? Or was I going to grow up as Sage Lindman, marry some white-collar guy in California and start a new generation of *Lindmans*, erasing Blackmore from the universe completely.

If my parents hadn't died, and my uncle hadn't denied the state's request for placement, who would I be right now?

I go for the bookcase again, plucking out the book that has *2001* on the spine, then I flip it open.

The Hallows Games—October 31, 2001.
Members—Andrew Blackmore, Aaron Blackmore, and Benjamin Gilmore.
Female selection—Megan Gallagher
Details of entire night to follow, **written by Christine Spencer.**

I know I need to read this one, even if it makes me sick, so I go back to my spot on the ground and turn the page. As I read it, it plays like a movie in my mind.

CHAPTER 19

Christine Spencer—Halloween 2001

The night is cold, and the cemetery is empty, save for a few animals that are still brave enough to be out this late. Even through the darkness, I can find my way here now like it's my home away from home. It pretty much is. This is where we feel the most comfortable to be ourselves, me and Andrew. His brother and Benjamin too, who I sometimes belong to as well.

I've crowned the name of the Hallows Girl, even though Andrew says he never imagined their group involving any members outside of the three of them.

I guess that's what you get when you fall in love, right? All your expectations fade away and become something different.

You end up sharing your life and your space with the person you hold dear.

That's what he is, Andrew, he's my everything—my life and my soulmate. But instead of being cruel to me now, he lets me wear the crown of his queen and lead alongside him.

Aaron and Benjamin didn't like it much at first, but since Andrew isn't selfish with me, they've learned to accept me into their family too.

When the boys told me I could be chosen again this year, it sounded like a good idea. That is, until I started to really think about it.

The games are supposed to be about being free for one night a year, aren't they? Why waste our one night on activities that we engage in any other day of the year?

No, we needed to choose someone else, find someone to bring into the darkness with us, create a story to tell the future generations that will inspire risk in them.

Megan was the obvious choice—my best friend who needed to see that I wasn't crazy for falling into this world. I presented the idea to Andrew, and when he accepted it, we told Aaron and Benjamin together.

We will bring Megan into this world, show her exactly why we're here, and she'll finally accept me again. After a decade of friendship, don't I at least deserve the chance to speak my truth to her? It shouldn't have been so easy for her to walk away from me.

Andrew had the idea for me to come into the crypt after they'd already captured Megan, surprise her and make her feel more comfortable.

He needed that element of power beforehand, though. That I know. Andrew is nothing if he isn't in control, leading, commanding.

As I reach the back edge of the cemetery, where the old Blackmore crypts are, I hear screaming. My blood heats, and my feet move quicker.

Surely, Megan must know no one will hear her out here.

We're too far out, it's too late, and the walls are thick. She's completely at our mercy, and I think that's the most exciting part.

Pushing into the crypt, candlelight hits my face at the same time I see Megan, and her eyes seek me out. She's tied to the bed, her arms and legs restrained, in nothing but her panties and bra, and she has tears sliding down her cheeks.

"Christine!" she shouts as I step into the crypt and close the door behind me. "You have to help me!"

My panties turn slick, so I breeze across the space and kiss Andrew, my hands finding his bare chest burning hot.

"Hi, my love," I breathe, looking up into his dark, bloodshot eyes.

His fingers tangle in my hair, but he looks over my head at Megan. "She's a screamer, it seems."

Giggling, I nod. "I heard her from outside."

"Christine!" Megan shouts again, and I pull from Andrew to look at her. "Please…"

I smile at her, love warming my gaze. "It's okay, Meg." Walking across the space slowly, I climb atop the bed in between her legs, making the old mattress creak under my weight.

"Just let me go, I won't tell anyone." Megan cries now, her heavy breasts lifting and falling.

I snuggle down with her, putting my head in the crook of her neck and wrapping my arm around her center like we used to do when we were little. "Tell anyone what, Meg? It's okay, I promise. I'm here now. I'll never let anything happen to you."

"Chris—they took my clothes; they tied me up. Please. Just let me go," Megan whispers, and I stroke her skin with my fingers.

"I can't, Meg. We need this, okay? You and me. Don't you love me?" I say, then I feel Andrew kneel on the mattress next to me.

"Enough, please, Christine. Get up and go sit down," Andrew says, and I find his searing gaze. He points across the crypt, where Aaron and Benjamin are seated on one of the couches. "Now."

Nodding, I kiss Megan on the cheek. "Everything is okay, Meg."

I get up, walk across the space, and sit down on the couch.

Benjamin and Aaron are holding hands, both in only their tight briefs, and I lean my head down on Aaron's shoulder as we watch Andrew climb between Megan's spread open legs and start removing the last of her clothing.

"No!" Megan screams, and thrashes against the restraints. "No!"

"*Meg, please,*" *I whisper under my breath, praying, hoping she accepts him, lets him inside her and falls into this world we've created. I need her— I need my best friend back.*

"*Christine,*" *Andrew says, turning to look at me,* "*maybe it'll be better if you help me.*"

My mouth waters, and I stand up to walk back over to the bed.

"*You'll need to talk to her,*" *Andrew says into my ear quietly, so no one else can hear him, like it's our secret to share.* "*Persuade her to say yes.*"

Nodding, I lie down with Megan.

Her big blue eyes find mine, tears streaming down her face.

"*Meg, please, I promise everything is okay. You'll like it, I promise. I miss you so much, and all I want is for you to be back in my life.* Please. *Just say yes.*" *I put my hand around her jaw and kiss her forehead.* "*I love you so much. I would never let anyone hurt you.*"

"*You've let him brainwash you, Chris,*" *Meg cries softly,* "*I don't even recognize you anymore.*"

I smile at her. "*Do you miss me, Meg?*"

She nods reluctantly, pressing her lips together.

"*So do this with me. Let me show you how good it can be. Let me back into your life.*"

She's silent for a long moment, then she nods, her voice a small whisper that feels forced. "*Okay.*"

I feel heat blooming on my cheeks as I slide my hand down her stomach slowly, between her legs and through her pussy. "*Spread your legs, Meg. I'll get you ready for him, okay?*"

Megan's teeth press down onto her lip, but she spreads her legs for me slowly, letting me stroke her clit. I tease her until she's a whimpering mess, her pussy gushing fluid that coats my fingers.

I don't notice Andrew positioning himself between her legs until he's sliding inside her, then she's groaning louder.

Andrew pushes my hand away from Meg, and I find his eyes as he thrusts between her legs. He smiles, his face creasing with pleasure as he fucks her.

Giggling, I bring Megan's face to mine, "doesn't he feel good? He'll make you come so hard, Meg. Just let go."

Megan tugs on the restraints, her back arching, then Andrew is grabbing her throat until her face turns red.

"Go sit down, Christine," Andrew grunts, and I feel moisture drip between my legs as I get up and walk back to where Benjamin and Aaron are watching from the couch.

I sit down, watching from the small distance as Andrew thrusts into Megan.

I can't see much. I can only hear the slickness between them and the sounds from their mouths. It turns my panties to a drenched mess, and as Aaron gets up to cross the space and join his brother, I grip onto Benjamin's forearm and bite my lip.

Closing my eyes, I let darkness wash over me as my other senses take the driver's seat—the sounds of two of the Hallows Boys with my best friend, the smell of the burning candles, the faint taste of beer in my mouth from the kiss I shared with Andrew only moments ago, the feel of Benjamin's skin under my fingernails.

It isn't so much about being in this round of games, as I don't need to be touched or do the touching—I just thrive in this setting. The erotic darkness, the intense thrill of need that runs through me in this place.

Benjamin kisses the top of my head as he gets up to join his brothers and Megan, and I'm left sitting on the couch by myself.

Opening my eyes, I watch the best I can from this angle.

All three of them touching her, using her for their own pleasure. I feel so fucking proud, so loved and in charge, like I'm finally going to get my best friend back. Like she'll finally be a part of this family. I start to imagine where she'll fit into our relationship. Will we be together too? Or will the boys enjoy her like they all enjoy me?

Will we all grow old together, raising kids and blending our families to create a new Blackmore? A Blackmore who's rid of judgement, of hate, one who Aaron and Benjamin can be together in and be proud of?

I'm pulled from my thoughts when I hear a shout, and I realize I've

closed my eyes again as my fantasies took over like their own universe.
"Christine! Oh my god, Christine, get over here! Oh my god!"

My eyes snap open, and I fly across the room to where Benjamin is
shouting. How long have I been sitting there in my own world? All four of
them are naked, except for the blood that covers their skin—red and dark and
everywhere.

Benjamin is pressing his hands to Megan's neck, to the slit that's now
sliced into her milky skin, where blood is spurting. My stomach turns leaden,
like it's going to fall straight from my gut out my ass.

I look around, finding Aaron's panicked gaze, his face splattered with
blood as he screams, then I seek out Andrew, looking for strength, but I find
his face dripping with a sheet of blood, his mouth spread into a smile as he
continues to thrust between Megan's legs, a knife in his hand.

CHAPTER 20

SAGE

I RUN FROM THE CRYPT SO FAST THAT I GET DIZZY, THEN I SPILL the entirety of my stomach onto the grass.

I'm violently sick again as the story from the notebook plays on a loop in my mind. It's almost as if I'm there, the way my mother wrote the story, her mind dark and so obsessed with my father that it almost feels childish.

This is worse than I imagined when the boys told me the information about these games. I assumed it wouldn't involve anything that felt as personal as this. I start to wonder as I'm walking back inside the crypt if every journal is like this one. Maybe there're other girls throughout the years who have written the story of their time in the games.

I close the door behind me and walk across the crypt to the wall where the girls' names are carved.

The first name, right at the top, is Christine Spencer —my mom.

The last name, right at the bottom, is Sage Lindman.

I feel like I'm going to be sick again, but my stomach aches with emptiness.

Pulling out my phone, I type out a message to Beckham, one that I feel deep in my soul.

ME:

> Do whatever you have to do to end the Hallows Games.

As tears pool in my eyes, I walk to the bookcase and pull down the next book, dedicating the rest of my night to reading every single word on this shelf. I want to learn it all, understand it all, picture it all. Because there's no way any year that followed my parents' last one is any worse.

CHAPTER 21

BECKHAM

With Sage spending the night at home with her grandmother, Kai takes the opportunity to call a Hallows Boys meeting.

We're nearing the new year, which means we'll have to induct the next generation soon, then teach them everything we know about the games.

I'm sick to my stomach, though, especially after receiving Sage's message.

Do whatever you have to do to end the Hallows Games.

It makes me wonder what she learned tonight. Did her grandmother have information that she shared with her that we don't know about? Maybe she started looking through her family albums again and started hating everything about the games.

I'm worried, sure, but most of all, I'm more inclined to end this shit tonight.

Even though I've been sitting here in Kai's garage and

listening to him and Vinny flip through social media profiles, I haven't said anything yet.

I don't want to involve Sage in this. I don't want Vinny and Kai to get pissed off at her for feeling like this, because they are dedicated to the Hallows Games and the tradition it holds. I don't know how either of them will react.

I'm toying with a loose thread on the edge of my t-shirt when Kai pulls my attention. "Becks, what do you think about these three?"

He's holding his phone out to me, showing me a photo of three boys he wants to induct into this sick tradition, and my heart thumps harder.

His brows pull down when I don't answer, and he snaps his fingers. "Hello? Earth to Becks? Care to fucking participate?"

"Not really," I say, and both Kai and Vinny's expressions turn confused.

"What do you mean, B?" Vinny asks, crossing his arms over his chest. "We need to get this done. It's almost January."

I feel the words burning in the back of my throat like vomit, and when I open my mouth, they come flying out.

"We don't have to fucking do this, you know." I sit up a little straighter. "We could just *not* bring anyone else into this shit."

"What?" Kai asks. "What are you talking about?"

"Did that thought ever cross your minds?" I spit, my voice getting angrier. "Just *not* creating another generation, letting the games die with us? We don't *have* to keep this fucking tradition going!"

"Becks, of course we do. Those are the rules. We don't get to just decide not to finish our job," Vinny says, his emerald eyes filling with curiosity.

"The founders are dead!" I yell. "Who's going to know if we don't?"

When Kaiden starts cracking each knuckle slowly, I know

I'm pissing him off. His voice is calm when he finally speaks again. "Beckham, we're going to pick another generation, and the Hallows Games will continue past us, so get on board or get the fuck out."

I scoff, shaking my head as I stand up and clap my hands together once. "I'll *get the fuck out*, then."

"Becks," Vinny says, standing.

"Let him," Kai says, rolling his eyes and looking back at his phone like the careless bastard he is. "He'll be back. He's nothing without the Hallows Games."

I laugh, half hoping Vinny leaves with me. He doesn't, though, he just looks at me like a confused little boy, trying to pick between his two favorite toys.

Shaking my head in disbelief, I storm out of the garage, one place on my mind.

———

IT'S AROUND TWO IN THE MORNING WHEN I GET TO THE cemetery, the air freezing cold and dry.

The darkness is so thick that I'm almost frightened, or I would be if I wasn't so angry and dedicated to my plan. My Nikes crunch against the leaves as I walk through the graveyard, careful not to spill any of the gasoline that's in the cans I have in either hand. I didn't bother putting on a coat, instead just wearing a thin t-shirt that hugs my chest. I want to feel the cold tonight. I want to feel everything as I move through my favorite place—*our* favorite place—and I destroy it.

Do whatever you have to do to end the Hallows Games, Sage had said, and I don't know any other way besides this.

Destroy the crypts, all the evidence. The journals and the names on the walls and the rules and *all of it*. Then the games won't exist anymore.

When I reach the crypt, I put down the gas cans and step back to look at the structure. I take a moment to say a silent goodbye to the games, to my memories, and to the boy who used to love this game. He's dead now, gone from someone who thrived in the darkness to someone who's afraid of the nighttime because of nightmares.

I spit on the crypt, saliva landing against the concrete, then I fish out my wallet to get the key for the crypts. When I slide my finger into the slot I keep it in, though, it's empty.

Not wanting to waste time going home to see if the key fell out somewhere there, I decide to just douse the outside concrete and hope the structures come crumbling down.

I grab the first can and start drenching the walls, the steps that lead to the door, the whole area around it, then I grab the second can and do the same thing to the other crypt.

Throwing the empty can at the edge of the crypt, I put my hand in my pocket and pull out a lighter.

As I ignite the lighter, then throw it onto the gasoline covered cement, I feel the anger in my veins dissipating a little. As the first crypt goes up in flames, I watch as the fire travels to the second, igniting that fire as well.

And just like that… the Hallows Games die before my eyes, alongside all the anger I've been carrying in my chest.

CHAPTER 22

VINNY

I wake up early the next day, hoping I'll have a message from Becks waiting for me. When I see my phone has no notifications, I sigh and throw myself into a hot shower.

After Beckham stormed out of Kaiden's last night, we decided on three boys who fit the role as Hallows Boys perfectly, then I went home, hoping to find Beckham there waiting for me. Unfortunately, he didn't show up, so I texted and called him until midnight, but then fell asleep waiting for a response.

It isn't like him to shut me out, but maybe this whole next generation thing is really getting to him. As I shower, I make the decision to walk over to his house.

It's New Year's Eve, anyway, and we need to figure out what we're doing tonight. I'm hoping we're driving into the closest city to see some fireworks, maybe grab a hotel and spend the night giving Sage fireworks between her legs.

I'm hard and full of tension when I get out of the shower,

and as I get dressed, I hope maybe Sage is done with breakfast with her grandmother earlier than she said after all.

The walk to Beckham's is short, but my wet hair makes me colder in the winter chill. His dad's car isn't on the driveway, so I walk into the house without knocking, heading straight for Beckham's room.

He's still asleep, curled under his blankets, so I kick off my shoes and climb under them with him to wake him up.

Kissing his jaw, I smell the faint scent of gasoline, but when he wakes up and runs his hands down my back, every thought in my mind disappears.

He moans as I kiss him. "Good morning."

"Morning, B," I breathe, sucking his neck. "I've been worried about you."

He grinds his pelvis against me. "Oh? Why's that?"

"You didn't answer your phone all night, not to mention the crazy anti-Hallows Boys rampage you went on at Kai's." I groan, but at my words, he freezes.

"*Crazy?*" he questions. "That's what you think?"

He sits up, and I follow him. "No, I mean—*yeah*, you were acting kinda crazy, B, but I get it. You've been through a lot. We just need to talk about this."

"I'm not crazy for wanting this sick tradition to end," he snaps, running his hand through his hair.

"If it wasn't for this *sick tradition*, we wouldn't be together, and we wouldn't have Sage. Is that something you want to imagine? Because I don't."

"Of course not, V." He sighs, his blue eyes tired.

I feel angry, like he's ashamed of what we are, who we are, and everything we've done together. "What the fuck, Beckham? You would rather have not found us?"

"I didn't say that Vinny!" he shouts. "I'm just saying it needs to fucking *end*."

"Before now, being a Hallows Boy was a huge part of our personalities—it basically *was* our personalities." My brows pull down, confusion and anger and malice inside of me burning so hot that I want to yell.

He shakes his head, shuffling closer to me and wrapping his arms around my center, pulling my head against his shoulder. "Stop getting mad at me, Vinny. I love you, I'm sorry."

I take a deep breath in, smelling him again. "Why do you smell like gasoline?"

Beckham leans away from me. "What? I don't."

"You do." I eye him, and his face goes white as he swings his legs over the side of the bed and stands up.

"I'm going to take a shower. Do you want to come?"

"Becks." I stand up, following after him, something gnawing at my gut with how he's acting. "What's going on?"

He turns to look at me as I approach him in the doorway, and his gaze has hardened. "I burned it down."

My brows pull down, having no clue what he's talking about. "What?"

"All of it," he says, his fingers pulling at his curly hair. "The crypts. I burned them down. The games are over."

"*What?!*" I gape, unable to find any other words to say right now. My mouth opens and closes twice before I can take a breath. I swear my heart stops beating. "Becks, *what?*"

The doorbell rings then, making me jump. My skin has turned prickly with goosebumps, and I follow Beckham as he goes to answer the door.

When he pulls it open, there are two police officers standing on the porch, hands on their belts. The older of the two speaks. "Beckham Bentley?"

My heart drops, my stomach turns to liquid, blood going cold with panic.

"Yeah?" Becks says, holding on to the door like he needs it for balance.

"We got an anonymous tip that you had something to do with the fire at the Blackmore Cemetery last night, do you know anything about that?" the officer asks, and my head spins.

I do my best to walk to Beckham's side, even as my legs wobble, and he looks at me for a brief second before he looks back to the cop.

"I don't know what you're talking about," he says, and when the cops both move their gazes to my face, I know they can read his lies on my skin.

The officer pulls a piece of paper from his pants pocket, unfolding it and holding it out for us to see. He points to it with one finger. "Can you explain this image, then?"

Pulling my top lip into my mouth and under my teeth, I bite down painfully, studying the photo of Beckham in the cemetery, a gas can in either hand.

Moisture fills my eyes, and I grab onto the back of Beckham's t-shirt like it will somehow save him from being taken away.

When Beckham doesn't say anything, the police officer pulls his handcuffs from the side of his belt. "You'll need to turn around for me, son. Put your hands behind your back."

Beckham chokes on his words, turning to look at me with pain shining in his eyes. "*Vinny.*"

"What are the charges?" I ask, desperate to delay the inevitable. "No one is even alive to press charges. All the Blackmores are dead!"

The officer looks at Becks, answering my question. "They found a body in the crypt. You're under arrest for murder."

"*What!?*" Beckham screams, shaking his head. "No, no, there's no way. There was no one there!"

"Turn around," the officer says, sadness in his eyes. "Don't make this harder on yourself than it needs to be."

Beckham turns around, putting his hands behind his back, then he twists his head so he can look at me, tears streaming down his face. "Vinny, call my dad."

I'm shaking violently, nausea twisting in my gut, and I reach over to hold Beckham's face between my hands as I demand answers from the cops.

"Who was it? Who was inside the crypt?! You can't just take him without telling us!" I yell, desperate to keep him with me for longer.

The officer takes a breath, the handcuffs clicking into place around Beckham's wrists, then he looks at me. "The body was identified as Sage Blackmore."

My body suddenly numbs, and my hands drop from Beckham's face.

Beckham goes rigid, and he shakes his head rapidly. "No, there's no way it was Sage." He looks at me, words shaky and distressed. "Call her right now. It wasn't her. There's no way."

I push through the door, shoving one of the officers out of the way in time to puke all over the sidewalk violently. My shaking hands go to my knees, and I throw up until my stomach is empty, then I dry heave for a minute before I stand up straight.

"Vinny, it wasn't her," Becks says urgently. "Call her, she'll answer, she was home all night."

The officer that isn't holding on to Beckham's handcuffed wrists puts a hand on my shoulder. "Her body was identified by the family. I'm sorry."

I look up, past the cops, and Beckham turns to look at me. When our eyes connect, it's pain unlike anything I've felt before.

If I wasn't so dizzy, I would launch myself at him, instead I just lean against the house and spit at his feet.

"You *killed her!*" I scream, my voice hurting my sore throat. "*How could you do this!?*"

Beckham's face goes sheet white, then he drops to his knees and screams at the top of his lungs, tears starting to stream down his cheeks in rivers that pull more anger from me. I want to hurt him, kill him, climb across the space and strangle him, but before I have a chance to act on my impulsive thoughts, the police officer pulls him back up to his feet. "Let's go, Beckham."

"Take him!" I scream, slamming my hand against the house as Beckham's gaze meets mine once more. "Don't come back! I never want to fucking see you again!"

CHAPTER 23

BECKHAM

"I'M GOING TO GET YOU OUT OF HERE, BECKHAM."

My dad is sitting across from me in the small interrogation room that the Blackmore Police Department has kept me in for the last eight hours. He's still dressed in a suit and tie from work, and he's typing away on his cell phone as he talks.

"I have Marten coming down—my lawyer. He'll cut you a deal and get you out of here, worst you're looking at is community service."

"Dad… are you delusional?" I ask, resting my cheek on my hand. "I'm being charged with murder; I doubt it's going to be that easy."

He still doesn't look up from his cell phone. "Don't you worry about that, son. It pays to have connections in this town, after all. You're lucky your old man is someone of power."

I roll my eyes, feeling sick to my stomach.

My father just so happens to be one of three people who sit

on the town's council, and he makes it seem like he's the president of the United States of fucking America.

"Okay." I sigh, putting my head down on the table. After eight hours of on and off interrogation, I'm exhausted.

No, I didn't know Sage was inside the crypt. No, I didn't have an argument with Sage. No, I never planned to hurt Sage. No, I didn't lure her out to the cemetery and murder her. No, no one helped me burn down the crypts. No, there was no specific reason I did it.

I'm spent, mentally and physically, and all I want them to do is book me and send me off to county jail. It'll be better there than here, sitting in this small room with no air and my father pretending he's POTUS adjacent.

At least in jail I can get this all out of my system, pick a fight with someone and get the absolute piss beaten out of me for killing the one girl in the entire world I've ever loved.

For betraying the man I love, the brother who has given me everything, the family we've built between the four of us.

I destroyed it all.

I fucking destroyed it all.

———

I'M STILL SITTING IN THE SMALL INTERROGATION ROOM A DAY later, since Blackmore doesn't have any holding cells, when my father and my lawyer come through the door with the arresting officer.

"Good news and bad news," Marten says in greeting, slapping a file folder down on the table. "You made bail, but they're putting you on house arrest until your hearing."

"Can't I just go to jail? I'm guilty," I say, looking up at my father.

"I don't want you to say that ever again, Beckham," Marten

says, then he looks at the officer. "Especially in front of police officers."

The cop tips his head. "I didn't hear a word."

"What the actual *fuck* is going on here?" I spit. "Why am I being let go?"

"I told you," my dad says, a smile pulling up his lips. "You're lucky your old man is powerful around here."

"Dad, *please!*" I shout. "You're on the town council in a small town in Georgia. Stop acting like you control the fucking senate!"

My dad's face goes red, but I'm too exhausted and angry and depressed to give a shit about hurting his feelings or ego. I don't *want* to go home. I want to be put behind bars for the rest of my life. The last thing I want is fucking freedom. I don't deserve freedom. I deserve to be punished for doing this to Sage. I should have gone inside the crypt before I set it on fire, but I couldn't find my key and I didn't want to take the time to look for it. I wanted to end the games more than I wanted anything else, and that was my mistake. I let my anger go to my head, and it got my girl killed.

In an effort to protect the future generations in Blackmore, I destroyed my entire world.

The officer approaches me. "Sit back, let's get these cuffs off of you."

I groan, but I lean back in my chair and give him access to where my cuffs are attached to the bottom of the table. When he's undone them, I stand up and look at Marten. "Do I need some sort of ankle monitor or something?"

"No, we made a deal with the judge that your father will keep a close eye on you. You're not to leave the house unless it's for court, got it?"

"Wow," I deadpan, "so much trust for an eighteen-year-old murderer. Did the judge get wasted at breakfast?"

"How about you just say thank you, hmm, Beckham?" my father says, turning up his lip in disapproval.

I take a bow, turning to all three men. "Thank you for keeping the streets of Blackmore safe."

———

WHEN MY FATHER AND I GET HOME, KAI IS WAITING ON THE steps.

My stomach turns to lead, weighing me down and keeping me in the front seat of my dad's truck.

He turns off the engine, sighing. "One minute. Then he needs to leave."

"Just tell him to leave, please. I don't want to see anyone," I mumble, grabbing my seatbelt with my fist and squeezing it. I can't get my body to move, can't get the strength in my legs or arms to stand up and face Kai.

My dad sighs, unbuckling his belt without another word and getting out of the car. He walks to the front door, says something, and then Kai's gaze finds mine. As he narrows his eyes, he nods and stuffs his hands into his pants pockets, then my dad breezes past him and goes inside the house. I feel like I'm going to be sick as Kai starts to walk toward the car, and I find myself wishing I could make myself invisible.

Kai pulls on the door handle, opening the passenger door and sighing. "You can't hide from me."

"I don't wanna talk," I mutter, looking at my feet. "Please."

"You think I owe you the respect of letting you avoid us?" Kai clicks his tongue. "The only reason I'm not beating you to death is because there's a witness."

I follow his line of sight, to where my father is watching from the living room window.

Kai gets closer, his voice dropping lower. "Let me make

something *very* clear, Beckham. You are no longer a Hallows Boy —you are no longer a part of our family, you will never see Vinny again, and you will never speak to me again. Show your face in school and I'll *end you*, got it?"

"Wow, big scary Kai," I deadpan, feeling exhausted and annoyed and numb inside. "You think I want any of those things? I'll put a gun in my mouth the second I get the chance."

"Good," he says, taking a step back. To my surprise, he doesn't say anything else or punch me in the face, he just walks away, taking the remainder of my soul with him.

CHAPTER 24

KAIDEN

It's one week after Sage's death that I check on Vinny again.

I'm half worried he'll try to kill himself, but part of me has hope that he won't. He lost everything in the flick of a lighter—both Sage and Beckham, the two people in the world he's ever loved, and all hope of a future for him was tied to them.

"Hey," I say, walking into his bedroom.

His front door was unlocked, and part of me wonders if he's waiting for Becks to show up and fix this. Maybe he's waiting for Sage to creep in and tell him this is all one big joke.

He's under the blankets in bed but answers me anyway. "Hey."

"Wanna go do something tonight?" I ask, sitting down next to him. His eyes peek out from under the blankets, and he narrows them.

"Why aren't you off in a depressive hole somewhere too? You loved Sage just as much as I did."

I shrug, not letting the thought of Sage seep into my mind. "We all have different ways to deal with shit."

"And yours is to pretend she never existed?" Vinny spits, sitting up and looking at me with daggers in his eyes. "She was a *real* fucking person, Kai, and you should be mourning her. We loved her. We loved Beckham. Everything is *fucked!*"

"Okay, *relax*," I growl, feeling defensive.

"No!" he shouts. "Why don't you give a fuck?!"

"I *do*, Vincent!" I yell, shoving his chest. "I've been helping her grandmother plan the fucking funeral!"

Vinny's face falls, and his eyes sparkle with moisture. "What?"

"Yeah," I spit, shoving him again. "So don't say I'm pretending she never existed, because I'm trying to make sure she's honored the right way."

He sniffles. "Sorry."

"Yeah." I stand up, crossing my arms over my chest. "So, are we going to do something tonight, or not?"

"Nah," Vinny says, lying back down under his blankets. "I just wanna get some sleep."

Heat spreads through my face as anger simmers in my chest. Stepping toward him, I rip the blankets off. "Vincent, get the fuck up! You can't just lie here forever. Get up, and let's find something to do to get our minds off this, at least for tonight."

"There's nothing, Kai. Nothing is going to make me feel any better." He looks at me with pain in his eyes, and my frustration fades a little.

Sighing, I sit down at the edge of his bed.

"I just want to know that Becks is in as much pain as me — I want to know that he's in *more* fucking pain than me," Vinny whispers. "Does that make me a bad person?"

Shaking my head, a small grin tugs at the edge of my lips.

"Not at all. Why don't we go make sure Becks feels exactly what you're feeling?"

———

I KNOW THAT MADNESS HAS ENTERED MY MIND WHEN I FEEL adrenaline pulsing through my veins as we walk to Beckham's. I'm excited. Excited to punish Becks for what he's done. And even though I told him to never speak to me again, I'm very interested in what he has to say for himself when he's faced with both of us together.

He was a shell of a boy the other day, and I didn't feel completely fulfilled after our encounter. He wasn't scared of me, just accepted the fact that he's dead to us and let me walk away without a fight.

Today will be different. I'll get him to feel exactly what we feel deep down.

Even though I won't show it, my world is shattered. He took the one person I've ever let under my skin, the one person who ever fit against me like the matching puzzle piece, and he's going to pay for it.

I thought maybe his charges, spending his life in prison, would be enough. But it isn't. I want him to taste the fear that Sage probably felt that night, when fire crept up on her and engulfed her, took her skin and flesh and bones.

Even though I've looked at Beckham as a brother since we could walk and talk, I will punish him like anyone else who's hurt me.

And I'll fucking enjoy it.

CHAPTER 25

BECKHAM

My dad went to work, even though we were told by the court that I essentially had to be babysat twenty-four hours a day. He said not to take things too seriously, that no one would come checking on me, since he's *powerful* and all that.

I don't bother leaving the house. Where would I go, anyway? Sage is dead, my brothers hate me, and I burned down the one place I've always gone to when I needed clarity.

I decide to spend the day in bed, wearing a pair of Vinny's sweatpants that he left at my house, my chest bare. I consider slitting my wrists, but I think I want to see how this all plays out, and I want to get the chance to apologize to Sage's family. I owe them that. I owe Kai and Vinny my apologies too, but I know that I need to give them time to grieve before I approach that.

As far as grieving goes, I don't think I will. I lost so much in the flash of my eyes that I can't feel a fucking thing anymore. I haven't been able to cry since I got home from the police station, and my entire body and soul feels numb.

I'm on my seventh episode of some show about storage units when my doorbell rings. Pausing the TV, I swing my legs over the side of my bed to get up. As I walk through the house, I half hope it's the cops coming to make sure I'm abiding by all my rules so they can drag me to jail after all.

The cold of early January hits my face as I pull open the front door, and I find Vinny and Kai standing there, both in black hoodies.

My mouth falls open a fraction, a small gasp squeezing through my lips. I take a breath in, studying both of their faces and reading the anger and grief etched in their skin. The air feels sharp and ragged as I finally speak.

"Hi."

Kai pushes through the door, shoving me backwards as he and Vinny both step into the house, the door shutting loudly behind them.

I stumble back, catching myself before I fall. "What the fuck?"

Kai grabs me by the shoulders. "Let's talk."

Pushing his chest, I try to get him to step away from me, but his face twists with a pleased smile as I struggle to get away.

"Talk, then," I growl, my cheeks heating. I haven't had a chance to get angry about all of this yet, and part of me wonders if Kai is here to pull that reaction from me — like maybe deep down he's doing me a favor.

I find Kai's eyes, so dark but so tired, and he smiles from ear to ear before he shoves me down onto the couch. "Oh, not me. I have nothing to say to you, *bitch*."

Vinny steps into my line of sight then, like a scared little mouse coming out from behind the big, bad wolf, and I shake my head at him. "What is it, V?"

His teeth smash together, his jaw going tight enough that the vein in his neck bulges out. "You destroyed everything, Beckham."

"I know," I breathe, looking up at him from the couch, tears filling my eyes. He looks so fucking sad, like there's nothing but a dead soul behind his exhausted eyes, and it makes me want to die all over again. If I'm the reason Vinny feels like this, I don't deserve to be left breathing at the end.

His strong hand goes around my throat then, and he uses the hold to lift me up until I'm in the right position for him to punch me across the face. I grunt, my head snapping to the side as I heat pulses through my cheek.

"You fucking destroyed *everything*," he growls, then he punches me again.

I cry out this time, swallowing hard around the hold he has on my throat. "*I'm sorry.*"

He punches me again, and again, and again, until he notices there's blood coating his knuckles, then he drops the hold he has on me and takes a step back.

"Don't stop," I say, crying, wiping the blood from my nose and lip as I stand up. "Keep going, I deserve it."

Vinny's eyes find mine, emeralds that I looked into during the best moments of my life are now empty, and I feel a sob clawing up my throat. I swallow down the noise before I can show both of them that I'm broken, then I take a step toward Vinny.

"Hit me again, V."

He clenches his jaw tighter, then storms toward me and throws his fist again. Grunting, I fly back down onto the couch, putting a hand to my bloody nose. "*Vinny.*"

He climbs on top of me, his knees going either side of my ribcage on the couch as he hits me across the face again, my blood spraying onto the upholstery. "Fuck."

I smile at him, because I can feel the blood covering my

teeth, and his green eyes flare as he looks down at me. That's when I feel it — *he's hard.*

Running my tongue over my teeth, I let my lips pull up at the sides a little higher. "You *like* seeing me like this? Covered in fucking blood?"

As the realization hits him that I've noticed he's turned on, his face curls into disgust and he grabs my face in his big hand, squeezing my jaw. He spits on my face, "Fuck you."

I smile, his saliva dripping down my cheek. "I know you want to, baby."

Before he can react, I punch him across the face, knocking him off balance so he falls to the floor. I hear him swear under his breath as he catches himself, and I sit up to look at him. "Get the fuck out of my house."

Kai laughs, and I'd almost forgotten he was here, standing in the corner like some lurking fucking gnome.

"What the fuck do you guys want? Huh?" I bark, standing up and moving away from them, the blood dripping from my nose and mouth, making it hard to breathe. "Just get the fuck out and leave me alone."

Kai takes a slow step closer, like a lion teasing their prey. "*Careful,* Becks."

I chuckle, spitting on the floor as the taste of blood becomes overwhelming, and then I look at Vinny. "Is this what you want? To hurt me? *Kill me?* Teach me a lesson? Well, lesson fucking learned, V, I mean nothing to you anymore. Now fucking *leave!*"

"That's the lesson you think I want to give you?" Vinny sneers, standing up and prowling toward me, his face a mask of hate that makes my stomach dip.

Before I can answer him, he's grabbing me again, slamming me against the wall and pressing against my back. His dick is still hard in his pants, and a small twinge of panic runs through me when a desperate, angry whisper slivers from between his lips on his next words. "No, Beckham, that isn't the lesson I want you to fucking learn."

I feel him twist as he holds me, then he calls for Kai to come over. "Hold him down."

As I wriggle in his arms, fear settles in my gut that I haven't felt in a long time, one that tells me he's unhinged, that this isn't really him, that I need to get *far* away from whatever Kaiden-shaped monster is inside my soulmate before he does something he regrets. Something he can't take back.

"Vinny," I say, struggling against him as Kai comes over and puts himself on top of me, then they're dragging me back over to the couch, my arms bent behind my back like they were the other day when I got arrested, totally at their mercy, left with no defense to get away.

As I'm shoved down on the couch, I feel Kaiden hold me in place, using my arms to keep me pinned against the upholstery that smells like detergent and old smoke, then he's laughing, his voice unrecognizable. "Teach him a fucking lesson since he really wants one, Vinny."

Vinny chuckles, my sweet and caring and handsome love, and it feels foreign and far away, then he's yanking my sweatpants down to my knees, my boxers following soon after.

I shout, "*Vinny*! What the fuck!"

He doesn't say anything, but I can hear how heavily he's breathing as he puts himself behind me, then I hear his zipper sliding down before he frees himself from his pants.

"Why don't you at least use some of the fucking blood to lube yourself up, Vin, huh?!" I scream, desperate, angry, hating him. "This is what you want?! Me scared of you? Hating you?!"

He spits on my asshole, then pushes inside, making me scream as pain slices through me.

"Yeah," he says softly, his voice tired. "This is what I fucking want, B."

I feel the tears rolling down my face before I even realize I'm crying, then my body is turning numb as he thrusts into me, his hips hitting my ass punishingly. Biting down on my lip, I refuse to give him any more satisfaction than he's already getting.

Kai is still on top of me, his weight holding down my top half and my arms as Vinny fucks into me from behind, and I let every muscle in my body fall lax in an effort to relieve some of the pain.

I know I deserve it, though, every ounce of pain they can give me, because I took everything they loved. I destroyed the lives they had.

So as the man I love thrusts into me from behind, and the brother I would give my life for holds me down as punishment, I press my eyes closed and take it.

CHAPTER 26

VINNY

I HATE THE PLEASURE ROCKING THROUGH ME, I HATE THE FACT it's from *him*, Beckham, and I hate that I'm enjoying taking something from him that he didn't want to give me.

I hate that I hurt him, and I hate that I fucking loved it.

I want to scream, pound into him harder, faster, until my orgasm barrels through me and makes me shake.

It isn't fair that, even as I destroy him, I still fucking love him, still hate myself. Every single moment, every single thrust of my hips feels wrong and right at the same time.

Becks cries under me, his body trembling, his strangled voice making my heart pound. "I'm sorry, *baby*. I'm sorry."

My hips thrust harder, my cock driving into his ass until finally my climax slams into me, making me grab his thick ass and hips, a loud groan pouring from my mouth.

After his ass is full of cum, I pull out and smack his ass harshly before I pull my pants up and walk across the room.

"Let him go."

Kaiden looks at me, still sitting atop Becks and holding his wrists in place, even as Beckham doesn't struggle to free himself. "You're done?"

"I'm fucking done. Let's go," I say, unable to look at either of them. "I don't want to see him ever again."

Kaiden lets go, then comes and stands next to me. He grabs the back of my head and he puts his forehead to mine. "Do you feel better?"

Tears fill my eyes, and I shake my head. "I feel worse."

Kai sighs, his lips twitching. "Maybe you should punch him again."

"No," I say, barely holding myself together. "Can we just go?"

I hear Beckham crying through the white noise in my mind, so I look over at him. He's pulled his sweats back up, and he's sitting upright on the couch. When his ocean eyes find mine, my heart cracks in half. He has blood on his face, from his nose and mouth and a small cut on his cheekbone, and I want to cross the space and wipe him clean.

I don't, though, even as tears make clean lines in the blood.

"Let's go," Kai says, slapping a hand down on my shoulder.

I nod, but then the doorbell rings, making all three of us look to the front door. In a panic, Beckham jumps up and runs to the bathroom, and a second later, he's coming out with a wet towel against his face in an effort to clean off the blood.

"Go sit down," Beckham growls to us as he passes, nodding to the couch as he throws the bloody towel on the floor against the wall. My heart pounds, and my legs turn to frozen blocks, so Kai has to drag me the short distance to the couch.

When Beckham opens the front door, I spot an older man on the porch dressed in a dark blue suit who I don't recognize.

"Marten," Beckham greets the man. "What's up?"

"I called your dad, but wanted to tell you in person," the man, Marten, says. "Can I come in?"

Becks holds the door open and steps to the side. "Sure."

Marten eyes me and Kai, and I feel nervous as he turns back to Beckham, clearly taking in his injured face. "Could we talk in private?"

"Just tell me, Marten." Beckham sighs, closing the front door and facing all of us.

"Well, I have some great news!" Marten says, his tone turning cheerful. "The murder charges have been dropped! You'll only be charged with arson, and that'll be easy to get rid of in court, since there's no proof you lit the fire!"

"Wait, what?" Becks questions, stuttering. "Start over—why are they dropping the murder charges?"

Marten sits down at one of the chairs at the little table in the room, then pulls a folder out of the briefcase I didn't notice he was carrying. As he opens the folder, he holds a piece of paper out to Becks. "Sage Blackmore's autopsy. She was already dead when the fire started."

"*What?!*" I shout, Kai and I both shooting up from our seats at the same time, but Becks walks to the table and grabs the piece of paper with shaking hands.

"How did she die?" Kai asks, voice tense, his hand turning into a fist at his side as the other grips the paper. We both walk to where Beckham is reading the autopsy and look over his shoulder to read alongside him.

AUTOPSY REPORT

PATIENT NAME: Sage Grace Blackmore

DOB: 01/14/2003

DOD: 12/31/2020

CAUSE OF DEATH: Gunshot wound to the chest.

NOTES: Although there was present burning on 60% of the body, there was no indication of smoke inhalation. Victim was deceased at the time of fire.

Before I can read any more, I feel bile sliding up my throat.

"I didn't kill Sage," Beckham breathes, dropping the piece of paper to the ground. "I didn't kill Sage."

Kai shoves past me, out the front door, then I hear him throwing up onto the grass.

I can't breathe, oxygen feeling too far and too thick and my lungs feeling small and drenched in anxiety.

Beckham whispers again, turning to look at me. "I didn't kill Sage."

I find his blue eyes filled with tears, and then I take a step away from him, shaking my head. "You didn't kill Sage."

Beckham turns to look at Marten, who's sitting at the table watching this information destroy our reality, and he clears his throat.

"Thanks for letting me know, Marten."

Marten nods as he stands up to leave. "Sure, son. Your house arrest was terminated. Just don't leave the county till we get you into court, got it?"

"Sure," Becks says, walking Marten to the door as Kai comes back inside, his arm over his mouth. "Thank you again."

Marten turns to look inside before Becks closes the front door, and it feels like he's looking at all three of us when he speaks now. "Try to stay out of trouble, okay?"

"You got it," Becks says, his voice still shaking from shock, then he closes the front door and puts his back to it. "I didn't kill Sage."

"You didn't fucking kill Sage, but who did?" Kaiden says, his features showing his renewed rage.

"Oh my god," I say, putting my fingers to my lips. "Oh *my god.*"

They both look at me, and my eyes fill with tears as a wave of anxiety passes through me. *"Oh my fucking god, what did I do?"*

I look across the room to Beckham, and his eyes are an ocean of sadness and pain. Taking a step toward him, tears stream down my face. "Becks."

"Don't," he says, shaking his head, trying to back up away from me, but he's already against the door. I feel a stabbing pain slice through my chest, and then Kai's hand comes down on my shoulder.

"Go sit down, Vincent."

Shaking my head, I look at Kai and find something serious in his eyes, so I turn and go to sit on the couch.

"Becks," Kaiden says, walking toward Beckham. "Let's talk, okay?"

"No," Becks says, shaking his head. "Can you guys leave? I don't want to do this."

"Beckham," I plead from the couch, and his eyes find me. "Please."

"What is there to say?" Beckham asks, putting his arms around his torso. "You can't just expect me to be okay right now, not after everything."

"I know," Kaiden says. *"We know.* But we need to talk about this, and we all need to stick together and figure out who killed our girl."

My lungs are burning with panic, and I gasp for air.

"Just… please, leave," Beckham says quietly, sidestepping both of us and slowly walking backwards to the hallways, like he can't take his eyes off of us, like he's worried we're going to attack him. My head feels light and dizzy, and I want to scream at the top of my lungs.

Digging my nails into my palms to feel the sting, I stand up again. "Becks, I'm sorry."

"Don't," he stops me before I can say any more, shaking his head as he continues to back away.

As Becks disappears into the bathroom, Kaiden looks at me, and I notice his face has gone pale. He doesn't say anything, just lets me read the pain and confusion and silent words in his eyes, then we both sit on the couch and take a deep breath.

CHAPTER 27

BECKHAM

I CRANK THE HOT WATER IN THE SHOWER AFTER I'VE CLOSED myself inside the bathroom, then I look in the mirror.

My face is already blooming with purple, and there's remnants of blood on my skin. I'm surprised Marten didn't say something, but I guess that explains the cautious look on his face when he first saw Kai and Vinny in the living room.

I feel a throb between my ass cheeks, but the pain is welcomed—because I know that it's what Vinny needed. Even though the entire reason for his actions was just dismissed, I know he needed to take that control from me.

I wish I could say I'm okay, though, and as I strip my clothes off and step into the burning shower, a sob rolls through me.

How do we come back from this? How can we possibly pretend none of this happened? How do we move on?

Sitting down on the tiled ground under the spray, I wrap my arms around my knees and pull them to my chest as I cry.

Sage would know how to handle this—she would know how to make me feel better. She would say the exact right thing to put the pieces of all three of us back together, and the reminder that she'll never be able to makes me cry harder.

Sage is gone, and Vinny has changed, and Kaiden is dead inside, and none of us will ever be okay again.

The water beats down on me, and I drop my head between my knees and gasp for air. I feel so broken, so torn apart from the inside out, like my organs are being held tight in someone's fist and I can't find the strength to breathe.

Everything hurts, from my face to my muscles to my chest. I just want the pain to stop, I want my piece of happy back. I want to move back in time and protect Sage from whoever hurt her, to shield Vinny from the pain of thinking it was my fault, to take back the violence I've created with my own hands.

Suddenly, the shower curtain moves to the side, making me jump. I look up, finding Vinny looking back at me, a tormented expression pulling down his handsome features.

"Can I get in?" he asks, his voice gruff and low.

Running my hands over my face, I nod silently.

The shower curtain falls back into place as he strips, then he's stepping into the shower and sitting down behind me, his legs going around my body so he can put his front to my back.

I feel another sob overcome me as his arms wrap around me, and his face falls to the back of my head.

"Becks..." he says, holding my body as it shakes.

He tightens his arms around me, and I fall back against him.

"I'm sorry..." he says, voice cracking as he kisses my hair. "I'm so sorry."

My cries taper off as I relax in his hold, sliding my hands up over his forearms. He sighs in relief, my touch softening his tensed muscles before he kisses down the back of my neck. "I love you. Tell me you can forgive me. Tell me everything is going to be okay."

Shaking my head, I squeeze his arms. "Nothing is okay, V. Nothing will ever be okay again. You get that, right? I killed your dad, and someone killed Sage, and everything is fucked."

"I know," he says softly, putting his face against my shoulder. "I know."

———

A HALF HOUR INTO SITTING UNDER THE HOT SPRAY OF THE shower, the water goes cold, forcing Vinny and I to get out.

I don't say anything as we both wrap towels around our waists and move to my bedroom. Kai has made himself comfortable on my bed, his legs crossed, arm behind his head and phone in his hand.

"We good?" Kaiden asks without looking up from his phone, and I catch Vinny's eye as I walk to my closet in silence to pull out some clean clothes.

"Fine," Vinny says, sighing.

"Cool," Kai says, standing up and slipping his feet into his shoes. "I'm heading to Sage's grandmas. Try not to kill each other while I'm gone."

"Sage's grandmas? What for?" I ask, my brows pulling down in confusion.

"I've been helping her with the funeral stuff. She's going through a lot."

I throw a pair of sweats and a t-shirt to Vinny, and then look at Kai again. "Can we come?"

Kaiden stares at me for a moment, then he looks at Vinny, who's getting dressed in silence. "Can you behave? She's not doing too well."

"We aren't children," I snap, and Kai's jaw goes tight.

Vinny pulls the t-shirt over his head, which is a little too tight and shows off his muscular arms. "We want to help too. We'll be fine, okay?"

"Fine," Kaiden concedes, heading for the door. "Let's go."

I quickly put on a pair of jeans and hoodie, and after Vinny has thrown his own hoodie back on, we all head out into the cold to walk to Sage's neighborhood.

The air smells fresh, and it makes me feel a little calmer as I take a deep breath. The trees have all long shed their leaves, the grass a crunchy mess of brown and green that makes the whole town look like it's out of a fall time magazine. I follow behind Kai and Vinny, my nerves still on edge, even as the sun warms my skin.

After five minutes, we're nearing Sage's neighborhood, and Kai slides his hands into the pockets of his pants. "So, what are we going to do about who killed her?"

Immediately, my pulse speeds back up, and I'm filled with a silent rage that burns my cold cheeks.

"The cops will find who did it, and then we'll figure out what to do," Vinny says, his hood up as he walks in front of me.

"Whoever did it is going to fucking die," I grit out between my teeth, trying to rein myself in, since I feel like I could scream.

"*Jesus*, Becks," Vinny says on a breath, turning around to look at me. I don't bother meeting his concerned gaze; I just keep my eyes ahead, ignoring the judgement in his tone.

"Agreed." Kaiden nods, and Vinny turns back around to send him a *what the fuck?* look.

We approach Sage's house before anyone can say anything else, and Kai skips up the steps to the terrace to knock on the front door.

"Let me do the talking. I don't think Sage's grandma will

appreciate the thought of her granddaughter having three boyfriends," Kaiden mutters just before the front door opens.

A small woman stands on the other side of the door, her hair grey and her face wrinkled with age, and she smiles when she looks at Kai.

"Kaiden Thorne, lookin' more handsome than ever." Her eyes graze over me and Vinny, then she looks back at Kai. "Who're your friends?"

Kai chuckles as he takes the time to introduce us. "This is Beckham and Vincent, Ms. Spencer, remember we talked about them?"

"I ain't senile, boy," Ms. Spencer says, grinning from ear to ear. "And haven't I told ya to call me Joyce?"

"Yes, ma'am, I'm sorry," Kaiden says, smiling.

"Well, come on in, boys." She holds the door open, stepping to the side. "You can tell me all about how ya know'd my Sage while I put on a pot of coffee."

Vinny and I share a nervous glance as we follow Kai into the house, and I close the door behind me before we all head into the homey kitchen, sitting down at the little table. Sage's grandma moves around slowly, getting to work on the coffee she promised.

When she turns around, she eyes Vinny first. "How'd ya know my granddaughter, son? School?"

"Yes, ma'am," Vinny says, clearing his throat. "I play football, so Sage and I knew each other from when she was cheering."

"Sad ya lost that playoff game, isn't it? My Sage only got that one game with y'all," Ms. Spencer says, sighing before she looks at me. "And you?"

"I had a few classes with her," I say, looking at Kaiden, though I'm not sure why. "We were all friends."

"I won't bother askin' what happened to your bruised up

face, and I'll assume you do some sorta boxin' club or something, okay?" Her face splits into a playful grin. "I'll also pretend like you ain't the boy who was goin' away for killin' my Sage until this morning."

I swallow hard. "Okay. I appreciate that."

"You two are friends with Kaiden here, so I'm sure you're just as sweet and pure hearted and looked out for my Sage," Ms. Spencer says, and I almost choke on my spit. I start to wonder how much time Kai has spent here, how much this woman knows about him and his relationship with her granddaughter. "So, I'll just say thank you, from the bottom of my heart, for makin' her feel at home here in Blackmore for the short time we had her here."

She starts to get emotional, so she turns and faces the coffeemaker again. I feel my heart swell, and so I clear my throat and speak. "Sage was one of a kind. She deserved better than this."

"She did," Ms. Spencer says, "and whoever did this to my girl is gonna get what's comin' to 'em."

"Did they say anything about any leads, Joyce?" Kai asks, like the two of them are best friends.

As she hands out empty coffee mugs, Ms. Spencer sighs. "A few, but nothin' credible. Just a few fingerprints and fibers at the scene they still gotta process."

I look at Vinny. "All of our DNA would be in the crypt, right?"

Kaiden shoots daggers at me with his gaze, and I sink down in my chair a little as coffee is poured into all the mugs. Ms. Spencer clicks her tongue at Kai. "Don't act like I'm some naive woman, Kaiden. I know what happens out at that cemetery. No need to pretend."

A small laugh sneaks out of my lips, so I grab my coffee and take a sip.

"Sorry, Joyce," Kai says, still glaring at me.

Ms. Spencer sits down, grabbing her own mug of coffee. "To answer your question, Beckham, yes, they found all of your DNA there."

"So, are we suspects?" Vinny asks, fear in his eyes.

"No," Ms. Spencer says, but she doesn't elaborate, and I don't think any of us have the balls to ask why not. We're just thankful none of us are under arrest.

The room falls into a silence that, surprisingly, isn't uncomfortable, and after a minute, Kai speaks again. "So, what's left to do for the funeral?"

"Well," Sage's grandmother says, sighing, "I think we've just about done everything besides pass out the invitations. That I'll leave to you boys, since I never met no one but Juliet who Sage was hangin' round."

"Has anyone spoken to Juliet? Told her what happened?" I ask, looking around the table. Sage and Juliet hadn't spoken in weeks, as far as I know. We managed to take over all her time after Halloween, bringing her into our circle and keeping her there with us. I almost feel bad for the loner girl.

"No," Kai says, looking at Ms. Spencer.

She shakes her head. "Only person I've spoken to is her uncle and a few of my distant relatives, all of whom said they won't be makin' it to the funeral. We didn't have no one else left."

"None of them are coming?" Kai asks, his brows furrowing with what I can tell is anger. "What about friends from California?"

"I don't know how to get in contact with none of 'em. Sage's phone burned up in that fire too." Ms. Spencer eyes me, and I sink down in my chair a little.

"Sorry," I mutter, chest tightening as I try to hold it together.

Vinny clears his throat. "When is the funeral?"

"A few days, on her birthday. She woulda been eighteen." Her eyes start to water as she chokes on sadness. "It ain't fair that she's gone."

Kai puts his hand on top of hers on the table to comfort her. "No, it isn't."

CHAPTER 28

VINNY

THE DAY OF SAGE'S FUNERAL, MY HEAD IS POUNDING SO HARD that I can barely stand upright. I haven't gone to school in a week. I don't know if Kai and Becks are going to school. I haven't spoken to either of them since we handed out funeral invitations three days ago.

It was hard to find people to come, since Sage's life solely revolved around us ever since she arrived in Blackmore. Juliet was nowhere to be found either. Her mom wouldn't even answer the door when we knocked and no one from school knew how to contact her. We can just hope she still has love inside of herself for the friend she once had, and she shows up to mourn her with everyone else.

Most of the cheer squad and football team agree to coming, save for a few of Rachel's loyalists. I don't blame them—why mourn someone they never knew and give up their friendship with someone who's still here? Whatever.

I manage to dig out a black button-down shirt from the back

of my father's closet, and pair it with black jeans that hug my thighs, then slip my feet into some black sneakers. I still haven't retained access to my father's bank accounts, so I'm not sure how I'm going to keep living on my own. I'm hoping I won't have to sell the house, but unless my dad had been smart with money and I didn't know it, then it's looking like I might have to.

A high school diploma feels impossible now, after everything that's been taken away from me, and what's the point in graduating high school when I'll never have enough money to go to college?

I'm filled with an endless pool of grief as I walk down the quiet streets toward the cemetery. The sky is dark grey, like it's going to downpour at any moment, and it's the perfect weather for today. It's how I feel inside—empty, dark, *dead*.

Kai is standing with Sage's grandma as I make my way into the cemetery, next to a few other people who I recognize from school.

I don't know why we're having the funeral here—it's not like she's going to be buried here. What was left of Sage was cremated after the autopsy and the ashes have already been delivered to her grandmother.

I also don't miss the irony that we're having her funeral in the place she was murdered. Or at least, the place her body was found.

Kaiden runs his hand through his black hair, a sad smile pulling at his lips as I say hello to everyone.

Ms. Spencer wraps her arms around me, and I feel how frail and cold she is under her thick black sweater. I rub my hands over her arms. "How are you, Ms. Spencer?"

She smiles at me, her hazel eyes tired. "I'm alright, Vincent. How are you, darlin'?"

I give her a smile, my eyes becoming blurry. "I miss her."

"Me too, honey. Me too." She hugs me once more, and as she releases me, I turn to see Beckham walking into the cemetery. He's wearing a black button-down, a coat over the top, and a pair of black dress slacks. He presses his lips together as he steps onto the grass where we're all standing, and he shoves his hands into his pockets when he reaches us.

He doesn't say anything, not even to Sage's grandmother, and that makes my heart throb with pain. He's so broken, every piece of him unrecognizable shards that I wish I could put back together.

Kaiden steps toward him, then wraps his arms around Beckham's shoulders to hug him. I want to cry, I want to scream, I want to be the one hugging Beckham, but I can't. I can't be that person for him right now because parts of his broken pieces are because of me, and he deserves time to heal from what I did to him.

I find his gaze after Kaiden has let go and stepped back, and there's indescribable pain behind it, making my stomach drop.

Although I can tell he doesn't want to talk to anyone, he steps closer to Sage's grandma and says hello, then says he's sorry for her loss. I think she can tell that he's in a lot of pain too, because she reaches for him and embraces him before she apologizes for his loss as well.

I'm not sure if she's under the impression Beckham was Sage's boyfriend, or Kaiden, or maybe me, and she didn't ask for clarification, but part of me feels like she knows what was going on, that we all loved her and that's all that matters.

As the cemetery fills up, I make myself busy saying hello to everyone I know, accepting whatever condolences people share for the sake of it.

Sage's grandmother organized for one of the pastors from the church to come down and lead the funeral—which is kind of more of a celebration of life without an official resting place

—and as he steps up to the small podium set up at the edge of the walkway, we all fall silent to listen to him.

"I want to thank you all for being here today to celebrate the life of Sage Grace Blackmore as well as mourn this sudden loss. Sage was new coming back to Blackmore, but this is where her life began. Although she moved to California when she was just a baby, she had Blackmore blood in her veins, and that makes her family to each and every one of us. In a small community like Blackmore, losing someone makes a huge impact on the whole town, and as a whole, we will mourn her beautiful soul as she returns home to God."

He puts his hands flat on the surface and looks out to the crowd, smiling. "As I look at all of you, I see that Sage has touched all of you separately with her golden aura and beautiful smile, and in return, her soul was touched by each of you, and that is more powerful than her loss. Knowing Sage was enough, even for the little while she lived here in Blackmore, and it isn't in vain that we say goodbye to her today, but in happiness that she's united with our Lord and Savior, watching over her loved ones."

I almost roll my eyes so hard that I black out, and I want to scream at the pastor that I'm sure Sage would rather be here, alive, with us, instead of wherever the hell or heaven she is now. I certainly wish she was here, and that none of this ever happened.

As the pastor continues with his speech, I tune him out, not wanting to hear about how Sage *touched us all*, when no one knew her the way we did. Instead, I stare at Beckham, the cemetery a perfect backdrop behind him, and I wonder if we'll ever be able to get past all of this. Will we ever be able to heal from everything that's happened? Or will it be like when parents lose a child, and they can't stay together because of the constant reminder of that pain?

I don't realize someone else has stepped up to the podium until Beckham's face drops into a state of shock, then I'm jerking my attention back to the podium in time to see Aaron Blackmore shake the hand of the pastor, then clear his throat and speak to the mass of people, a tiny smirk kissing his lips as he gives a brief second of his attention to Kaiden, Beckham, and I.

Aaron Blackmore smiles to the crowd, an arrogant aura around him as everyone admires his handsome face and perfectly styled hair. "Hello, everyone, my name is Aaron Blackmore, and I'm Sage's uncle. I wish it was under better circumstances that I'm here with you today… I'm glad I have the opportunity to honor the life of my niece, though, who for eighteen years was like a daughter to me."

I almost laugh, thinking of how Aaron sent her packing when her parents died and she needed somewhere to live. However, if he had taken her in, we never would have met her.

He twists the ring on his thumb mindlessly as he continues. "Sage brought so much sunshine and so much laughter into the world, and everyone she met was affected by her beauty and her kindness. She had a passion for learning, for leading, and for endless growth. Sage was the future, and it breaks my heart that we won't get to see her succeed how she dreamed of."

Aaron chokes up, so he takes a moment to pull a ragged breath between his lips before he continues. "I can't believe I'll never see my girl again. I'll never get to hug her again, and I'll never get to see her grow into a woman. I loved her with my whole heart, and I always will. Thank you."

He wipes a hand across his face, although I don't spot any tears on his cheeks, then steps to the side. The pastor steps up to the podium once more and gives us all a warm smile. "Now, I'd like to open it up for anyone who would like to say a few words about Sage."

The small crowd is still quiet, and I peek at Sage's grandmother, who's holding onto Kai's arm like she needs the support. He slowly walks her up to the podium, and a twinge of sadness runs through me. I know she can get herself around fine, so it means that she's so heartbroken by the loss of her granddaughter that she needs the extra help today.

"Hello, everyone, and thank ya for bein' here today to honor my Sage," Ms. Spencer starts, a small smile kicking up her lips. "Mostly everythin' has been said already, so I wanted to share a piece of Sage with y'all from when she came here to Blackmore a few months ago."

I feel warm thinking about the short months ago Sage arrived here, when we chose her for the games, when we didn't know she would mean the world to all three of us.

"I hadn't seen Sage since she was a baby, since her mama and daddy had moved to California to give her a better life, and when she got outta that cab all those months ago, I just knew this girl was gonna change my life." Ms. Spencer smiles again, closing her eyes as she thinks over the memory. "She was exhausted, skinny and broken, with three suitcases to her name, and she showed up on my doorstep and threw a wrench into my silly little routine. It didn't take long for me to get some meat on them bones, feedin' her good southern cookin' and makin' sure she never went to bed without dessert, and soon after she got here, we was the best of friends. She was just like her mama, sassy and playful and always makin' jokes."

My eyes well with tears, so I take a page out of Ms. Spencer's book and close my eyes as I continue to listen.

"Sage was one of a kind—she truly was. And I am very thankful I got to know her."

I open my eyes in time to watch as Kai helps Ms. Spencer back to where she was standing, and as I look around the group of people here, I realize there's a lot more people crying than I thought there would be. I don't know if it's the reminder of death, or the speech from Sage's grandma.

The pastor steps up to the podium again, beginning whatever closing statements he has prepared. I've already checked out, though, my mind going fuzzy at the edges and making white noise ring in my ears. I stare at Beckham again, memorizing his face just in case this is one of the last times I'll see it—because after this, what is there for us? Although we've been together since we were kids, Sage became the glue that held us all together. Will we all be able to keep going as normal one day?

I don't know how to get things back to normal, and I don't know if it's possible.

As the funeral wraps up, I watch Beckham's face, admiring how he gives the pastor all of his attention out of respect, even though I know deep down he's hurting so badly that he probably wishes everyone would just leave. I feel my lips twitch when Becks licks his lips, his hair moving under the small breeze running through the cemetery as the storm rolls in, then his eyes wander across the small area that separates us and they find mine like I'm pulling his gaze with a magnet.

I don't smile, I don't do anything, I just stare at him, aware that I probably look like a stalker, watching him simply exist in the same place as me.

His face doesn't change either, he just stares right back, a sliver of longing behind his expression.

I want to move across the cemetery, wrap my arms around him, and tell him I love him, that everything is going to be okay, that it's him and I until the end, even after everything that's happened. But I don't. We just stare at each other, almost as if there's something blocking our paths.

Kaiden steps up beside me, and I finally pull my attention from Beckham, realizing the pastor has stepped down from the

podium and the small gathering has turned more social as
people get ready to leave.

"You okay?" Kai asks, his brown and gold gaze laced with
concern.

"Fine," I lie, sliding my hands into the pockets of my pants
as I realize that my fingers are frozen. "You?"

"Fine," he says, and I know he's lying as well.

None of us will ever be okay, not without Sage here.

A small breeze blows again, and a shiver spiders down my
spine, and I regret not wearing a coat. There's a bad storm
rolling in, it seems, and part of me hopes that it starts to
downpour while I'm still out here in the graveyard. Maybe the
rain will turn to ice and freeze me in place.

"The Hallows Boys, I assume?" A cold voice cuts into my
mind, and both Kai and I look to the right to see Aaron
Blackmore, his face twisted into a smile that reeks of superiority.
"What a *pleasure* it is to meet my shit-stained legacies."

Kaiden snorts, his eyebrow pulling up. "Excuse me?"

I press my lips together, then Beckham appears behind
Aaron's back, his voice powerful and sharp when he speaks.
"You need something?"

Aaron turns, stepping backwards a foot so he can keep an
eye on all of us. "Just telling your brothers that it's an honor to
meet the boys who destroyed my legacy."

Kai laughs, "Says the sole member of your generation still
free from death or prison, one of the ones who pissed on
everything this game was supposed to mean."

Aaron speaks between his teeth. "You have no idea what this
game was supposed to mean, you little shit. And now you've
gone and burned it all down."

"Actually," Beckham interjects, a small smile kissing his lips,
"that was just me."

With fire in his eyes, Aaron glares at Beckham like he

may fly across the few feet that separate them and beat him to death. Before he has a chance, I pull his attention with a question. "What are you doing here, *Aaron*? You abandoned Sage all those months ago, after she lost her parents, and now you feel like you can come here and put on a show?"

Aaron's expression settles back into one of superiority and calmness. "Sage was meant to come to Blackmore. Don't you three know that better than anyone? As far as my appearance today, I'm in town to collect my daughter, who has already left to go back to California to attend a private school."

"Your daughter?" Kaiden asks, trying not to show how badly the curiosity is burning him.

"Yes, I think you may know her? Juliet McIntosh? She took her mother's name as to not to draw attention to herself. She was flunking out of school, so I stepped in to help. Poor girl was drinking herself silly as well," Aaron muses, something I can't figure out glistening in his eyes.

"Juliet is your daughter?!" I gasp, eyes widening, even as I try to tamp down my reaction. "Sage's cousin?"

"Yes," Aaron says, and I expect him to give some sort of explanation as to why no one knew anything about this, but he doesn't say anything else. I look at Becks, then glance at Kai, hoping one of them asks him for more details, but I'm sure both of them are too caught off guard to think up anything worth asking right now.

"Well…" Aaron says as the silence starts to swallow us up. "I'm going to get going—I have a plane to catch. You three stay safe now."

His words feel ominous, like there's something laced between them, and if I wasn't so exhausted, I may be able to figure them out. Instead, we all stand in silence as he walks away, his lips curved into a smile so small I almost miss it.

When we're alone, I look to Becks, hoping he'll say
something to me.

He doesn't, just slides his hands into the front pockets of his
coat and gives us both a tight-lipped smile in goodbye, then he
walks away, toward where the road meets the cemetery.

Sighing, I turn to Kai. "He hates us."

"No, he doesn't. He'll come around. Just give it some time,
Vincent." He shakes his head, running his hand through his
messy hair before he holds a hand out for me to grasp. "I'm
going to have dinner with Sage's grandmother. I'll call you
tomorrow."

Nodding, I say goodbye to him, then head deeper into the
cemetery. I almost want to go all the way out to where the crypts
are, where the Hallows Crypt used to be, to see if there's
anything left of it, but when I think about Sage being murdered
there, I feel sick to my stomach.

It shouldn't be possible to be this empty, but I feel like a cup
that can't fill up, like there're holes all over me that everything
leaks from. My soul hurts, my heart, my fucking entire body. I've
felt so much loss in my life, but this time, it feels so fucking
different that I'm not sure how to process it.

I sit down at one of the headstones with a Blackmore last
name, tracing my fingers over the carved letters a few times
before I drop my head against it. I know this isn't Sage's grave,
that she won't have one here, but maybe this is as close to her as
I'm going to get—an ancestor who might be able to connect
with her.

"Hey, princess," I say softly, feeling a little foolish. "I don't
know how we all got here, but I know that if you were here, you
could make it all better. You made everything better. You made
Kai softer, you made Becks stronger, and me? You made me feel
loved in a new way and hopeful for the first time. Like maybe I

was worth something after all. Like I'm not just some dumb jock who let his dad beat his ass every day."

I shake my head, tracing the word *BLACKMORE* one more time with my fingers.

"You made us better—you made us whole. And I'm scared we'll never feel complete ever again."

I sigh, feeling tears spring to my eyes. "I miss you, princess. I love you."

Standing up, I brush the grass from my pants, then make the decision to *try*. I'm going to try to make one thing better. I'm going to get Beckham back.

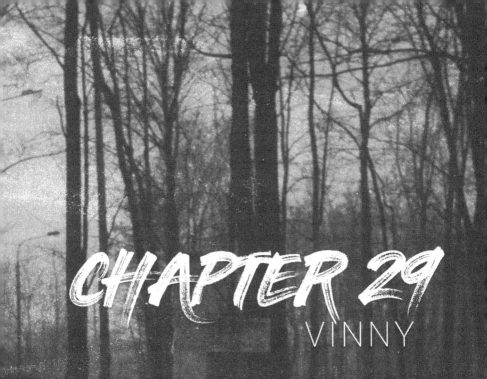

CHAPTER 29

VINNY

I walk across town slowly, even as the storm rolls in, and rain starts to pelt down on me. It's freezing cold, but it's welcomed. It feels refreshing, like I'm washing away the bad and letting the good back in. The sky has turned to a dark grey that blocks the sun and makes it feel later than it is, and even without the rain, the thunder overhead would be enough to clear the trees of birds.

Lightning splits the sky in two, and the rain comes down harder, soaking me as I walk down the middle of the road slowly. My body is freezing, and every drop of rain feels like a pellet of ice hitting my tender skin.

When I reach Beckham's driveway, I'm drenched to the point my hair and clothes are all dripping, my eyes blurry from the rain and my teeth chattering from the cold. Wrapping my arms around myself, I make it to the front door and hit the doorbell with my shoulder.

Beckham opens the front door a moment later. "Oh my god!

What are you doing? You're going to freeze to death, get in here!"

He holds the door open, ushering me inside, and I chuckle as I step into the house. I'm thankful he typically runs cold, because his heat is on inside and it feels good against my cold face.

"Stay there," Beckham says, shuffling quickly through the house. When he comes back, he throws a towel at me, and I wrap it around my shoulders. "What're you doing here, V?"

"I miss you." I shiver, wiping the towel over my face. "I needed to see you."

He sighs, looking off into the distance. "Vinny—"

"I know, you hate me, I know," I say, cutting him off. "But I *fucking love you*, Beckham Bentley, and I can't stay away anymore. I need you."

Beckham's mouth pulls down into a frown, and he presses his eyes closed. "You really fucking hurt me."

"I know," I say in a rush, and he looks at me with searing anger in his eyes.

"How am I supposed to forgive you?"

"You just are," I answer, swallowing roughly. "Because I love you, and you love me, and we're meant to be together. We're meant to use each other for strength right now, because we lost our girl, and we can't just let everything go that we've built together. You're my best friend, my soulmate, my whole life, and without you, I have no one else. Without you, I don't want anyone else. Because you are my world."

His gaze slowly lifts to mine, and as I find tears in his bright blue eyes, I realize my chest is heaving. He moves toward me, his hands sliding into my wet hair and squeezing. He doesn't do anything else, though, still hesitant and scared and hurt.

I drop my eyes closed, breathing through my lips as I

whisper. "I love you, Beckham. I'm so sorry for everything I did. I'll never fucking hurt you again, baby..."

His mouth finds mine, pressing softly, and I freeze in place.

He hesitates at first, nipping my bottom lip a few times before he uses more pressure and kisses me harder. When his tongue slides against mine, I grab his sides and squeeze his shirt between my fingers as I moan. His hand goes around my jaw, and he turns my head so he can deepen our kiss, then he's feasting on my lips like he's been starving for me, like the time we spent apart turned him ravenous and malnourished for my kiss.

He groans deep in his throat, his tongue playing with mine as he grabs me by the shirt.

As he pulls back, he looks me up and down. "C'mon, let's get you outta these freezing cold clothes."

Nodding, I let him grab my hand and drag me through the house into the bathroom. He turns the water on, then pulls the shower curtain straight before looking back at me. As Beckham prowls closer, he smiles.

Fuck, I've missed seeing that smile.

Beckham unbuttons my shirt slowly, his eyes locked on mine, making my heart race. When he's undone the last button, he slides his hands under the fabric and pushes it over my shoulders and down my arms until it falls to the ground.

Before I can reach for him, he drops to a crouch and starts to unlace my sneakers, then he looks up at me as he pats my foot. "Up."

I lift my feet one by one so he can pull off my shoes and socks, then he reaches for the button on my jeans and unfastens it. My cock thickens and hardens as he drags the zipper down, then he's yanking the denim over my hips. My cock pushes on the thin material of my boxers, and Beck's eyes flick back up to mine as he pulls on the waistband of my underwear and lowers them down to my knees with my jeans.

Before he continues to pull off my clothes, he licks a line down my shaft, then suctions around the head of my cock, making me hiss between my teeth. *"Becks."*

His eyes are still on me, even as he slides down on my cock and swallows me whole, and I thread my fingers into the back of his curly hair. Moaning as he bobs his head, he grabs my balls and rolls them in one hand.

"Fuck, B," I moan, my head going back as ecstasy covers my vision.

He can read my body better than anyone, so when I thrust my hips against him, he knows that I'm chasing my release and he pulls off. Groaning, I squeeze his hair.

"Not yet," he says, pushing my jeans and underwear down over my knees to my ankles, then he lets me step out of them before he stands up and yanks his shirt over his head. "Get in the shower."

I nod, grabbing his sweatpants and yanking them down until he can step out of them, too, then I follow him into the hot spray of water, pulling the shower curtain back into place behind us.

He pushes me under the spray, then threads his hands into my hair and leans my head back as he massages my scalp. "Are you warming up, baby?"

I grin, looking at him. "I'm hot."

Chuckling, he grabs a bottle of shampoo and squeezes some onto his palm, then he massages it into my hair. My cock is pulsing with pleasure still, precum coating the head and growing messy as he teases me with his touch.

After he's rinsed my hair, he grabs the conditioner and squeezes some into his palm. His gaze finds mine, then he grins. "Turn around, V."

I watch as he uses the conditioner to make his cock slippery, then I turn around quickly and brace myself against the wall, arching my back and looking over my shoulder as water rains down on my backside.

His eyes darken as he grips himself roughly and positions the head of his cock at my asshole. "Take a breath, baby."

I do as he says, breathing in, and then as I blow out, he slides into my ass slowly.

"Fuck!" I slap my palm down on the tiled wall, pushing back against him so he presses in farther.

Beckham's hands grab my hips, then he kisses a line up my spine until he's at the back of my neck. "I love you, Vincent."

I moan at the sound of those words from his lips, grinding my ass against him. My voice is an indistinguishable noise that is mainly moans and breathy pleas. "I love you so much."

His hand glides up my side, over my shoulders and into my hair, then he threads his fingers into the strands and yanks, pulling my head back as he starts to thrust his hips with more force.

"Fuck!" I yell again, feeling him stretch me from behind as his cock strokes against my prostate again and again.

He moans, his free hand reaching around and grabbing my pulsing cock, and it only takes three swipes of his fist before I'm coming, shooting my load onto the wall and floor, yelling and pounding my hand against the tiles.

"God, your fucking ass is so tight, baby. I'm gonna come. Do you want it?" he moans from behind me, and I'm blinded by my orgasm, so my answer is an unintelligible set of moans that has him pounding into me harder.

"Take it, take it, take it," Beckham chants, spreading my ass cheeks and slamming into me through his climax, his cock filling me with his seed as he does. "There you go, take it."

I feel his cock start to soften as he shoots the last of his release deep inside of me, then he's pulling out and falling to his knees behind me.

"Can you come again for me, baby?" he asks, then he slides his tongue into my ass, his palms spreading me wide.

"*Becks*…" I moan, my whole body shivering at the sensation. Grinding my ass against his tongue, my cock fills with blood again as he starts to slurp down his own release.

Pulling back, he uses his hands to spin me around, then he's sliding down my cock until I'm hitting the back of his throat.

I shout, the sensation too much and not enough and exactly perfect all at once as he bobs his head and gags around me.

My hands slide into his hair so I can hold him in place as I begin to thrust my hips against him, my cock slamming into the back of his throat over and over, until a few minutes later, I'm exploding into his mouth, shouting his name as my eyes water from pleasure.

———

LATER THAT NIGHT, BECKHAM AND I ARE WOKEN UP BY A LOUD bang outside the window. The rain is still pelting down in sheets, thunder shaking the sky. As we both wipe sleep from our eyes, we sit up in bed and look at each other through the darkness.

Another bang on the window makes me jump, and Beckham stands up to walk across the room. When he pulls the curtain back, he reveals Kaiden's face through the glass and groans. Unlocking the window, he lifts it so Kai can climb through.

"What's with you two? You're going to catch a fucking cold," Beckham shouts.

Kai shakes his head as he steps into the room, kicking off his soaked shoes and ripping his shirt over his head. "You got a towel?"

Beckham laughs, walking to where we left one of our towels

from our shower earlier on the ground, then he throws it to Kai, who's stripping out of the rest of his soaking wet clothes.

Walking back to the window, Beckham slams it closed as I shuffle back in bed, putting the blankets over my naked lower half. "What are you doing here, Kai?"

"You guys didn't answer your phones, and this couldn't wait," he breathes, using the towel to dry his hair. It's then I start to worry that something is really wrong, wrong enough that he had to trek through the cold storm to talk to us in the middle of the night.

"What's the matter?" Becks asks, sitting back down in bed as palpable fear passes over his features. "What happened?"

"Someone murdered Sage's grandmother tonight," Kaiden says, eyes distant, and my heart stops.

"What…?" Beckham sucks in a breath, his whole body going still at my side.

I've stopped breathing altogether, though, my mouth falling open as shock runs through me and I try to speak. Nothing comes out, as I just stare at Kai in disbelief, even as he continues.

"They think it's the same person who killed Sage. Someone trying to wipe out the whole family, maybe," Kai says, and I shake my head, finally finding words.

"Sage's grandmother isn't a Blackmore, though. She's a Spencer. What's the point in killing her?"

"What's the point in killing Sage?" Kai asks, and it's a good point. It's not like anyone would have had a reason to kill our girl. She had just moved here—no one knew her.

Kai slips his boxers off, then wraps the towel around his waist before he comes to sit down in bed with us. "What the fuck is going on? That's what I want to know. Who killed Sage, and who killed Joyce, and who is next?"

"Who's *next?!*" Beckham asks, scooting toward me an inch

without realizing it. "You think someone else is going to get murdered? Like we have a serial killer or something?"

"We need to look at this logically," Kai says, sighing. "Sage gets killed and Beckham gets blamed. Now Joyce has been killed —Sage's grandmother. Maybe it has to do with the Hallows Games? Maybe someone is wiping out anyone who has anything to do with the Games and the Blackmores."

My brows furrow, eyes narrowing. "Which would mean *we* would be next."

"That's my theory," Kai says, and Beckham scoffs.

"It's a stretch, an assumption. You don't actually *know* what the fuck is going on," Becks says, shaking his head. In a bit of denial, I think.

"That's why I said *theory*," Kai snaps, giving Beckham a dirty look.

"Okay," I say, cutting off the argument between them before it can begin. "We can't do anything right now, so let's sleep on this information, then start fresh tomorrow."

They both nod, and I stand up to grab Kai a pair of sweatpants from one of the drawers in Becks' dresser. Throwing it at him, I sigh. "Put some pants on and lay down."

As Kai stands up and slips the sweatpants on, Becks gives me a look that tells me he's scared and tired, and I think if one more insane thing happens, he might completely lose it.

Sliding back into bed, I curl around Becks and kiss his forehead. "We'll get it all figured out, baby. I promise."

CHAPTER 30
KAIDEN

Over the next few days, the cops find nothing to hint at who committed both murders.

All the fingerprints found at the crypt where they found Sage's body end up belonging to Sage, and the only other thing they found was DNA that belongs to me, Becks, and Vinny. We're all brought in for questioning, but my dad provides an alibi for all three of us for the timeframe when Sage was murdered. It's easily explained to the police why our DNA was found in the Hallows Crypt, especially because one of the officers was a Hallows Boy once upon a time.

They do ask for our keys, though, so we can prove that we're telling the truth, and all but Beckham's key is turned in. It turns out that he lost his. Maybe it was stolen by whoever killed Sage, or maybe even Sage herself.

Since Blackmore is such a small town, any evidence they find has to be sent to the county sheriff for examination, and it takes days for answers.

We're brought into the station again that following Monday for questioning about why our fingerprints were found at Sage's grandmother's house.

"We had been helping Joyce plan Sage's funeral," I say, crossing my legs. They haven't bothered to put us inside the one small interrogation room they have here, instead sitting us at the desk of the investigating officer.

"Why?" the officer asks, his face bored but thoughtful.

"*Why?*" I repeat, taking control of the conversation as Becks and Vinny listen. "I don't understand the question."

"*Why* were you helping Joyce plan the funeral? What is your connection to Sage Blackmore?" the officer clarifies, now looking annoyed.

"Oh," I say, twisting my lips to the side. "We were all friends with Sage. She was—*is* important to us."

"Got it." The officer scribbles something down in his notebook, nodding as he does. After a minute of thick tension and silence, he speaks again without looking up from his paper. "Doesn't look good that you're tied to both scenes."

"You'd had to have done a shit job investigating if you *didn't* link us to both scenes." The officer looks up at me, eyebrow quirked slightly. "We've explained everything you've brought to us, so are we free to go?"

I'm surprised Vinny and Beckham have sat without a word this whole time, but I think after everything they went through with Beckham's previous arrest, they don't want to make a slip of the tongue or make things worse. It's easier when I just control the situation.

The officer clears his throat. "If you three are linked to another murder, I'll have to bring you back in."

Chuckling, I stand up and brush my hands down the front of my jeans, dismissing myself. "Maybe do a better job at making sure your residents don't get murdered."

Vinny laughs, and he and Becks stand up to follow me out of the room before I have a chance to hear the retort the officer throws my way.

We exit the police station and step out into the day, heading down the quiet road toward my neighborhood. Becks and Vinny are walking with three feet separating them, and part of me wants to interject myself into the tension between them, since it's partly my fault, but I'm too emotionally exhausted from my head to my toes to take on one more thing right now.

I feel like someone has scooped out my insides, all the good parts that had started to grow when Sage came into my life now thrown away, leaving me the person I *used* to be. Hard, angry, mean, *empty*.

Sage was that spark inside of me, the one that lit me up and turned me into a brighter color some days.

She changed everything, and I know my brothers are feeling the same way.

When we step onto my street, Vinny speaks. "How are we going to find who killed them?"

"I don't know." I say, feeling hopeless and shaking my head as I stare up into the sun. "Where do we even *start* looking?"

No one answers me, and we all walk down the street in more silence.

As we approach my house, I decide to go inside to grab something to eat while Vinny and Becks go directly to the garage to hang out. My father isn't home from work yet, and I'm thankful. I don't want to have to explain why I'm not at school again or tell him that I was speaking to the cops.

My dad wouldn't be disappointed in me, he would be *furious*. There isn't anything he wants more than my future, I don't think, and it makes my stomach hurt thinking about telling him what's been going on lately. I haven't checked in with teachers or coaches, and I haven't cared to. Maybe they're still giving everyone that small grace period after we lost a classmate—whatever. I don't plan on going back. I don't care anymore. That part of me that used to be built for academics and succeeding is dead.

Just like Sage.

I make each of us a sandwich, grab a bag of tortilla chips and a few bottles of water, then I balance it all in my arms as I head out to the garage. When I reach the door, there's a letter-sized brown envelope, made of that thick paper you'd see in old movies, sitting on the mat, and my brows lower in concern. I don't have a free hand to grab it, so as I kick through the door, I call for someone.

"Hey! Was this here when you came in?"

Vinny looks up from his phone, stands up and walks over to me to grab a sandwich, then he looks down at the envelope. "Nope."

Beckham appears a second later, and he bends down to pick up the envelope so I can close the door and shut us inside the garage.

As I go across the room and put everything down on the table, Becks and Vinny follow me. When my hands are free, I grab the envelope.

Flipping it over in my hand, I examine it. There's no writing on it, and only one piece of tape holds the flap closed. Shrugging, I slide my finger under the tape and tear it open.

"What is it?" Becks asks before I've even pulled anything out, and I ignore him.

Pushing the envelope open, I look inside.

All of a sudden, oxygen becomes too thin to bring down into my lungs, and I stand motionless as I stare into the envelope.

"*Kai,*" Vinny says, stepping closer to me. "Your face just turned white. What is it?"

I swallow thickly, pouring the contents of the envelope onto my palm so they can see what's inside—a necklace, the pendant on the end in the shape of a *K*.

The necklace Sage was wearing when she died.

A small piece of paper falls out as well, but I don't manage to catch it in my numb hands, instead letting it fall to the floor. I'm too stunned, too fucked up and bruised from seeing her necklace, the necklace she barely got to wear for a week before someone killed her.

Vinny bends down, though, picking up the paper and unfolding it.

When he reads the note, his voice sounds foreign and far away.

"You should have protected her."

CHAPTER 31

BECKHAM

"*You should have protected her?!* What the fuck does that mean?" I shout, grabbing the piece of paper from Vinny's hands and reading it again.

"Oh, *god*," Kai groans, putting his head back and his hand on his chest. "I feel like I'm going to fucking puke."

"You should have protected her? Who the fuck sent this?" I snap at Vinny, realizing he's just standing frozen, staring at where Kai is squeezing the necklace in his hand. "Vinny?"

"What?" he whispers, looking at me slowly, like his mind is somewhere else entirely.

I shake my head, looking between him and Kai, suddenly forgetting the question I was going to ask. We all just stare at each other for a moment in silence, trying to piece together what's going on.

After a while, Kai finally speaks. "Someone's taunting us. Someone knew about us and is using this to taunt us. But *why*? And *who*?"

Vinny shakes his head. "We need to go to Sage's house and snoop around."

"I think it's still closed off as a crime scene," Kai says.

I grin, shrugging. "So we'll be really, *really* careful."

———

WE WAIT UNTIL LATER THAT NIGHT TO SNEAK OVER TO SAGE'S house, since we're less likely to be seen in the dark, and climb up the side of the house to enter through Sage's room.

The window is still unlocked, like she had been waiting for Kaiden to sneak in, and the thought makes me sadder. I know that was their thing, what made Kai feel okay with our arrangement—the moments in the night when he could take her body and claim it.

No one says anything about it, though, as we all drop down onto the carpet, and Kai slides the window closed behind him.

"Don't turn the lights on and be quiet," Kai says, walking to Sage's bed and sliding his hand over the blanket.

"How are we supposed to see anything in the dark?" I ask, hating how scared I sound. The idea that maybe someone is here, waiting in the dark to jump out at us, makes my skin crawl.

The darkness used to be our escape, our comfort zone and safe place—and now it's all fucked. I would give anything to have that sense of security and safety back, but now I'm just worried we're going to come face to face with danger.

Kai takes his backpack off and puts it down on Sage's bed, then he pulls out three flashlights, turning them on one by one and handing them out.

Using the flashlight, I look around Sage's room, my eyes skating over her empty desk before I move to the closet. Her clothes still hang neatly like they're waiting for her to return home, and my gut churns.

"This is miserable," I whisper, running my hands over the different fabrics.

"Looks like the cops took her computer," Vinny says, and I look at where he's sitting at her desk. He pulls open the top drawer and rifles through it. "Nothing but old homework in here either."

"What is it that we're looking for?" I ask, walking to where Kai is digging through her bedside table.

"I don't know yet," he says, but doesn't stop what he's doing. He's on a mission. "Anything that hints towards who's responsible."

Nodding, I get on my knees and look under the bed, pulling out a box about the size of a shoe box. Lifting the lid, I look inside and find some old photos and papers. It almost feels wrong looking through her secret stuff like this, but I know we need to. I know she would want us to get to the bottom of this.

Using the flashlight, I flip through the stack of photographs in my hand, recognizing her parents from the pictures I've seen, and a few of Megan Gallagher from back in the day. These must be the photos she found in her grandmother's closet all those months ago.

Setting them to the side, I look through the papers next. There are a few old birthday cards from her parents, keepsakes that probably helped her deal with the loss of them, and then I come across an unopened envelope addressed to Sage, the return address belonging to her Uncle Aaron.

"Hey, look at this." I tap Kai on the knee with the letter. "Think we should open it?"

Kai takes it from my hand, reads it, then slides his finger under the lip of the envelope to rip it open. Pulling the letter out, he reads it aloud to all of us.

"Sage, you haven't returned any of my phone calls, even when I manage to get your grandmother on the phone, and so I've been forced to put all my

thoughts down the old-fashioned way. I can only hope you find the courage and forgiveness in your heart to open this letter.

I need to start by saying that I love you. I always have, and I always will. You'll always be my favorite girl; nothing will ever change that, Sage Grace. I'm sorry things happened the way they did, but I need you to understand a few things before you completely decide you hate me forever.

I couldn't let you come live with me in California. I saw what this place was doing to you and your parents, and it made me sick. We're Blackmores, and the only way I was going to be able to explain that to you is if you ended up there. Your parents would have never allowed it if they were alive—they wanted to be Lindmans forever, live far away from anything that resembled Blackmore, but it was wrong, Sage.

We belong to Blackmore, and we were stupid, foolish kids to run away from it.

Your parents didn't understand, Sage, but I do. And I know that it's you who can put the good back into the Blackmore name, bring pride to our ancestors, and restore everything our family has lived for. I've known since you were a little girl, and you would kick and scream when your mother made you wear frilly pink dresses when all you wanted to do was play in the dirt with the boys. You weren't made to be this… California princess. You were made to be a Blackmore queen—someone who is comfortable in the dark cemetery like we all used to be.

So, please remember that, because all I've ever wanted was the best for you, Sage. I needed to get you back to Blackmore, and we need to find the life we were meant to live all this time.

I hope one day I can explain everything to you better, but until then, I hope Blackmore is teaching you everything it can.

I love you,

Aaron."

My stomach churns with anxiety as Kai looks up from the piece of paper, his mouth curled up in disgust.

"What the fuck?" Kai mutters, looking from me to Vinny, then back down at the letter. "Why didn't Sage open this?"

"She was really mad at her uncle for refusing to let her live with him in California. Maybe she just didn't want to forgive him yet," I suggest, even though I'm wondering if there's another reason too.

"Now I guess it's too late," Vinny adds, shaking his head.

I watch Kai as he silently reads over the letter again, then he looks up at me. "Something about this just isn't sitting right with me. Why was he so obsessed with getting her back to Blackmore? He makes it sound like he would have done anything to get her here."

"Does it matter?" I ask with a shrug. "She's dead now, and this just crosses one more person off our suspect list. Why would he kill her as soon as he got her back here?"

I grab the letter from Kai, fold it up, and slide it back into the envelope to put it back where I found it. There's something in his eyes, though, like he's lost in a thought that he just can't shake.

Vinny closes the last drawer in Sage's dresser, coming up empty, and sighs. "Let's go downstairs. There's nothing else in here."

Putting the lid back on the box, I slide it under the bed and stand up. Kaiden is staring at where his hand is resting on Sage's blanket, and his thumb is slowly moving over the fabric.

"Kai? You coming?" I ask, and when he looks at me, his gaze is still distant.

"Yeah, I'll meet you down there."

Nodding, I follow Vinny out into the hallway and down the stairs, using our flashlights to lead the way. The house doesn't get any less scary the farther we go, and I'm walking with every nerve on edge as we creep into the kitchen.

Only a few days ago, we were sitting here with Sage's grandmother, chatting over coffee about Sage's funeral. It feels surreal, like a dream maybe, and it's hard to believe that now Ms. Spencer is gone too.

There's a coffee cup in the sink, with residue of Ms. Spencer's last cup of coffee in the bottom of it, and I feel sad. She probably put it in there on her last day, telling herself she would wash it up in the morning.

"Do you think she'll have a funeral?" I ask Vinny, and my voice makes him jump as he looks around the kitchen.

"I don't know," Vinny says. "We don't really know any of her other family."

"Yeah," I sigh, feeling even sadder now. Everyone deserves an appropriate goodbye, and it isn't fair that there's no one left to mourn the kind woman we had started to know.

Vinny and I both look around the kitchen for a little while, then the living room—both rooms coming up empty.

We still aren't sure what we're looking for. Clues, blaring red flags, a flashing sign that says the name of the murderer, maybe? I know we aren't going to find anything; I think we're more here so we can say we tried everything. If the cops aren't going to find something, then neither are we. And clearly, the killer did a good job at covering their tracks.

No, we're more likely to find a psychological connection. Maybe someone who had been in Sage's life, someone who was quietly watching in the shadows.

Kaiden joins us in the living room by the time I finally say something again. "Her grandmother said her phone burned in the fire, right?"

Kai looks at me, eyes narrowed. "Yeah."

"And the cops took her computer," Vinny adds, sensing where I'm going.

"What about the cloud? Could we hack into her cloud account on a different computer, and access her information that way?" I ask, feeling stupid that we hadn't thought of it before.

Both Kai and Vinny stare at me for a moment, and something clicks into place.

"Let's go," Kai says, turning to lead us back up the stairs so we can exit through Sage's window again.

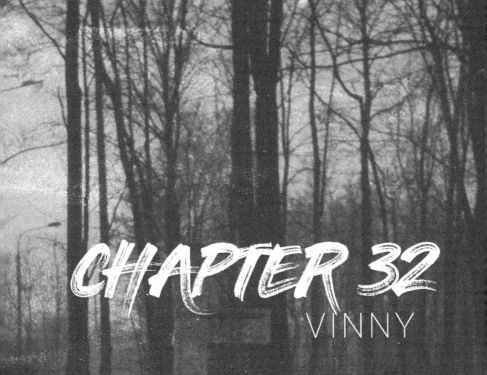

CHAPTER 32
VINNY

DESPITE IT BEING MIDNIGHT, THERE'S AN ENVELOPE SITTING ON my doorstep when we get back to my house. This one is bigger than the first, and I grab it as we go inside, stomach clenching with nerves.

"Open it," Kaiden orders the second the front door closes, and I rip the top of the envelope off in a hurry.

The only thing inside the envelope is a photograph—in it, Sage is walking through the cemetery, her blonde hair hanging loose down her back in waves. My entire world seems to flip on a tilt at seeing her, and everything vibrates at the edges.

"That's Sage," Becks breathes. "That's on Christmas. That's the dress she wore to dinner with her grandmother."

"Really?" Kai asks, snapping his gaze to him.

Becks nods, swallowing roughly. "Yeah, I remember it."

"So, she went to the cemetery on Christmas at some point, and someone was following her?" I say, less of a question and more of an observation. "Who? The person who killed her?"

Out of nowhere, Kai slams his fist into the wall, making me and Becks jump. "*God!*" Kai shouts. "I am *so sick* of getting more questions before we get fucking answers for the ones we already have!"

I nod, understanding his frustration. "I know."

"Flip the picture over." Becks points to my hand. "It looks like something's written on the back."

I flip the picture, revealing thick, bold, red letters written on the back in marker—*YOU WERE SUPPOSED TO PROTECT HER.*

"*We* were supposed to protect her?!" Becks spits. "We didn't even know someone was after her!"

"Maybe that's the point. Maybe that's why we're being taunted. Because we didn't pay close enough fucking attention and didn't notice she was *being fucking followed!*" Kai screams the last few words, and I flinch when he punches the wall again.

We don't stop him, though, even as he smashes his knuckles into the wall so hard that a picture falls down the hall and shatters, because afterwards, he collapses to the ground and heaves for breath, his bloody hand against his chest and tears sliding down his cheeks.

"We should have paid closer fucking attention," Kaiden cries, and my entire body goes cold. "This is our fucking fault."

Becks gives me a worried look, and I know he's thinking exactly what I am. *Kai has finally broken.*

In my eighteen years of life, I have never seen Kaiden Thorne cry, and that's how I know I need to drop to my knees as well. Becks follows me to the ground, and we both put a hand on Kaiden. Mine on his shoulder and Becks's on his back, and we sit that way and let him cry.

Kai cries silently, but his tears never slow, streaming down his cheeks like he's turned on a faucet, and it splits me in two. If the strongest one of us is breaking, what's left? Who's going to hold us up when more shit hits the fan?

After about five minutes, Kai wipes his hands across his cheeks and looks at me.

There's an unspoken respect between me and Kai—there always has been. Like any Alpha and his Beta, we understand each other better than him and Becks. Becks is rebellious, emotional, but me? I can fall into line when I need to, and the glimmer of control in Kaiden's eyes makes my spine straighten.

"It's time to find this motherfucker," Kai growls, his gaze hardening as his tears dry up. "And it's time to fucking end this."

———

THE NEXT MORNING, WE WAKE UP AT THE CRACK OF DAWN, JUST as the sun is kissing the day, and head for the cemetery.

It's cold as shit, but the sun is shining, so that keeps my face warm as we walk through town. We see a few kids heading to school but manage to avoid any wandering gazes that might want to ask questions.

The principal will be calling for us soon, maybe even getting the courts involved for truancy. Maybe we should officially un-enroll. That might help things.

Well, I could. Becks and Kai might have a hard time getting their parents on board, although when they get expelled for skipping, they'll have no choice.

Even though Sage isn't buried here, I say a silent hello to the Blackmore grave I've named hers as we pass by, and a small smile pulls up the edges of my lips. It's been a while since I've smiled a real smile, but feeling closer to Sage makes me feel better. Maybe we should be coming out to the cemetery more often. No one from school comes out here right now, since they're afraid they're going to get murdered, so we would have privacy.

I follow behind Becks and Kai, wanting to be last to have some sense of space while I'm thinking about Sage. It's intimate and personal, and even though my friends are closer than anyone else, I still want this time to talk to Sage in my mind as we walk.

We get farther out into the cemetery, the headstones old and brittle, and the leaves turning dry from the shade of the trees, making them crunch loudly under our feet.

I close my eyes, savoring the memory of this place—the smells, the sounds. It's familiar and foreign all at once, and part of me misses it. Part of me misses the nights in this dark, empty, echoing place.

My eyes open when Becks hisses under his breath, and I get an eyeful of his handiwork for the first time.

Half of the first crypt is still standing, only the front half caved in and burnt, like maybe the other half was too strong to come down even with fire. Unless the fire department got here before the whole thing went down, but that seems unlikely since the second crypt, the one we used for the games, is completely gone, only rubble and unrecognizable pieces left.

"Jesus Christ, Becks." Kai laughs, and it triggers my own laughter, even though it isn't funny.

Beckham, however, doesn't laugh. He just walks over to Hallows Crypt and stands at the edge.

"Be careful, Beckham," I say, my eyes flaring. "That thing could come down at any minute."

"I'm fine," he says, stepping into the broken pieces and debris. "I won't touch the walls."

Kai and I silently watch as Becks moves through the rubble with caution, his eyes directed down at the dirty ground. After a minute, Kai speaks.

"What are you looking for?"

"Anything," Becks answers mindlessly, his gaze still wandering around the ground.

If he finds anything the police may have missed, it would be a miracle, but I don't want to rain on his parade, and it seems neither does Kai, because we both just stand and watch.

It's a few more minutes before Becks shouts, making us both jump.

"Here!"

"What?!" I move toward the crypt in an instant, Kai hot on my heels.

Beckham shakes his head, pointing to the back wall. "It isn't about what's *here*, it's about what's *not*."

My brows pull down, and I look at an equally confused Kai for a moment before we both look at Becks again. "Okay?"

Becks laughs. "Maybe it's because I was always the one to get this crypt ready for the games… You guys don't notice what's missing?"

We're silent for a minute, then Kai clicks his tongue. "The notebooks… they're gone."

My eyes trail to the bookshelf, which is still intact at the edge of the crypt, and even though it's covered in dust and dirt and mildew from the rain, there's something else that's different about it.

It's empty.

"Who would have taken them?" I ask, bewildered. "The only people who would know they existed were former Hallows Boys."

"Yeah," Kai says, a small twitch to his lips. "That makes the suspect pool a hell of a lot smaller."

"There's only one generation that has incriminating shit in theirs." Becks smiles, huffing a laugh that holds no amusement.

"And only one person I can think of who would want to hide all the evidence of the games."

"Aaron," I breathe, feeling sick as I look at the dirty wall, still intact with names carved into it—names of all the Hallows Boys, all except the first three, which have been scratched out so they're unreadable.

Kai and Becks follow my gaze, noticing the same thing I do, and all the pieces start to move into place as we stare at the wall. All except one.

"But why kill Sage when he was trying to get her here all this time?" Kai asks the question on my tongue, and we all look at each other, the sun hitting our faces from the holes in the ceiling. "It doesn't add up."

"We don't know what happened that night before she ended up in the crypt. None of us were with her," Becks says, and I can hear the regret in his tone.

"I want to get out of here," I say, walking backwards toward the gaping hole in the side of the crypt, my skin crawling with the thought of this place. "We aren't going to find anything else; we might as well go home."

"C'mon," Kai says to Becks as he follows me back out onto the grass. "Let's go."

Becks eyes scan the messy, half-shattered remains of the Hallows Crypt one last time, maybe looking for something else that might help us, or saying goodbye to that chapter of our lives, then he looks up at me and presses his lips together.

This is where we really found each other—the first place we touched, kissed, loved—and it's almost bittersweet that now it's gone. I smile at Becks softly, hoping he can read the words behind the gesture.

Losing this place doesn't mean the loss of us.

CHAPTER 33

KAIDEN

A WEEK LATER, THE COPS STILL HAVE NO LEADS, WHICH ISN'T surprising since they're a bunch of idiots. We're closer to finding out the truth than they are, and it makes me angry but almost thankful. Part of me is glad no one is looking at Aaron, so we can deal with things the way we want to. I want the opportunity to rip him limb from limb, and I don't need *Blackmore's finest* interfering.

There isn't much we can do besides hop a bus to California and track Aaron down, so we spend Monday morning scrolling different websites to try to get the best deal for the three of us.

I think all of us have grown so angry and bitter that it's an impulse to push away the depression of loss. Focusing on revenge makes things easier to swallow.

The only thing we want now is for Aaron to pay for what he's done, and we want answers for *why* he did this to his niece and her grandmother. After that, we'll see what happens.

Becks, Vinny, and I are discussing our best plan of action for getting to California, when there's a bang on the door to my garage. Becks, who's sitting closest to the door, jumps a little, and Vinny laughs.

"Grab that, would you?" I ask, scrolling one of the travel websites on my phone.

Becks goes and opens the door, and after a few seconds, he calls for us. "Uhh, guys?"

I look up, finding him standing in front of the open door with a large envelope in his hand, something thick inside. Sweat beads at the back of my neck, and I jump up, run out the door, and try to catch whoever dropped it off.

"Fucking no one," I growl under my breath, then Vinny is behind me, breathless and equally as annoyed that whoever just dropped off our newest present of torment is already in the wind.

When we walk back inside, Becks has the envelope on the table, and he's sliding his finger under the paper to rip it open. Lifting it, he lets the contents fall out.

"This is mine," Becks says, looking at the photo album that's now sitting on the table, and as he tosses the empty envelope to the side, he runs his fingers down the front of the book. "This is the polaroid book Sage got me for Christmas."

"What?!" Vinny questions in a panic, now sitting next to Becks on the couch. "You're sure?"

"Yeah, I'm positive," Becks says, and I watch in silence as he flips open the front page of the book.

The first two slots are filled with polaroid photos of the entrance of the cemetery, the front sign that says *BLACKMORE CEMETERY, 1812*. Both images are from the same angle, but one was taken during the day and the other at night.

The next pages follow the same theme, except they're all of the crypts. Some of the polaroids are from *before* the fire, hinting that whoever has Beckham's camera had it before Sage's death.

Most of the polaroids, though, are from after the fire, showcasing the extensive damage the flames made in the grass, the concrete, the furniture, the walls, and everything else.

As Becks slowly flips through the book, my blood freezes. Why taunt us with this? There is no changing what Becks has already done.

When Becks gets to the last couple of pages, the messages in red ink start.

YOU TOOK MY LEGACY is first, written on the border of a polaroid of the wall in the Hallows Crypt.

The next page finishes the sentence.

SO, I'M GOING TO TAKE YOURS is written on the border of a polaroid of a blonde head of hair.

"Sage?!" Becks screams, his shaking hand going to the photo, but my stomach has turned leaden, and my mouth is watering painfully.

"Turn to the last page, Becks," I croak, my vision going spotty with panic.

Becks turns the page, then I drop to the ground, because in place of another polaroid, is a small piece of photo paper.

An ultrasound of a baby.

PART THREE

REVENGE

CHAPTER 34

KAIDEN

"That says *going to take*," Vinny breathes. "*I'm going to* take *yours*. Future tense, like he hasn't done it yet."

I can't breathe. I can barely see anything, the whole room is spinning, and the sound of Becks choking on sobs is making me want to claw my skin off.

"Sage is dead," I say mindlessly, my lips feeling numb as the words pass through. "We were at her funeral. I saw her ashes at her grandmothers."

Becks flips back a page and slams his hand down on the photo. "So, who is that?!"

I look at the polaroid, trying to keep the bile down that's rising in my throat.

A baby, a baby, a baby. My baby, Sage's baby, our baby.

"Sage is dead," I say again, my voice nothing but a whisper, and I'm not sure if I'm saying the words to convince myself or to convince them. "Sage is dead."

"Kai." Vinny grabs me by the shoulders, and I finally look at him, letting some clarity back into my vision. "Snap out of it."

My teeth shake, so I grit my jaw for a moment before I take a deep breath and blow it out. Vinny's green eyes are serious, and I pull some strength from them. "What the fuck?"

He shakes his head. "I don't know."

"Should we go to the cops?" Becks asks, ripping the polaroid of the blonde out of the case and looking at it closer. "This is Sage. This is Sage *alive*."

I'm starting to feel a little more present, so I look at Becks. "That could have been taken weeks ago."

He flips the page in the book, points to the ultrasound photo, and looks at me. "And this? What do you have to say about this?"

"It could be fake," I answer, and Becks narrows his eyes at me.

"You're a miserable, hopeless, pathetic bastard, Kai," Becks spits, waving the photo of the blonde in the air. "*This* is Sage, and I'm going to fucking find her."

"*How?*" I yell, throwing my hands up in the air. "We have no idea where she could be, *if that's even her!*"

"And your plan is to just assume it *isn't* her?" he shouts back, standing up.

I look at Vinny, trying to gauge who's side he's sitting on right now, but he's staring at the ultrasound photo like he's seen a ghost. Tightening my jaw, I take a breath through my nose, then slowly blow it out, flaring my nostrils.

"Vincent, what should we do?" I ask, trying to stay calm.

"We need to figure out if Sage is alive, and if she's fucking pregnant," Vinny answers, then he puts his hands on his cheeks. "Oh, God. *Pregnant*."

A wave of nausea passes through me, so I sit down on the couch. "Where do we start?"

"We need to look for Aaron," Becks says definitively, and Vinny nods at his side.

"Let's go."

CHAPTER 35

SAGE

It's been days, weeks, months… I don't know, but the pale beige walls of this bedroom are starting to make me dizzy. There's a small TV in the corner, but it isn't connected to the internet or anything, so I only have a stack of Halloween-themed DVDs to keep me occupied, all of which I ran through within the first few days of being here.

Food and water show up just inside the door while I'm asleep, as well as a change of clothes. The bathroom attached to this room has a toilet and a small shower, but the window is boarded up, so no sunlight comes through.

I just want to go home.

I want to see my grandmother; I want to see my guys. I can't imagine how worried they are. I know they're looking for me, though. They wouldn't give up, Gran too. There's no way she's giving up on me.

I'll be rescued any day now.

Until then, I'll lie on this musty mattress with its light pink sheets and watch the same five movies on a loop.

Blackmore is a small town, so whoever has taken me must know they can't get away with it. That is—if we're still even *in* Blackmore, and because of my involvement with the Hallows Boys, they can't think they'll be able to hide me for very long… right?

My blonde hair is matted and tangled, since I haven't been given the gift of a hairbrush, and after I get out of here, I'll never take for granted the small luxuries again—like conditioner, and skincare, and soft pajamas.

I've been given shampoo, and a bar of soap, but apart from that, I'm living with nothing else.

Most nights, I try to stay awake, waiting for the moment that the door to my bedroom opens so he can replenish my food and water, then I'll jump, fight, run, and scream. But every night, I'm unsuccessful, taken under by sleep so deep that it almost feels uncontrollable.

There is no window in my bedroom, so as I watch Hocus Pocus for the 30th time, I try to imagine it's sunny outside, the earth growing green as winter leaves and spring creeps in. Maybe it's raining, feeding the trees and grass and plants enough that they can flourish through the mild chill still clinging to the air.

I want to go outside. I want to smell the rain and earth and dirt in the cemetery. I want to listen to the birds in the distance, singing songs meant for only me. I want to breathe in my three guys, kiss them and touch them and tell them everything I've learned. I want to tell them I'm sorry, that I can't let them bring a new generation into the games, because the Blackmore name can't carry on like this. I want to tell Gran I love her, and kiss her cheek, and smell her soapy perfume that clings to her skin and clothes.

It isn't fair.

Tears roll over my eyelids as I smash them shut, refusing to let myself get worked up again. I promised myself I would stop giving whoever this is the satisfaction of my misery, because he doesn't deserve it.

I am strength and wildfire and power, and I can get through this. I am Sage Blackmore, and I will survive.

———

I'M NOT SURE HOW LONG I'VE BEEN AWAKE, ALL I KNOW IS THAT skipping food all day has been my saving grace. I have more energy now than I've had any other day, which makes me believe there's been something slipped into my food this whole time.

Sitting up on the bed, I leave *Scream* playing on the TV, letting the sounds fill the room so it isn't immediately obvious I'm awake when he comes in. I usually fall asleep with a movie on anyway.

I pull my knees to my chest, wrap my arms around my legs, and rest my cheek against my kneecap to watch the door. A small shiver of fear wraps around my spine, and I press my teeth into my bottom lip so I don't cry.

It's a couple more hours before someone comes to the door, the movie credits running on the TV as I listen to a key sliding into the lock and twisting. I hold my breath, scared and hopeful and *terrified*. Then the doorknob twists, and the door opens slowly. I see his shadow before I see him, a large black shape stretching across the carpet for a few seconds before his face comes into view and he peeks into the room.

His eyes go wide when he sees me sitting up in bed, wide awake, and a loud gasp escapes me. I feel relieved for a moment, thankful someone is here to save me, his name passing through my lips like a prayer.

"Uncle Aaron, *thank God*. How did you find me?!" I whisper-shout, climbing to the edge of the bed, but when he doesn't push the door open farther and step inside, my brows furrow in confusion. "Uncle Aaron?"

"Sage," he says, a small smile curling the edges of his lips. "Why aren't you asleep?"

His eyes travel across the room to the table where my uneaten food and water for the day sits, and he clicks his tongue in disappointment. "Oh, Sage. You must be hungry."

A small glimmer of mischief twinkles in his eye, and he pushes into the room and closes the door behind him.

"Uncle Aaron?" I say quietly, still confused, but growing more uneasy by the second.

"This isn't how I wanted to do this, sweetheart." He shakes his head, a sad smile on his face as he walks toward me.

I shuffle back on the bed on pure instinct, my knees curling to my chest again like they're a bulletproof vest. "What are you doing?"

He sits down on the edge of the bed, but he doesn't touch me. "Let me just explain everything. Okay, Sage?"

"You're the one keeping me in here?!" I breathe, heat spreading through my cheeks. "*Why?*"

"I had to," he says, shaking his head. "You were in *danger*. I was trying to protect you."

"*Danger?!* I was in danger from *what?* Where are we?" I gasp for breath, my heart racing to the point I'm feeling dizzy. "Uncle Aaron, you need to let me go. Gran will be looking for me. My friends."

"Your *friends?*" Uncle Aaron spits. "You mean those boys you spread your legs for in the cemetery? They couldn't protect you, Sage. Only I can protect you."

My face burns with embarrassment, even as I spit my next words in anger. "The Hallows Boys. You know all about them, though, don't you?"

"You were never meant to get mixed up with them. That isn't why I made it so you were sent here. You were supposed to *rule* this town, not blend in with three troublemakers." He scoffs.

"You *made it so I would end up here?*" I repeat, my stomach clenching. "What does that mean?"

He ignores my question and stands up, walks across the room, and picks up the water bottle from the table. When he comes back, he holds it out to me. "You need to at least drink some water. You're probably dehydrated."

I stare at his outstretched hand, at the bottle of water, and shake my head. Rolling his eyes, he sighs. "There's nothing in it, only the food."

When I still don't reach for it, he twists the lid off and takes a mouthful, then gives me a look that says '*see?*'

To get him to shut up, I take the bottle and drink a sip of the water before I put the cap back on. "There, happy?"

He smiles, his brown eyes crinkling at the sides. "Thank you."

Silence coats us like a sickness, but I find some courage deep in my gut and speak. "You guys killed Megan Gallagher."

Uncle Aaron sighs, shaking his head. "No, Sage."

"I read the book. From your games with Megan," I say, disgust in my tone. "You can't lie."

"You read the book, so you know your *father* killed her, Sage. No one else. And he made Benjamin take the fall because he was arrogant and horrible and *selfish.*"

"Stop," I say, and he stops talking. Pressing my eyes closed, I feel moisture lick at my eyelids. "Don't talk about him like that."

"I want you to know every truth, Sage, I do. I just want you to know the reasons behind them all first. And you need to know that your parents weren't the people you thought they were," Uncle Aaron says, then he runs his hand through his perfectly styled brown hair. "They were always ganging up on me, even when we were in high school and playing the games. No one was ever as good as your dad. It wasn't fair. Benjamin and I tried to get your mom to love us as much as him, but we were never *Andrew*."

He spits my dad's name like it's a dirty word.

"I said stop," I growl, then I clear my throat as tears fill my eyes. "*Please.*"

"I can't, Sage! You need to hear the story!" he shouts, making me jump.

Sighing, he runs a hand over his jaw in thought, then he starts talking again. "I loved Benjamin so much, and it wasn't fair that your parents made him take the fall for Megan's death. It *still* isn't fair that he's in prison and they got away with it, but decisions had to be made so I could get you here. For that, I'm sorry. They never would have let you come; they wouldn't even let me *talk* about Blackmore."

"What decisions?" I whisper, afraid of the answer.

He grabs my hand and squeezes. "I *had to*, Sage. I had to get rid of them to get you away from them! They were turning you into something you weren't."

I rip my hand from his, my entire body shaking with a tremor. "What…? You… you killed my parents?"

When he nods, and a sad smile touches his lips, I feel nauseous, like I might fall over and drown in a sea of my own grief.

"I had to, Sage. It wasn't right what they did. They deserved to be punished for what they did to Benjamin, to Megan, to *me*, and eventually, they would have destroyed you as well."

My hands go to my face, and I shake my head. "Oh my god."

"Listen, Sage. Listen, listen, listen," Uncle Aaron pleads as he moves closer to me, his hands reaching out for me. I move back before he can touch me, though, feeling nauseating anguish roll through me.

"You wouldn't even speak to me after my parents died. Where have you been all this time if this was all some big plan to get me to Blackmore?" I ask, putting my fingertips to my lips.

"I couldn't bear to face you after what I'd done. I wanted to give you some time to mourn, so I didn't have to see what I'd done to you. I was a coward—I *am* a coward. I only came to Blackmore now because of what Juliet had been doing. I had to protect you from her!"

"Juliet?" I clarify, voice shaky. "What does Juliet have to do with any of this?"

He sighs as he gets up. "It'll be better if I show you."

I'm a mix of confusion, anger, and sadness as he leaves the room, closing and locking the door behind him. It's a while before he comes back, but when he does, he has a big box in his hands.

Putting the box down on the bed, he takes the lid off and shakes his head. "Such a troubled girl. I guess she had been following you."

I peer into the box, which is filled with hundreds of photographs, all of them of me.

"What the hell?" I whisper, reaching for some of the ones on the top. It's of me and Beckham, in the cafeteria, having breakfast and laughing. The next one is me at cheer practice, stretching and watching Coach Steele ahead of the whole squad. The third one I look at is me and Kai, in my bedroom, his muscular arm holding me at a distance, his hips between mine, our bodies bare.

"What the fuck…" I grab another handful, and flip through

them, one after the other making me feel like the room is closing in on me.

Me and Beckham in the library, with me bent over a stack of books.

Me and Vinny in his bedroom, our mouths tangled in a kiss so passionate I can feel it in my toes.

Me asleep in my bed, no one in the room with me.

Me in fifth period physics.

Me in the ladies' bathroom, putting lipstick on in the mirror.

Me at the library.

Me in the cemetery, sitting at my favorite old Blackmore headstone.

I throw the photos back into the box and look at my uncle Aaron. "How did you know?"

"She sent me some… I guess to taunt me," he says. "Juliet's mother gave birth the same year you were born. We had already left Blackmore, so I didn't know she existed until much later. She never took the Blackmore name. She was following you to get to me. She was going to hurt you. I *had* to protect you from her."

I close my eyes, slowly shaking my head in confusion. "No, no, no, no, no."

"I'm sorry, I really am."

Putting a hand to my forehead, I press my lips together to keep myself from crying. After a moment, I look at my uncle again. "We need to get Juliet the help she needs. She deserves it. She's *family*."

He looks at me for a moment, and a small smile touches his lips as he reaches for my hand. "You're so kind, Sage. That's one of the things that made me love you so much."

Pulling my hand back , I shuffle an inch farther away. "Why am I here, Uncle Aaron?"

"There isn't a straightforward answer to that question,

Sage." He sighs. "But as soon as I figure out the last three problems I have, we can join Blackmore again. Together."

"Can I call my grandmother? She's probably worried," I say softly, trying to be as nice as possible so he might let me.

"There's so much I still need to tell you, Sage." He presses his lips together and stands up. "But for now, I think it's best if you get some sleep, okay?"

"Wait!" I shout louder than I mean to. "Please, tell me everything now."

"I think you need time to process everything you've learned first before I throw more at you. Trust me." He smiles, then leans down too quick for me to dodge, and kisses my forehead. "I love you, Sage. Sweet dreams."

"No!" But I'm too slow as I chase after him, missing my chance to get through the door before he closes and locks it again. I scream, banging my hands on the door. "No! Let me out! Please! Please!"

I spend the next ten minutes shouting, banging and kicking, until I finally fall down on the ground, exhausted, wishing I was far away from this dusty room, the pale pink accents, and the stack of Halloween DVDs.

I need to get the fuck out of here. *Now.*

CHAPTER 36

SAGE

I SPEND THE REST OF THE NIGHT FLIPPING THROUGH THE BIG BOX of photos my uncle brought in and find that there's enough to document every day since I moved to Blackmore. I'm shown in all sorts of compromising positions, including on Halloween.

It's like Juliet was stalking me from the first moment she met me, and all I want to know is *why*. And why did she never tell me we were related? Things could have been so different—we could have been a real family, maybe.

The creeping feeling of Juliet watching me sinks deep into my bones, so I spend the early morning hours running through every conversation I can think of that I had with her. Nothing stands out, though, and it makes me angry. I should be able to remember *one* thing she said that was a red flag, right? She was either incredibly careful, or I'm a terrible friend.

I did shut her out when I started to get more serious with the Hallows Boys, so maybe it's my fault that I can't remember anything. My whole world became my guys, and I need to apologize for that.

Turning on Hocus Pocus again, I roll myself up in the blanket and lie back on the bed, flipping through the pictures over and over again while I listen to the TV.

Most are taken from a distance, but some are closer. Especially ones where I'm with the guys. It's like she was more willing to get caught for the juicy photos, because there're more shots of us having sex than anything. The rest of the majority are shots of me from behind, walking through the hallways at school or through town or through the cemetery.

I fade into sleep with the feeling that I'm being watched, and my nightmares are filled with creepy-crawly sensations that cover my skin.

———

"SAGE?" MY UNCLE'S VOICE PULLS ME FROM SLEEP WITH A GASP, and I sit upright too quick, making myself dizzy.

"What?" I say, looking at my uncle.

"I brought some more stuff to help you understand what's been going on since you've been in here. Do you want something to eat first?"

Shaking my head, I run my hand down my face and sit up straight. "I'm not hungry."

"You're going to make yourself sick if you don't eat something soon," he says, putting a bag down on the table.

"I'm fine," I say, watching as he pulls a piece of thick cardstock out of the bag first and puts it to his chest.

"I don't want you to panic, okay? I will explain everything, and it will all make sense." He smiles, then extends the card toward me.

I choke on the spit in my mouth as I read the card aloud, heart dropping to my stomach.

"Please join us for the funeral of Sage Grace Blackmore, 1 p.m. in Blackmore Cemetery, January 14th." My eyes seek him out, and he chuckles, like it's one big joke.

"I don't understand," I say, my mouth hanging open. I search for something else I can say to him, but nothing comes out when I try to speak.

"I got to Blackmore on Christmas and tried to talk some sense into Juliet. I had recently tried to bond with the girl, and I thought maybe I could put an end to this whole *stalking* thing." He sits down on the edge of the bed. "She told me it stopped, but I caught her following you again. The night you snuck out of your grandmother's and went down to the crypts."

I sit and stare at him, speechless, unable to breathe, and wait for him to continue.

"She followed you through the cemetery, down to the crypts and waited. She was taking pictures of you, Sage. I didn't know what she was going to do. It was the middle of the night, and you were all alone, but I sat back and waited. I wasn't going to step in unless you were in danger." He sighs. "Then Juliet started going for the crypts, and I knew you had gone into the Hallows Crypt, so I cut her off and confronted her. She pulled a knife on me, and I had no choice but to defend us! I wasn't going to let some sick girl hurt you!"

My head slowly shakes in disbelief. "What happened...?"

"It all just happened so fast. I never meant for the girl to die, but all of a sudden, she was just bleeding out on the cemetery ground," he says, sighing and running a hand through his hair. I feel like I'm going to be sick, but shock takes over as I let him continue. "I knew you would get caught up in it. I knew it would hurt you. I wanted to save you the imminent pain of losing a friend like that, so I grabbed you and brought you here. I didn't know your Hallows Boy was going to torch the place till I went back and saw him with the gas cans, and at that point, I couldn't get Juliet's body back out of the crypt."

"*What?!* Which Hallows Boy? What happened?" I gasp, desperate for morsels of information about my guys. "Are they okay?"

"Beckham burned the crypt down while Juliet was inside, and I had to come up with some sort of explanation of where *you* were," he says simply, and my mind spins. "There's a former Hallows Boy who works at the police station. He's helping me try to get Benjamin out of prison, and I have a few more connections left in Blackmore after all, because it was easy enough to get them to lie on the death certificate and say it was you. All I had to do was sign my name and say I had identified your body—easy."

"*Easy,*" I repeat in disbelief. "Do you even hear yourself? Murder, corruption, faking my *death?!* What the fuck is wrong with you?!"

"Now, Sage, you need to let me finish the rest of the story."

I grit my teeth, anger simmering inside me. "Go on, then."

"So, everything was fine, right, but then I saw those *boys* at your funeral, and they had gotten cozy with Joyce Spencer, who knew far too much about all of us for her own good—"

"Wait, wait, wait—*knew?!*" I cut him off, standing up and backing away as my chest starts to heave with panic. "Did you do something to my Gran?"

He stands, holding his hands up. "Now, Sage, this one I can explain too."

I charge him, shoving his chest with my hands as I scream, "*What did you do to my gran!*"

He grabs my wrists. "Sit down and listen, Sage."

"No!" I shout, tears streaming down my face as sobs roll through me in painful waves. "Did you hurt her?!"

"It was an accident. I just wanted to talk to her!" he shouts, and I fall to the ground in a mess of tears and screams. "I *swear*, Sage! I would never do that to you, she slipped and that's it!"

I wail, my cries making it hard to breathe as I dig my fingernails into the carpet. *"Gran, no, no, no! Gran!"*

"I'll come back later, okay? When you aren't so emotional." Uncle Aaron grabs the bag he brought with him, and I don't bother to acknowledge his exit as he leaves the room, shutting the door and locking it. I just keep crying, keep calling for my gran, hoping the gaping hole in my chest continues to open up and swallow me whole.

I'M IN A STATE OF CATATONIA WHEN MY UNCLE COMES BACK, THE four beige walls around me officially suffocating me.

"Sage?" Uncle Aaron says softly, but I don't look up, my head feeling too heavy where it's lying on the mattress. My limbs ache with grief, and I want to turn myself to a mist that fades away from this place.

"Sage?" he says again, his tone kind and careful as he sits down on the edge of the bed. "Can I continue with the story?"

I don't move, and my voice comes out like gravel grating over the dry ground. "Okay."

He clears his throat. "I never meant to hurt anyone, Sage. They were all *accidents*, all necessary to protect you. The only thing I've ever wanted was to *protect you.*"

"Well, that will be easy to do within these four walls," I whisper, feeling helpless.

"Exactly!" Uncle Aaron says, not reading the dark sarcasm behind my words, like I've finally caught on to his insane plan. "Eventually, I'll need to figure out how to explain that you're alive, so we can reintegrate back into the town, but it'll all come together, Sage, okay? I just need to figure out a way to deal with those *boys.*"

I shoot up, renewed energy surging through me at the mention of my guys. I stare at my uncle, who still resembles the man I once knew—a friend, a safe place, my family—but I know that person is long gone. I won't find the person I used to know within his corrupted soul.

"Don't touch them," I growl, feeling angry and scared and protective.

He sighs, reaching for the bag he brought with him again. "I brought something that might change your mind about them, Sage."

My jaw hurts as I clench it, but I watch as he pulls a leather-bound book from his bag—one I recognize. One I swore I would never open and read. The journal from last year's Hallows Games.

"I haven't read this yet, so it'll be a new story for the both of us." He smiles, then cracks the book open to the first page and starts reading. "*The Hallows Games, October 31, 2019. Members: Kaiden Thorne, Vincent Donahue, and Beckham Bentley.*"

I cut him off, knowing the name of the girl is next, not wanting to know who it is or what they did. "Please, *stop.*"

"This is for your own good, Sage. You need to understand that you don't mean anything different to them than any of the other girls. You need this to get over them."

"I don't want to know," I cry, a tear sliding down my cheek as nausea curls around my gut.

"I know, sweetie." He scoots closer, putting a hand on my cheek. "But *we* need this."

Before I can plead any more, he turns back to the book and continues. "*Female Selection—Madison Marks.*"

I recognize the name, but can't pinpoint who it is, and I

don't have enough time to, because my uncle continues reading. *"The details of the night are as follows, written by Beckham Bentley."*

My stomach cramps as nausea rolls through me in waves, not wanting to hear the story. I smash my eyes closed as my uncle keeps reading.

"Although the rules for documentation of the games were set in place by the founders, as this year's generation, we will not be cataloging in detail what happened with Madison. It is our responsibility as Hallows Boys to grow and learn as the years go on, and I do not feel it's appropriate to put onto paper what happened during the Hallows Games."

My lips twist into a smile, and my uncle narrows his eyes. "What the fuck?"

"Surprised?" I ask my uncle, and he meets my gaze.

"They're supposed to document it," he says, shaking his head as his face goes red with anger. "They can't just change the rules and do whatever they want. That isn't how this fucking works! *We* created the game, they can't just change it."

He slams the book shut, stands up, and throws it across the room. I flinch, shrinking away from him as he starts yelling. "The rules are *clear!* They're supposed to document everything!"

My hands start to shake, so I squeeze them into each other as I watch him pace back and forth, his voice getting louder. "Entitled, arrogant, horrible fucking generation! I'll show them what happens when they break the rules!"

"What does that mean?" I ask, panicked as he looks at me again, rage burning in his gaze. His face splits into a smile, one that feels evil, and I stop breathing as terror snakes its way around my lungs.

"Oh, I'll show them," he says, his white teeth sparkling as his smile widens and he lunges for me.

CHAPTER 37

KAIDEN

After a day of searching Blackmore for any trace of Aaron—the cemetery, the asylum, the motel, the woods behind the school—by dinnertime, we retreat to Vinny's house to get some food and rest so we can start again the next morning, maybe hop to the next town and check there too.

We decide we don't want to head across the country to California until we know, without a doubt, that Aaron really did leave Blackmore. It isn't like he would have been able to transport Sage across state lines without raising some flags, so we're half-convinced that he's stashing her somewhere in town.

We just need to figure out *where.*

There's a plain cardboard box on the doorstep when we get to Vinny's house, our names written on the top in thick black marker.

I rip the tape off the top as soon as we're shut inside Vinny's living room, the box resting on the coffee table.

The box is larger than necessary, because inside there's only a few single polaroids sitting loosely at the bottom. Grabbing them, I hold them up so Becks and Vinny can see them clearly as well.

The first is a shot of Sage's face, her eyes shut and her nose bleeding, a hand grabbing her jaw to hold her head up straight.

"It's her," Becks breathes, his hand digging into my forearm. "It's Sage."

I flip to the next photo, which is Sage lying on her stomach completely naked, the same hand pressing on the back of her head, so her face is pressing into the mattress.

Nausea spirals through me, making me want to scream.

The third photo is Sage on her back, her blonde hair a mess on the pillow under her head, a hand around her throat and her face a shade of purple it shouldn't be.

I crumple that photo in my hand and stand up, not wanting to see the rest. "Let's go. We're going to find her."

"Where? We've looked everywhere, Kai!" Vinny says, grabbing my arm as I start to move toward the door.

A renewed sense of urgency rushes through me, though. Now that I have concrete proof that my girl is alive, it's like the surge of panic makes me think clearer, and pieces start to come together in my mind.

"I have an idea," I say, looking at my brothers. "We need to check Juliet's house."

CHAPTER 38

SAGE

A NUMB, ALMOST CALM FEELING SETTLED INSIDE OF ME A FEW hours ago, and all I want to do is close my eyes and never wake up. I've been kidnapped, my death faked, my grandmother murdered, and now… *now*… my last living relative has crossed a line that should never be crossed.

And he snapped photos of it the whole time.

Like father, like daughter, I guess.

There is no doubt in my mind that soon, my death won't be a made-up story. Soon, I'll be murdered by my uncle too.

I'm sure the moment he returns from delivering the photos to the Hallows Boys, his revolting way to punish them for staining his legacy and tradition, he'll end my life in a panic, unable to find another outcome for his actions.

Should I fight through it? Or just let the darkness take me one last time? Will death claim me in pain, or will I fade away gently? After everything I've been put through, I deserve for it to be quick, I think.

I'm thinking about Kai's cocky smile, Beckham's deep blue eyes, and Vinny's soft lips when sleep takes me into the dark.

———

"Sage? Sage? *Sage?!*" A voice startles me, my name on a loop, but I can't seem to completely rip myself from sleep. My eyelids are so heavy, and my limbs ache so badly from lack of sleep and water and food. I can't lift my head. I can't bring myself to open my eyes even a millimeter to answer whoever is now shaking me.

"*Sage,* you've got to wake up, baby. Please. You need to wake up *now.*"

Like some sort of miracle, my hands tighten in the sweat soaked sheets, and I manage to crack my eyelids open just slightly, letting the light in the room blind me for a half second before his face comes into view. Kaiden. *My* Kaiden.

Maybe I'm dreaming—maybe he isn't here at all. Maybe I've died, and this is my version of heaven, a place with the Hallows King.

Something inside of me feels real, though, telling me that this isn't a dream, that I haven't passed on. This is *real*—Kai is here, rescuing me.

"Kaiden?" I whisper, meaning to lift my arms, but finding no strength to do so. My stomach growls as if to remind me that I haven't had even a crumb of food in days, not since I learned my uncle was drugging me.

"Oh, God. Sage, please, please, wake up right now. I need you to wrap your arms around my neck, okay?" Kaiden says, his tone panicked and scared. It's not how I'm used to hearing him, and it makes my heart race. His hands go under my arms, and he drapes them around his neck before he slides his arms under my torso and lifts me. "Hold on, okay? I'm here. I'm never leaving you. Just hold on, Sage."

"Kaiden," I breathe, my face dropping into his neck, and I think it's the smell of him—the smokey, manly, earthly scent of his skin—that makes me find a tiny morsel of energy deep in my gut, because I tighten my arms around his neck and open my eyes.

He turns us as he takes a step away from the bed, and I spot Beckham and Vinny at the door, my stomach plummeting when I see the gun being held to the back of their heads.

I'm still out of it, though, dizzy and unable to scream, even as they continue to walk into the room and my uncle comes into view, his face angry and hateful.

"Put. Her. Down," my uncle grits out between his teeth, sliding his thumb against the metal so the gun clicks. "*Now.*"

Kaiden's body stiffens, and he takes a tiny step backwards until his backside hits the bed. "No."

My uncle shifts his arm, placing the gun on the back of Beckham's head.

Beckham doesn't flinch, standing strong, and my chest aches at what I might witness. "Don't let her go, Kai. No matter what he does. Let him kill me if it means saving her."

Before anyone can say anything else, my uncle pulls back the gun and slams it down on the back of Beckham's head, making him drop to the floor in an unconscious pile. Vinny spins, grabbing my uncle by the throat, but he's quicker, and he has the barrel of the gun pressed to Vinny's forehead before he's able to disarm him.

My uncle and Vinny stare at each other for a minute that seems to last forever, then he pulls back and jams the gun into Vinny's temple, catching him off guard. Vinny grunts, his grip on my uncle's throat wavering as he trips backwards, blood dripping from his head.

"Stop it!" I finally shout, my voice scratchy but forceful, bringing my uncle's attention back to me and Kaiden.

He gives me a small smile. "Are you okay, Sage?"

"Fuck you," I spit, and Kaiden's hands tighten around my body.

He sighs, like my words are a disappointment to him, and my head spins with anxiety as walks across the room toward me. As my uncle's eyes seek Kaiden out again, I feel sick to my stomach. "Put her down, boy. Now's your last chance to leave here without a body bag."

Panic snakes through me, because I don't know if Kaiden knows everything I do—and I know that my uncle will have no problem pulling the trigger. I look up at Kai, his dark eyes serious as the stare burning daggers at my uncle, and I lift my arms from around his neck.

He flinches, grabbing me, urgency in his tone. "What are you doing?"

"He's serious, Kaiden. He'll kill you, all three of you. You guys need to leave."

Kaiden shakes his head. "There's no fucking way you're leaving my arms, Sage. If I die, I'll die trying to save you."

My uncle clicks his tongue. "The big, bad, brave Hallows Boy. I know all about you, Kaiden Thorne… You were student body president, captain of the basketball team, most popular guy in school—a *classic Andrew*."

Kai squeezes his fists in my shirt as my uncle continues.

"But you'll *never be able to protect her*. You aren't what makes a king, *boy*. You'll abandon your morals and your loyalties the second they stop seeming like a benefit to you, just like Andrew did." My uncle laughs, the barrel of the gun pressing against Kai's forehead now once he reaches us. "Get your hands off her. This is your last chance. Don't be a fucking hero."

Kaiden's nostrils flare as he pushes his forehead against the gun, a twist to his lips. "You'll have to shoot me."

"No!" I shout, scrambling, pushing from Kaiden's arms until I'm slamming into my uncle. "I'll go with you. Just leave them alone, *please.*"

"*Sage.*" Kai reaches for me, but my uncle presses the gun against his forehead harder, holding him in place as I stand next to my uncle.

Beckham and Vinny stir on the ground behind us, so my uncle grabs me and shoves me in the opposite direction, then he takes Kaiden by the throat and shoves him toward Beckham and Vinny like he weighs nothing.

"Get on your knees, *Hallows Boy*," my uncle sneers, and Kaiden stands frozen, with Beckham and Vinny behind him, who are holding their head wounds and staring up at my uncle. "Show the Hallows Queen how much of a *pussy* the leader of this generation really is."

"Fuck you," Kaiden spits, and my uncle laughs before he slams the gun into Kai's temple, making me flinch.

As Kaiden grunts, his hand going to his head, my uncle yells, "On your knees!"

Kaiden looks at my uncle, his dark, golden eyes filled with so much hate, then he drops to his knees. The gun is pressed to his forehead a moment later, and even as Kaiden looks up at my uncle, there's no fear in his eyes.

"Look at you," Uncle Aaron chuckles, "a once dominating and fearless leader reduced to a pathetic little boy on his knees, begging for his life."

"I haven't *begged* for shit," Kaiden bites out, pressing closer to the gun. "If you're going to kill me, kill me, but it'll make no difference if I'm alive or dead. *She'll always be mine.*"

He slams the gun into Kai's head again, making him grunt

and fall back, then he cracks his neck before he lifts the gun to Kai's head once more.

All my nerves unwind, knowing what's coming imminently if I don't stop this. I find the last piece of strength I can muster, and I launch myself across the room, barreling right into my uncle, hoping the boys have enough sense to help me get him to the ground.

Everything moves in the blink of an eye then. Becks and Vinny are grabbing my uncle as I body slam him, sending him flying to the ground; Kaiden is reaching for the gun that slides over the carpet, then a gunshot sounds that makes my uncle's body drop into stillness.

CHAPTER 39

SAGE

I GO IN AND OUT OF DARKNESS FOR THE NEXT DAY, PIECES OF reality sticking and others fading away, like I can't keep the memories aligned in my brain for long enough to hold on to them.

A faint beeping pulls me from sleep, the cloud-white walls around me hurting my sore eyes as I crack them open. I groan, and then a hand is squeezing my forearm.

"Sage?"

Everything is fuzzy at the edges, and there's a pinch in my arm where a needle is sticking out of my vein, making me groan again as I try to bend my elbow to get myself upright.

"Sage?" the voice from before says again, and I finally bring myself far enough into the present to realize it's Beckham's voice, and he's the one squeezing my arm in his hand for dear life. "Can you hear me?"

I blink—*once, twice, three times*—trying to get my vision to clear, and everything comes into focus. I'm looking at Beckham's bruised face, his features worried and filled with emotion. Moisture licks at the backs of my eyes, forcing me to close my eyes again. My throat aches as I speak, finally getting his name out of my body like a prayer.

"Beckham?"

"Yeah," he says, his voice cracking as he grabs me with both hands now, like he's making sure I can't go anywhere, and I find his dark blue eyes glossy with tears.

"Where am I?" I ask, looking around slowly, having no memory of coming here.

Beckham leans closer, a hand going to my forehead. "You're in the hospital, Savage. You've been here since yesterday."

I shake my head, trying my hardest to find the memory inside my muddled mind. "What happened?"

"I'll explain everything, I promise." He pulls my hand to his lips and kisses it softly. "When you're better."

"I'm fine," I say, my voice a croak, so many concerns surfacing in an instant. "Where are Kaiden and Vinny? Are they okay?"

Beckham smiles at me, then he looks over his shoulder to the couch sitting at the edge of the room, where Kaiden and Vinny are fast asleep. "Do you want me to wake them up?"

"No." I shake my head, feeling a tear slide down my face. "Let them sleep."

"Why are you crying, baby?" Beckham puts the back of his hand to my cheek, and it makes the tears fall freely, like he's opened the floodgates. "What's the matter?"

I press my eyes closed again, trying to get the tears to slow. "Nothing, I don't know. I'm so tired, Beckham."

He huffs a laugh like he understands, brushing the tears from my cheeks before he kisses my forehead. "Get some rest, Sage. I'll still be here when you wake up."

"Beckham?" I say, opening my eyes to get a glimpse of his

familiar face to soothe the sadness soaring through my soul. "Will you hold me?"

He doesn't answer, just stands up and lifts my blankets so he can climb underneath them with me. I do my best to shuffle over, lifting a little so I can lie in his arms when he's settled beside me.

"Always," he says, and then I'm taken under sleep again.

CHAPTER 40

KAIDEN

Sage goes in and out of sleep, like her body is rejecting being awake to acknowledge everything that's happened. Beckham, Vincent, and I take shifts staying awake for the moments she comes into consciousness.

We do our best to answer questions from the police, but the only person who can really clue us in on what happened three weeks ago is Sage.

Forty-two hours after arriving at the hospital, on one of my shifts, she wakes up with renewed energy.

My hand is in hers, and I'm staring at the ground when her fingers squeeze mine, making me sit up straight to look at her, finding her eyes wide open.

I stand, grabbing her jaw carefully. "Sage?"

"Hey," she says, casual as ever, and I laugh lightly.

"How do you feel?" I question, sitting back down, but pulling the chair as close to her bed as I can get so I can continue to touch her.

Her chocolate eyes look around the room for a moment, studying her surroundings like curiosity is searing through her. When she looks at me again, she puts a hand to her stomach. "Starving."

Chuckling, I grab for the remote at her bedside. "Let me call the nurse so she can get you some food."

As I press the button to call the nurses' station, Sage grabs my forearm. "Is he dead?"

I look at her, finding her eyes sad. She has small bruises along her cheek, like he had hit her at some point, and it makes me burn with anger. "Yes, he's dead."

"Good." And that's all she says.

Beckham and Vinny wake up when the nurse turns on the lights, her cart banging against the table as she comes into the room.

"Sage? How are you feeling?" the nurse asks as she clicks through something on the computer on her cart.

"She's hungry," I answer, and the nurse steps toward Sage.

"Well, I'll get some dinner sent up here as soon as I finish my exam, okay, Sage?" The nurse looks her over, takes her temperature, and examines the bruises on her face.

I sit back, letting the nurse check her out, and Beckham taps on my shoulder to get my attention. Leaning back in my chair, I look at his worried face and lift a brow. He leans into my ear and whispers, "Has anyone told her yet?"

Shaking my head, I give him a warning look, and he sits back on the couch with Vinny.

A small sliver of fear runs through me, because I know now that she's awake, she's going to have to face everything that's happened, and she's going to have to learn everything we know —including the fact that she's pregnant.

When we first got to the hospital, we informed the doctor

what had been sent to us, and they ran a blood test to confirm Sage is almost twelve weeks pregnant.

The police ended up finding an ultrasound machine at Juliet's house. Apparently, her mom was a nurse or something, and I guess her uncle had used it on her when she was knocked out to get a picture to send to us.

How he knew that she was pregnant, I guess we'll never know.

Maybe after the rest of the investigation, we'll have answers, but who knows? Now that Aaron Blackmore is dead, we may never have every question answered. We might have to just live with the mystery of some things.

How did Aaron know *anything* he did?

As the nurse finishes her exam, I stand up and pull her attention. "Can I speak to you in the hall?"

I walk out before she responds, and thankfully, she follows me.

"Yes?"

Before I speak, I make sure Sage's door is closed.

"Who is going to tell her she's pregnant?"

The nurse looks at me for a moment, the question in her eyes that everyone here has probably had: *which one of you is the father?*

"The doctor will be by to speak with Sage about her condition when the time is right. Her mental state is fragile right now, and something else could send her off the deep end," the nurse finally says, and I chew on my cheek in thought for a moment before I respond.

"I think it would be best if *I* told her."

"I'm not sure that's smart," she says, her light eyes filled with worry. "Why don't we just wait for the doctor, and see what he thinks?"

Nodding, I put my hand on the door handle for her room.

"Please get her something to eat, and make sure the doctor is on his way."

Before the nurse can answer, I open the door and walk back into the room, dismissing her.

Vinny and Beckham are sitting at Sage's bedside now, and Sage is sitting up straighter in bed, some color returning to her cheeks as she talks with them.

I join them, sitting on the end of the bed and smiling at my girl.

There's a knock to the door before any of us can speak, and then a couple of police officers are pushing into the room.

"Sage? Is now a good time to ask you some questions?" one of the officers asks, and I recognize him from when they arrived at Juliet's house a few days ago.

Sage looks at me, almost like she needs a push, so I grin at her and nod.

"Sure," she says, swallowing roughly, adjusting her position.

Beckham, Vinny, and I don't bother moving, instead letting the police speak to all four of us.

The door shuts behind them, and they move to stand closer to the bed. "Can you tell us the first thing you remember from the last few weeks?"

Sage chews on her lip. "I don't really know. I think he was drugging me, so everything is super fuzzy. I... I remember him coming into the room and showing me pictures. He said that Juliet had been stalking me."

"Did he tell you why he took you?" the officer asks, and Sage stiffens.

"He said he needed to protect me," Sage says, and a chill runs down my spine.

"From what?"

Sage shrugs. "I don't know, but he said he killed my parents... and Gran and Juliet too, all to protect me."

"What else do you remember, Sage?" the officer prompts, and Sage grabs Beckham's hand and squeezes.

"He *touched* me," Sage answers, her voice a strangled whisper.

Anger burns through me, and I stand up. "Does she have to go through this? You saw the pictures. You already know what happened."

"We're just trying to get to the bottom of things, son," the officer says, and I want to punch him clear across the face.

I grit my jaw, and Vinny puts a hand on my arm to try to calm me down, but I want to burn the whole town down after everything that's happened to my girl. I almost wish I hadn't killed Aaron Blackmore, so I could see him suffer behind bars for the rest of his life.

The officer looks at Sage again, tone softening. "Can you tell us what happened when your friends showed up where you were being held, Sage?"

Sage swallows, looking at me. "The first thing I remember was Kaiden waking me up, but I was so tired and dizzy that I couldn't really focus. Then Beckham and Vinny were there, and my uncle had a gun, and after that, it's all blurry. I just remember trying to get my uncle's attention off of them, so he wouldn't hurt them."

The officers are silent for a moment, then one of them clears his throat and closes his notebook. "There's a lot of moving pieces here, Sage. But I'll just tell you what we know now, okay? Your uncle was sick. It seems he had some sort of obsession with you. We found lots of different things that hint at a sick-minded individual who had been planning this for a while. There was an immense amount of evidence that proves he was the one who killed your grandmother, and then there's the case of his daughter, Juliet."

Sage wipes a tear that's running down her cheek. "Is it true that she was my cousin? That she was stalking me?"

"We searched the house and found diary entries that proved she had been fixated on you for a while, Sage—even before you came to Blackmore. She was consumed by the fact that your uncle had a relationship with you and not her. We fear that she was getting close to you to hurt you."

"So, my uncle *was* trying to protect me?" Sage asks, and my blood boils. But I keep my mouth shut.

"In his own sick way, maybe he was, Sage, but he was desperate, and desperation always leads you in the wrong direction. He hurt a lot of people who didn't need to be hurt—your parents, your grandmother, his own daughter and her mother, all collateral damage in an attempt to get close to you."

"So all of their deaths are my fault," Sage says, despondent. It isn't a question, but a statement.

"No," I say, pulling everyone's attention to me. "It was your uncle's fault. Too obsessed with the past that he couldn't see the present clearly."

"I want to go home," Sage says, voice deepening with sadness. "I just want to go, please."

The doctor walks in almost at the exact right moment, just as I can see Sage start to break under the gaze of the officers, who are making her face everything all at once.

"I need to interrupt," the doctor says, and the officers give Sage a smile.

"We're done for now," one of the cops says. "Feel better, Sage."

It feels like her room has a revolving door as the doctor steps closer, a small smile touching his aging face as he looks at the three of us sitting with Sage on her bed. "Can we give the patient some room, gentlemen?"

Although I don't want to, I stand up, and Beckham and

Vinny follow my lead, going to the couch to sit down so the doctor has better access to Sage.

I don't sit, I just stand at the end of the bed and watch as the doctor sits down in the chair beside her bed. "How are you feeling, Sage?"

The doctor has a great bedside manner because Sage instantly warms to him. She shrugs. "I'm okay. Hungry, a little nauseous."

"I think the nurse was going to bring up your dinner," the doctor says, but from his tone, I know what's coming next. "There're a few things we need to discuss, and it's best we do it in private."

Sage looks at me, and I make a point to keep my face neutral. Even though I don't want to leave the room, I will if she's more comfortable that way. She glances at the couch at Beckham and Vinny, and I hope they're also staying neutral to support her, and when she looks back at the doctor, she shakes her head. "They can hear anything you have to say. They're my family."

"Okay." The doctor stands up and goes to the computer to click through Sage's chart for a minute, then he turns to look at her. "When you came in, you were incredibly dehydrated and on the verge of starvation. I'm assuming when you were being held captive, you hadn't been getting the nutrition you need right now. We ran a few tests, and we found out that you're pregnant. Did you know that?"

I keep my gaze on Sage and study the feelings that pass through her based on her features.

Shock comes first—of course. Then confusion.

Then she puts a hand to her belly and looks at me, her chocolate eyes filling with tears as she starts to understand the words better.

"Pregnant?" she says, her voice tight like she's trying not to panic. She looks at the doctor again, shaking her head slightly. "You're sure?"

"About twelve weeks." He nods. "You're still in early stages, giving you some options."

"No," Sage says strongly, a smile tugging her lips wider. "I don't need options. I'm keeping it."

She looks up at me again, then gives Vinny and Beckham equal amounts of her attention too before a tear slides down her cheek. A smile twists my lips up when she speaks to all three of us, and I realize I'm relieved by her decision. "We're keeping it."

CHAPTER 41

SAGE

I'M DIZZY AND NAUSEOUS AND EXCITED AS THE DOCTOR FINISHES talking to me and leaves the room. *Pregnant. I'm pregnant.*

Kai walks toward me, eyes searching mine. "Are you okay?"

"Twelve weeks," I muse, putting my hand back on my stomach.

"Halloween." Kaiden smirks, and Beckham appears at my other side.

"Our very own Hallows Baby." He smiles, threading his fingers between mine.

I squeeze his hand, then I lift my head and look across the room, where Vinny is still seated on the couch, his arms resting on his knees as he looks at me.

"Vinny, come here," I say, lifting a brow.

He stands, walks toward me, then puts a hand on my jaw. "Yes, princess?"

"A baby," I say, looking up at him, a tear trailing down my cheek that he catches. "*Our* baby."

He nods, his green eyes overcome with anxiety that I want to ease.

"What do you think about that?" I ask, putting my hand atop his on my jaw. As Beckham places a hand on his shoulder, I realize it's something they've probably talked about before.

"I think…" Vinny starts, giving me a small smile. "I don't want to be anything like my dad."

Lifting myself up, I put my mouth on his—my tough, damaged, kind boy—and I kiss him softly for a moment before I pull back. "You are *nothing* like your father, and you are going to be an amazing dad to our baby."

"I love you," he says, his eyes filling with moisture before he kisses me again, and then he pulls away, his hands going around my face. "I'm glad you aren't dead, princess. I can't live without you."

"Me, too," I whisper, my chest warming.

As Vinny sits, Kaiden and Beckham move in, and all three of them surround me, giving me the opportunity to admire each of them together.

All of them so different, but so similar—the three loves of my life who I never saw coming but am now tied to forever, through blood and love and trauma and possession.

Kaiden gives me a smug smile, and I return the look with a curious one of my own. "What?"

"You know that baby is mine, right?" he says, arrogant as ever.

Before any of the other boys can say anything, I grab him by the jaw. "It's *ours*. All of ours. Don't forget it."

His eyes flare. "If you weren't sitting in a hospital bed right now, *Little Rabbit*, I'd turn your skin red from neck to ass for talking to me like that."

"No, you wouldn't," I say, smiling. "Not when I have our baby inside me."

There's a knock at the door, and I notice that Kaiden has to adjust his erection as I call out for whoever it is to come in. A small smirk is touching my lips as an unfamiliar man steps into the room, and Beckham stands and puts his back to me like he's going on guard.

"Sage Blackmore?" the man asks, his eyes turning up in greeting.

"Yes?" I say, and Vinny joins Beckham where he's standing at my bedside.

"My name is Harvey Williams. I'm the lawyer in charge of executing your grandmother's will. Is now a good time?"

I sit up straighter, making a point to pat Beckham's back to get him and Vinny to stand down. "Sure, come on in."

The lawyer clears his throat, putting a leather folder down on the little rolling table that's sitting vacant at the side of the room, and he moves toward me. "First off, I'm sorry to hear about your grandmother's passing. She was a lovely woman."

He smiles at me, and I nod. "Thank you."

Pulling some papers out of the folder, he clears his throat again. "I really just need to get a couple of signatures from you today, Sage. Your grandmother left everything to you, and it's all very simplified. She did, however, leave a letter that she asked me to give to you after she passed."

He flips through his papers, takes out a white envelope, and hands it to me. Without a word, I take it and rip it open, pulling out a single sheet of paper to unfold, then I start reading the letter to myself.

Sage, if you're reading this, I've passed on. I hope you'll accept the house in Blackmore, and I hope you'll consider staying in it. I know you were hoping to get back to California, but maybe you'll consider staying in our little town if you have your own house.

I've left instructions for Harvey to take care of everything else. My accounts

and retirement and all of that will go to you, I just wanted the chance to give
you some last words that I've never said to you.

I pray you can forgive your parents one day. I know you'll never get the
chance to hear their side of the story, but just know that they loved you,
Sage. They always wanted to protect you, and they did what they thought
was best by leaving Blackmore. I don't hate them for that. The only
resentment I have is that I didn't get to know you sooner. You changed my
life, Sage Grace, you really did. I know that if you hadn't come back to
Blackmore and disrupted my life, I never would have passed on with the
happiness and joy I have inside of myself right now.

You were the best thing to happen to me in a long time, and I'll always be
thankful that I got to know you.

Promise me that you'll live your life with pure intentions and always chase
your dreams, darling. You deserve to. Find what makes your soul burn with
unfiltered happiness and hold on to it.

I love you, Sage. I always have, and I always will.

Gran

I'm crying when I get to the end of the letter, so I fold it back up and put it back into the envelope before I set it in my lap. Beckham's hand slides into mine, and he gives me a soft smile.

"Thank you," I say to Harvey, and he nods minutely before he flips through his papers again and gets a pen out of his pocket.

"I just need you to sign the deed for the house, and a few more forms to put her bank accounts in your name. Insurance money will go directly to you as well."

I read over the papers he wants me to sign, and once I'm confident I understand them, I sign my name at the bottom of each.

Harvey gets them all back into his folder, then he folds it up and looks at me. "Again, Miss Blackmore, I'm sorry for your loss. I'll have all of this mailed over to you in a few weeks."

"Thank you," I say, feeling sad and overwhelmed as he leaves.

Beckham squeezes my hand. "Are you okay, Savage?"

Nodding, I take a moment to look at each of them before I answer. "Can someone see where that nurse is with my dinner?"

CHAPTER 42

SAGE

I GET TO GO HOME THE NEXT DAY, A REFERRAL TO AN OB-GYN and a little baggie of prenatal vitamin samples from the nurses in tow, and walk outside to find that Kaiden has gone to get my car from my house.

Beckham and Vinny settle me into the passenger seat, then slide into the back before Kai drives us to my house.

"What now?" I ask, and Kai looks at me out of the corner of his eye.

"What do you mean?"

I put my feet up on the dash and try to get comfortable. "I've been dead for weeks, so there's no way I'm going to catch up in time to graduate."

All three of them laugh, and Beckham answers me. "I'm sure they'll understand. You had a good excuse."

"And what about you?" I look at Beckham. "Aren't you still facing charges for burning down the crypts?"

Kai snorts, turning onto Main Street.

"The charges were dropped," Beckham says, and I give him a confused look. "The Blackmore family is still in ownership of the cemetery, and since all of you were dead, there was no one to press charges."

I laugh. "I'll have to speak to the police now that I'm alive, then."

Beckham rolls his eyes at me. "You love me too much to do that."

Kaiden pulls the car into my driveway then, and I turn to look up at the house. This will be my first time here as the owner, and part of it doesn't feel right to me. This house doesn't feel right without my gran.

My car door opens, making me jump, and Vinny reaches over me to undo my seatbelt before he kisses my cheek. "You okay, princess?"

Nodding, I look into his deep, emerald eyes and find the strength to get out of the car and face my new reality.

Kaiden leads the way, Vinny holding my hand and Beckham following behind us, carrying my bag. As Kai slips the key into the door, he turns back to look at me, a smile spreading across his face. "Welcome home, baby."

The lock clicks, he turns the doorknob, then he pushes into the house. I follow him, finding the entryway and living room decorated with an unnecessary amount of birthday decorations. There are balloons all over the staircase, streamers hanging from the ceiling, banners on every wall and confetti all over the floor.

I laugh, looking at Kai as he turns around to look at me. "Happy birthday."

"My birthday was almost two weeks ago." I laugh, admiring the decorations for a moment before I look at Kaiden.

He runs his hand over his jaw. "You were dead for your birthday, and we didn't have a chance to celebrate."

Vinny's hands go around my waist, his face falling into my

neck from behind. "We wanted you to still have an eighteenth birthday party."

Beckham laughs. "Yeah, to make up for the fact we actually went to your funeral on your real birthday, while you were locked in a bedroom by your deranged uncle."

I snort, looking at Beckham, who's still laughing. "Super dark."

He shrugs, and then Kai grabs my face to turn my attention back to the decorations. "Do you like it, baby?"

I stare up at him, his dark eyes so happy I could cry. "I love it, King, thank you."

He grabs me from Vinny's arms, pulling me into him so he can kiss me softly. When he pulls back, he smiles against my skin. "I'm so glad you're home."

Vinny grabs my waist again, yanking me from Kai's hold. "Share her, we all missed her."

I laugh, shaking from everyone's hands. "Alright, I'm going to take a shower. You guys can argue over me while I'm gone so I don't have to listen to it."

"Can I come with you?" Beckham asks, grabbing my hand, and I laugh again.

"No, and there better be a birthday cake for me when I get back down here."

———

After cake and lots of attention from my guys, we all curl up in my bed to watch a movie. It's like we had paused life, and now we're pressing play again, back to our normal. I guess it is—me and my three favorite people, locked in my bedroom, except now… we're finally alone for the first time.

There's no one sneaking photos of us, and even though we didn't know it was happening, I can feel a change in the air.

Contentment sets in, and all three of the boys fall asleep before me. I lie there as the closing credits roll, and listen to the soft song that accompanies them, as well as the sounds of Kaiden, Beckham, and Vinny breathing. Someone is softly snoring, probably Vinny, and it soothes me enough that I start to drift away into sleep.

———

A SMALL SHOUT WAKES ME UP A FEW HOURS LATER AS nightmares haunt my sleep, a cold sweat dripping down my back and between my breasts.

"What is it?" Beckham says, grabbing me by the shoulders as he looks around the dark room. "Are you okay?"

"Shh…" I say, not wanting Kaiden and Vinny to wake up too, and I drop my face into Beckham's warm chest to whisper to him. "Just a nightmare."

His arms go around me, his large hands running up and down my sweaty skin. "You're okay. I'm right here."

I kiss his breastbone. "Don't let me go."

His arms tighten around me. "Never, Savage."

Kai curls against my backside, his hands grabbing my hips under the blankets and turning me hot. Safety sets in, and as Kai rubs my waist and Beckham strokes his fingers against my back, I find sleep again.

———

A FEW HOURS LATER, I WAKE UP AGAIN. THE SUN IS RISING outside the window, and there're small beams of light stretching over the room. Beckham is awake, staring down at me as I sleep, and I smile up at him. "Hi."

He runs his fingers through my hair and tilts my head back to look deeper into my eyes. "Hey, baby."

"Are you watching me sleep?" I ask playfully, wrapping my hands around his waist and pulling his body against mine.

He grins, kissing my forehead. "Yeah."

"You can't sleep?" I ask, looking at him again with a furrowed brow.

Beckham shakes his head, sadness and worry lining his features, and something inside of me feels scared. I breathe him in, his own personal scent of amber calming me a little.

"What's wrong, B?" I whisper. "Why aren't you sleeping?"

"I just can't. Too much in my head."

"Like what?" I press, trying to read whatever is hiding in his eyes.

Vinny starts to stir, so Beckham puts a finger to my lips to silence me. Putting his mouth at my ear, he whispers against my skin, "You wanna go for a walk?"

Nodding, I pull back to slide under the blankets and out of the bed with him. Kaiden and Vinny are fast asleep, breathing deeply. I grab a pair of sweatpants and a hoodie from my closet in silence, then creep out of the bedroom with Beckham, who has a hand secured around my waist.

I pile my hair on top of my head in a messy bun as we walk down the stairs, and Beckham grabs a hoodie where he left it in the kitchen while I slip my feet into my sneakers at the front door.

"Ready?" Becks asks, putting a hand around my waist again, almost like he can't stand to let go of me.

I stare at him for a moment, then I lean forward and put my lips on his. His fingers press into my waist, and he walks me backwards until my back is against the front door. A small moan escapes my lips as his hands slide into my hair, and he takes the opportunity to slip his tongue into my mouth.

He feeds on my kiss, his warm body pressed against mine and my back digging into the solid wood behind me as I get lost in his touch. I'm pressing my nails into his waist when he pulls away an inch, his breath fanning over my wet mouth. "I missed you so fucking much, Sage. Everything was horrible without you."

Nodding, I look up into his deep blue eyes. "I'm never going anywhere ever again."

"C'mon." He grabs my hand, pulling me from the door so he can open it. "Let's walk."

It's still cold from winter, but with the sun rising in the east, my skin feels warm as we step onto the porch and out into the day. I'm reminded of the days when I would walk to school, downtown, or to the cemetery in the crisp early mornings. Beckham threads his fingers between mine and guides me along the road as we walk in peace, the only thing in the air is the distant sounds of birds in the trees and the occasional breeze that makes the leaves blow.

After a moment, I start to realize Beckham is leading us toward the cemetery, and I turn to look at him. "Where are we going, B?"

His curly black hair is a mess, like he was running his hands through it all night as he tossed and turned, and his blue eyes are lifeless and lonely when he looks at me. "I need you to see what I did, and I need to talk to you about everything that followed."

"The crypts?" I ask, and he just nods as he keeps walking.

I'm not nervous about seeing the crypts. I'm not nervous about seeing anything in the cemetery. I know that regardless of whatever has happened, this was always the place that all four of us felt most at home, like we belonged to the sadness that clings to this place. The openness of the graveyard was always a playground for this town, and it was the first thing that made me truly feel like I was a Blackmore.

As we step onto the sidewalk that connects with the cemetery, a calm, distant feeling settles into my gut, like I'm returning home after being gone for so long.

I have a feeling Beckham is feeling the same way when I look up at him and notice there's a small smile pulling at his lips.

We continue to walk in silence, hand in hand, the ground solid and dry under our sneakers, and I run my free hand over the headstones that are within my reach as we move.

After a few minutes, a chill is settling inside me as we walk under some of the larger, older trees that make the graveyard dark even in the daytime, then the crypts are coming into view.

Well, what the crypts used to be.

They're in pieces now, broken and cracked and blackened from the fire that Beckham set, and it makes me sad.

This is where we fell in love, where our baby was conceived, and now it's just chunks of concrete that hold all our secrets.

"Beckham..." I breathe, and he turns to look at me.

Shaking his head, he runs a hand down his face. "End the games—that's what you said, Sage. That's what I did... If I had known all of this would have happened because of it..."

He lifts his hands to his sides, his face turning angry. "I didn't know you were here that night, Sage. I wouldn't have done it if I had fucking known all of this would happen because of me!"

"Hold on." I step toward him and grab his waist, shaking my head. "None of this happened because of *you*, Beckham. *I wasn't inside the crypt when you burned it down!* Aaron had already taken me then, and Juliet was already dead, you get that, right?"

"I don't know!" Beckham yells, pulling from my arms. "Maybe if I hadn't made such a public display out of destroying this place, he wouldn't have kept you. He wouldn't have had to make up a story that you were dead when they found Juliet's body in there!"

I move with him, grabbing him again, this time by the face. "Stop it, Beckham! You can't blame yourself for everything that's happened. Aaron was *sick*. And I'm *fine!* I'm here, and I'm never fucking going anywhere again!"

He shakes his head, his blue eyes filling with tears and turning into a sea of despair. "You don't know everything that happened when you were gone, Sage…"

"So tell me," I say, pulling him against me and kissing his mouth. "Tell me everything."

Beckham sighs, his hands sliding over the top of mine where they're still resting on his cheeks. "Let's find somewhere to sit down, and I'll tell you."

I give him a smile that I hope comes off as supportive, and he leads me to the Hallows Crypt. He steps over the broken entrance until we're under the shadow of the concrete still standing, right where the empty bookcase is still against the wall with our names. He pulls me down to the floor with him, our backs against the dusty wall.

His eyes seek mine out. "I guess you can't have a cigarette for our talks anymore, huh?"

I chuckle. "Not for a few months."

Heavy silence settles over us this time, and we stare at each other for a moment, then Beckham grabs my hand and kisses it. "Who do you think the dad is?"

I narrow my eyes at him. "None of you have very strong pull-out game, so there's really no way to know."

Beckham laughs, then grins at me. "I bet it's mine."

Rolling my eyes, I shake my head. "I don't want to know who the biological father is. He's *all* of ours."

"*He?!*" Beckham balks, a small wave of shock passing over his features. "Did you find out it's a boy?"

"No," I laugh. "Not yet, I just have a feeling."

He hums between his lips, then looks over my head at the names carved in the concrete.

Kaiden Thorne, Vincent Donahue, Beckham Bentley.

"Would you believe that it was only a few months ago that we were here together?" he says, reaching over my head and tracing the outline of Vinny's name. "Everything is so different now."

I grab his arm, smoothing my fingers over his skin until I'm threading them through his. "What happened when I was gone, B?"

He shakes his head and sighs. "None of us knew how to handle it, Sage. I can't really blame them for what happened."

"What happened?" I ask again, feeling protective over my soft Hallows Boy.

Beckham's gaze finds mine, and the look in his eyes makes me uneasy about what truths I still don't know. "I got arrested for your murder. They thought you had died in the fire, and there was a photo *anonymously* submitted to the police department of me with the gas cans in the cemetery."

He shakes his head, and I swallow over the lump in my throat. "Vinny was there when I got arrested, and I can't blame him for hating me then... I would have hated him for killing you too. It made sense."

"Okay..." I say shakily, watching him as his face saddens.

"I sat at the police station for days, then finally got bail. Came home and Kai was here waiting for me. He basically just told me I was dead to them, *blahblahblah*, tough-boy Kai shit, you know how he is."

I nod, and he continues. "A few days later, him and Vinny show up on my doorstep, push inside, and Vinny beats the shit out of me."

He chokes on the last word, and a tear slides down his cheek before he quickly pushes it away. I tighten my grip on him and scoot closer, trying to give him the comfort he needs to continue.

"I don't blame him, Sage," he says, his voice cracking with sadness. "He was so fucked up that you were gone. He thought I killed you, and he wanted to fucking punish me. I know that he needed to do what he did to show me that he *could.*"

Beckham brushes another tear from his cheek and clears his throat before he meets my gaze.

"Vinny told Kai to hold me down so he could *fuck* me."

I squeeze my eyes shut, shaking my head as nausea overcomes my senses, twisting like a knot in my stomach, the memory of my own recent assault coming back to me.

"I can't get the fucking memory out of my head, Sage. I can't fucking stop thinking about him like that, the fucking boy I love—taking advantage of me because he wanted to show me he was more powerful than me. I know that I deserved it, b—"

I cut him off, opening my eyes and putting a hand to his cheek. "You didn't deserve *that.*"

He looks at me, and he's so fucking sad I want to scream. I want to make it better, make *him* better, but most of all, I want to show him that he's not fucking alone in this. He doesn't need to suffer in silence with this.

"We are going to get through all of this leftover trauma, Beckham." I move closer, putting my legs around his waist as I scoot onto his lap to plaster my body to his. "We are going to fucking survive this. We are here, and we are together, and I will never let anything happen to you again."

He shakes his head softly, then he kisses me hard enough that I groan on impact. My mouth opens, and he angles his head to mine to deepen our connection, his hands threading into my hair to control the movements of my lips. After a minute, he pulls back, his chest heaving. "I love you, Savage. I love you so fucking much."

I slide my hands under his shirt to feel his burning skin. "I love you too, Beckham."

He kisses me again, his fingers pulling my hair softly as we fall back into the chaotic mess of our kiss, and that's how we stay for a long time, our bodies pressed together in the shadow of the broken crypt, our trauma pooled around our feet as we kiss like long-lost lovers coming back together again, once and for all.

———

I FEEL ANXIOUS AS WE LEAVE THE CEMETERY, THE IMAGE OF Beckham being taken advantage of on a loop in my mind. I want to make it better for him. I want to find a way to help him heal from what was done to him, and at the same time, I want to find a way to heal from my own assault.

There are a few things mixing around in my mind as we make the walk home, and by the time we're back inside my house, I know how to handle the feelings that I have left over from everything my uncle did to me.

Before we left the cemetery, Beckham made me promise I wouldn't say anything to Kaiden and Vinny about it, even though I'm so angry I want to tear them apart. It's his trauma, though. He gets to decide when it's brought up, and I understand that.

Kai and Vinny are sitting at the kitchen table when we get back, both of them eating a bowl of cereal.

"Morning," I say, kicking my shoes off and pulling my hoodie over my head.

"Where have you two been?" Kai asks, and there's anger in his eyes.

"We went to the cemetery," I say, feeling angry for my own reasons too. "Is that okay?"

Kaiden gives me a look, one that screams *trouble*, and then licks his lips as he takes a breath through his nose. "Maybe you shouldn't disappear without a word a day after returning home from being kidnapped?"

"She was with me," Beckham cuts in, sitting down and grabbing the box of cereal in the center of the table.

Kaiden shoots daggers at Beckham, and I sigh as I put a hand on his shoulder. "I'm sorry."

His hand slides around my thigh and he pulls me onto his lap so he can speak into my ear quietly. "At least take your phone if you're going to go somewhere, okay?"

The tone of his voice tells me that he was genuinely worried, the fear of me leaving hitting a nerve I didn't even think to consider. I can understand why he was freaked out—he woke up and I was gone.

"I'm sorry, King," I say, kissing his throat. "It won't happen again."

"Good," he says, putting some dominance back into his tone as he slides his hand up my back and into my hair. "Now give me a kiss good morning."

I grin, putting my mouth on his so he can kiss me, and his hands tighten in my hair for a moment before he pulls away.

He pats my ass, signaling for me to get up, and I stand so he can take his bowl to the sink.

Vinny reaches for me, grabbing my hand and pulling me closer so he can kiss me as well. It's quick, closed-lipped, and over too soon, so I lean back in and grab his jaw, sucking on his lower lip for a moment before his large hands slide around my thighs and grab my ass.

He pulls away again, groaning, "*Princess.*"

"I want you," I breathe. "So bad."

A hand threads into the back of my hair and massages my scalp lovingly, and then Kaiden's voice cuts through the tension.

"There's no time for that, baby. We need to be at the school in twenty minutes to re-enroll you."

I groan, leaning my head back to look at Kaiden. "Seriously? *Today?* I just got home."

He chuckles. "It's almost February. We can't afford to miss any more time."

I roll my eyes, and Kai pulls my hair, making me hiss. "*Kaiden.*"

"Go get dressed. We're leaving in ten." He kisses my lips, then lets go of my hair and walks back to the sink. "All of you."

CHAPTER 43

BECKHAM

WHILE KAI TAKES SAGE TO BLACKMORE HIGH TO RE-ENROLL, Vinny and I go to his house to pack some of his stuff so he can stay with Sage for a while.

I think it's better she has someone there for now, and since Vinny is the only one who also lives alone, it makes sense that it's him.

Even though Kaiden and I are eighteen, we still have to answer to our dads. It's just easier not to fight that. As soon as we graduate, we'll figure out a more permanent situation with Sage. Maybe we'll all move in together.

I'm daydreaming about what it would be like to fall asleep between Vinny and Sage every night, and wake up in the same place every morning, when Vinny calls my name to get my attention. He's packing a duffle bag that's sitting on his bed with clothes, a small backpack next to it that he put his laptop, and some other stuff into. I look up at him from where I'm seated across the room at his desk. "What?"

"I said, *are we okay?*" he repeats, rolling a pair of jeans and putting them in the duffle.

"We're fine, Vincent," I say, looking down at my nails so he doesn't see the lie in my eyes.

"*Vincent?*" he questions, taking a step toward me. "Since when do you call me Vincent?"

I look up at him again, and he has an eyebrow lifted as he stalks closer. "That's your name."

He tilts his head, a humored smile spreading across his face.

"I know that's my name, Becks, but you've never called me that." A thoughtful look passes over his features as he reaches me. "It's Vin, Vinny, V, Baby, *oooh-daddy-right-there*—but never *Vincent.*"

I laugh, smacking his hand away as he goes to grab me. "I don't think I've ever called you *daddy.*"

He steps even closer, so close that my legs spread so he can step between my thighs. His pelvis brushes mine, and he grins down at me as he slides a hand around my jaw and into my hair. "You could, though. I'd like to see you on your knees, begging *daddy* for his big cock."

I swallow hard, heat spreading through me—desire and anxiety mixing together so quickly that I start to breathe faster, and I flinch just hard enough that Vinny notices.

Vinny raises a brow, then takes a step back to scan his gaze over me. "What's wrong?"

Shaking my head, I go to grab him, but he moves out of my reach. "Nothing, V. Come here."

"Should we talk about whatever's bothering you, B?" he asks, his features going soft. "You can't keep pulling away from me and expect me not to notice."

"I know," I say quietly, pressing my lips together for a moment. "I'm sorry."

"You don't need to be sorry. I just need you to communicate with me."

Nodding, I run my hand down my face as I take a breath. "I'm just still fucked up from everything that's happened."

"I think we all are, B. But we stick together. That's how we've always gotten through shit." Vinny bites his lip, eyes on mine.

"It's different this time," I whisper, wanting to curl up inside myself, make myself so small that he can't see the shame I feel for everything I've done, for everything *he's* done.

"What do you mean?" Vinny presses, and when I look back at his face, he looks hurt enough that I want to cry.

"I'm just having a hard time letting you back in," I say hesitantly, hating the way the words taste on my tongue.

Vinny nods, pressing his lips together in thought for a moment. "Tell me what I need to do. Tell me what you need."

"I just need time, V," I answer, standing up to meet him. "I still love you, and I still want this life with you, I just need to get over what you did."

"Okay," he whispers, his gaze keeping mine captive, and I get the urge to kiss him. So that's what I do. I wrap my arms around his neck and kiss him softly, savoring the taste of his lips and the smell of his skin and the feel of his hair under my fingers.

When I pull back, I smile at him. "We're okay, V. Just give it time."

He kisses me one more time. "I love you, Beckham."

"Me too, *daddy*," I say, making him laugh.

———

It's deep into the afternoon when we get back to Sage's house. Kai and Sage are on the porch, sitting in the little rocking chair Sage's grandmother had set up out there, and Kai is whispering something into Sage's ear through her hair.

When they notice us walking up the driveway, Sage's face splits into a smile that spreads from ear to ear.

Kai's hands are on her bare thighs, her shorts riding up, and when we're stepping onto the porch, she jumps up to hug both of us.

"Hi."

"Did you get back into school?" Vinny asks, tilting her head back by her chin.

"Yes," she answers, her deep brown eyes narrowing. "Now it's your turn."

I laugh, smacking Sage's ass playfully as I walk past them to take Vinny's bag inside. "Yeah, good luck."

"Kaiden is going back with me," Sage says, looking at me over her shoulder. "Are you?"

I throw Vinny's bag down in the entry, then run back outside and grab Sage by the waist, lifting her and carrying her inside.

"Hey! Be careful with her!" Kaiden yells after me, and both Sage and I laugh.

"She's not going to break!" I shout behind me, then I start taking the stairs up to Sage's bedroom, dead set on throwing her into bed and climbing between her legs to feel her heat against my skin.

As I walk through the bedroom door, Sage giggles and grabs my cheeks. "I know what we need to do, Beckham."

"Oh yeah?" I say, dropping her down on the mattress playfully and standing between her open thighs. "What's that, Savage?"

She curves her back slightly, looking up at me through her lashes. "We need to take back the power."

Sliding my hands over her waist, I squeeze her thighs and hips. "What power?"

She spreads her legs wider. "What happened to us was fucked up, Beckham. But we can take back control of our lives, our feelings, our fucking *sexuality*, and we can have the goddamn power again."

I hum between my lips, kissing down her neck in a wet, sloppy kiss that makes her head fall back. "Tell me what you want, then. Take the fucking power, baby."

CHAPTER 44

SAGE

I spot Kaiden and Vinny walking through my bedroom door behind Beckham's head, and I smirk up at them. This is for Beckham, but it's also for me. I deserve to feel like I'm in control of my own decisions again after everything my uncle did to me. I don't want to sit here and lick my wounds, having flashbacks and nightmares of when I was powerless and weak, I want to be strong and *powerful*.

Beckham looks over his shoulder at Kaiden and Vinny, a smirk pulling up his lips. "Our girl wants to be in control. Does anyone have a problem with that?"

Before they can answer, I answer him myself, looking at Kaiden and Vinny. "I want both of you to come sit on the bed, against the headboard."

Vinny chuckles. "Whatever you want, princess."

I see a twitch in Kai's jaw, but he complies regardless, following Vinny around the bed to sit down against the pillows.

Sliding my hand around Beckham's jaw, I bring his mouth

to mine and capture his lips in a powerful kiss that makes him groan. Ignoring the other two boys who are sitting in the bed, I slide my legs around Beckham's waist and pull him down on top of me, grinding my hips and arching my back.

Beckham pulls back, heated gaze locking onto mine. "What is it that you want, Savage?"

My answer is simple. "Fuck me. They can watch."

He chuckles, but kisses me again, sliding his hands under my arms to lift me farther across the bed so my legs are no longer hanging off the edge. I moan as he brings his knee between mine and spreads my legs wider, his pelvis pressing against mine so hard that I feel his cock against my clit through my jeans.

I smooth my hands under his shirt, desperation rising within me. "Take this off."

He lifts, rips his shirt over his head, then tosses it onto the floor before his lips are consuming mine again. His warm skin presses against mine, and I trail my fingers all over his body. After a minute, he strips me of my shirt and bra, then kisses down my chest.

As hard as it is to ignore Kaiden and Vinny, I want this moment with Beckham. I want to feel like we have the control, that we can find our confidence and sexuality within each other again. This is fucking important for both of us.

"So fucking beautiful," Beckham murmurs against my skin as he kisses between my breasts and around my nipples.

"Beckham…" I whisper, heat spreading from my head to my toes.

My fingers tangle through his curly hair, and I pull his mouth back to mine so I can kiss him. Pressing my bare chest against his, I savor the feeling of our skin rubbing and sticking together.

Beckham pulls back once more, his deep blue eyes finding

mine as he reaches between us to undo my jeans. "You want this?"

Nodding, I do the same, reaching for the button on his pants and undoing them. "I want this." I feel a hand thread into my hair and realize that Vinny has moved toward us on the bed, and I shake my head. "Not yet. Sit back down and wait your turn."

He pouts, but listens, moving back to where he was sitting at the head of the bed. I take a second to look at Kai, finding his face pressed into frustration, his arms crossed over his chest, but he doesn't move. He doesn't disobey me, just stares at where me and Beckham are horizontal on the bed.

Beckham slides the zipper on my pants, pulling my attention back to him, and I continue my efforts to undo his pants and slide them down far enough that I can free his throbbing erection.

He stands up, rips my jeans and panties down my legs, then he falls back down on top of me, lifting my legs up against his ribs.

I stroke my hand over his dick again, my gaze meeting his as I guide him between the slit of my pussy, and his ocean eyes flare with heat as I roll my hips against him to impale myself on his length.

"Fuck, Sage," he moans, kissing me as he thrusts, his hands tightening in my hair.

Pleasure rolls through me as he slowly but powerfully drives into me, his hips grinding against mine. I'm a symphony of moans and pleas and cries against his kiss as he feasts on my mouth and tongue, his cock massaging me from the inside as he makes love to me.

After a few minutes, he moves faster, still making tight and precise circles with his hips that have my clit throbbing every time he rubs against it, his hands grabbing my hair and jaw and face and neck.

"*Beckham,*" I cry, pulling my wet lips from his as my back curves up so my nipples press harder against his solid chest. My arms spread to my sides so I can grip the blanket between my fingers, heat rushing over my body as Beckham continues to fuck me thoroughly.

His mouth suctions on the skin at my throat, my pulse point, my chest, my nipples, and my orgasm blossoms deep in my center. I grow restless and hungry, getting addicted to the slow and deep thrusts Beckham seems to have mastered, and my throat grows sore from moaning.

His tongue glides between my tits, up my throat and to my mouth, where he outlines the shape of my lips before he pulls me into a kiss that's wet and sloppy and slippery. I go dizzy, feeling pleasure so immense that my hands ache from gripping the blankets.

"Tell me," Beckham groans, and he moves faster, the wet sounds of our connection filling the room. "Tell me you love me."

I move my hands around his face, pulling his gaze to mine as he fucks into me faster. My voice is unrecognizable and throaty, coming out louder than I intend. "I love you, Beckham."

"*Ah, fuck,*" he moans, his face dropping into my neck. "Come with me, baby. Let me feel you fall apart for me while I fill you with my cum."

I moan between my lips, my orgasm ripping through me like my body knew exactly what he was asking for.

"Oh, Jesus fucking *Christ*, Sage." Beckham's hips move faster and faster as his climax takes over, his muscles going rigid as his lips spread and suction around the skin on my neck.

Even as we ride out, and then come down from our orgasms, he still rolls his hips between mine, his cock making deep strokes inside me that have me crying out his name on repeat. We're a soaked mess between our legs when he finally slows, both of our releases leaking from me and spreading over our skin.

He kisses me once more, and I caress his cheeks lovingly before he pulls back an inch, whispering so only I can hear. "Thank you, Savage."

Desire burns in my core all over again, even as his cock grows soft inside of me, and I lift up to kiss him before I grin against his mouth. "Thank you, too."

"I'm growing impatient, Sage," I hear Kaiden growl, and a small laugh escapes my lips before I can stop it. I give Beckham a look, as if to say *alright, get up,* and he lifts off me.

Beckham stands up, kicks his pants the rest of the way off, then he walks toward Vinny at the same time I lift onto my knees and crawl across the bed.

I keep my gaze shifting between Kaiden and Vinny, who are seated at the head of the bed fully clothed, and a small smirk pulls the corner of my lips up. I take a moment to look at Beckham, noticing that his dick has already grown solid again, and his hand is stroking it as he reaches Vinny.

Deciding to give them their moment, I focus on Kaiden and crawl the rest of the way to him, putting myself between his legs so I can reach forward and unbutton his pants.

"Take your clothes off, Kai," I breathe, my voice silky smooth and ready for whatever he's about to give me.

His lips turn up into a smile that makes my spine tingle, and he reaches for me, lifting me and placing me on his lap. "You don't get to be in control with me, Little Rabbit. You're *my* filthy fucking slut, not the other way around."

I narrow my gaze, putting my hand on his jaw and sliding down his skin until I'm circling his throat. "If I want to be in control, you'll fucking let me, Kaiden."

He blinks at me as I squeeze the column of his throat, then he lifts a brow and rests his hands on the bed next to his hips. "Take what you want from me then, baby, but you better hurry up and get on my cock before I shove myself so far down your throat you feel it in your lungs."

I smirk, taking a small moment to look over at Vinny and Beckham, who are kissing and moaning and running their hands all over each other.

"I want all of you," I say, pulling their attention and dropping the hand I have on Kaiden's throat. "All at once."

Kai rips his shirt over his head, then lifts me and places me next to him on the bed so he can take off his pants and boxers.

Vinny does the same, with Beckham's help, and before I know it, we're all naked and coming back together.

"Turn around, Sage," Kai says. "I want your ass."

Beckham fishes around in my bedside table for some lube while I position myself on top of Kai, my back to his chest, and then he's passing it to Kai, who's spitting into my ass and pressing his pointer finger against the hole.

A pinch of pain radiates between my cheeks, but Vinny crawls between my open legs on the bed and suctions around my clit to help me relax. I cry out as pleasure rocks through me again, Vinny's tongue flicking against my clit while Kaiden squirts some lube between my cheeks and adds another finger.

"Give me that," Beckham says to Kai, holding a hand out for the lube, and before Kai passes it off, he covers his cock in the slippery liquid.

Beckham kneels between Vinny's legs on the bed while he eats my pussy, and he spreads his ass cheeks apart before he drips lube from above. Vinny licks me faster, his hips rising a little as Beckham presses a finger to his ass, then I feel Kaiden slipping a third finger into my own.

"God, you're so fucking tight," Kaiden growls into my ear

from behind, pumping his fingers a few times and making me shout in pleasure.

Beckham continues to stretch Vinny's ass while he feasts between my legs, and watching him top Vinny is enough to turn me into a dripping mess. My head goes back on Kai's chest, and he kisses around my throat as he pulls his fingers free and swaps them with his cock.

"Take a breath, baby," Kaiden says, sucking my earlobe into his mouth as he pushes the head of his cock through the ring of muscle.

"Oh, fuck," I moan, and Vinny sucks my clit between his teeth and rolls it, pushing me into a climax so powerful that I scream and convulse, hands gripping the sheets below me until they ache.

Kai slips in farther as I fall into the chaotic bliss of my orgasm, and I reach up to grab at my bare breasts as greedy screams climb from my throat.

"That's my girl," Kaiden praises me, pulling me down on his cock until we're ass to thigh and he's fully impaling me.

"*Vinny…*" I moan, reaching for his hair and pulling. "Come here. Now."

Kai thrusts slowly as Vinny lifts from between my legs, wipes his mouth, and crawls closer to me. Grabbing his dick with one hand, I use the other to grab his jaw and pull his mouth to mine. "Fuck me."

Vinny looks between my legs and rolls the head of his cock through my dripping cunt, the overstimulation every time he hits my clit making me twitch. After a moment, he pushes inside me, and I drop my head back against Kaiden, who is grabbing my hips desperately as I squeeze his cock in my ass.

My eyes find Beckham over Vinny's shoulder, and he smiles at me as he pushes into Vinny's ass, making him thrust deeper into my pussy.

"Oh *my god*," I moan, doing my best to keep myself upright as pleasure makes my limbs shake. "*Yes, yes, yes.*"

"How does that feel, baby?" Kai whispers into my ear from behind, his fingers reaching around and pinching my nipples.

I don't have a chance to respond, because Vinny is kissing me hard enough to make my teeth shake. My eyes close as our tongues tangle, his cock moving in my pussy and rubbing against Kai's through the thin wall inside me.

With one hand, I grab Vinny's hair, and with the other, I reach behind him and grab Beckham, wanting to connect with him as well, and then we're all moving in unison like a perfectly timed orchestra. Beckham, thrusting into Vinny's ass while he thrusts into my pussy, my hips grinding against Kaiden's lap as his cock impales my ass.

Kaiden continues to roll my sensitive nipples between his fingers, and it's not long until I'm reaching the peak of my orgasm again, my pussy squirting and soaking Vinny from the front.

"Again," Kaiden groans, biting my neck as he reaches between my legs to pinch my clit. Screaming, I twitch and writhe against him, but with Vinny on top of me and Kai holding me down from below, I'm helpless to rip away from the overstimulation.

Pleasure-fueled tears stream down my face as another orgasm passes through my body, my mind spinning and my hand digging into Vinny's chest hard enough that he bleeds.

"Fuck, princess." Vinny drops his head into my chest and bites my skin as he starts to come, his hips pounding into me the best he can while all of us are moving with him, and then I feel Beckham reaching for me. When I look up at Beckham, I find his face splitting into euphoria as his own orgasm hits him, and Vinny's body starts to ram into me harder, faster, and wilder as Beckham fucks him with just as much passion.

My core lights up, and I squeeze Vinny from the inside as he chases the rest of his release, then he's falling against me in exhaustion, his mouth kissing my breasts languidly as Beckham also slows.

"Everyone get up," Kaiden says, his voice controlling and powerful, and his brothers listen to him, Beckham pulling away first, and then Vinny kisses me on the lips once before he pulls out of me.

"What is it?" I ask Kai, but he just lifts me by the hips and turns me around, dropping me back down on his cock.

My ass stretches again as he enters me until his balls are against my skin.

"Look at me," Kaiden says, his hands rubbing up my thighs, my hips, my stomach. "I need to see your eyes."

My gaze finds his dark golden one as his hands press into my hair.

He grips my head with both hands, pulling my chest against his to bring us closer together. "Ride me, baby."

I moan loud, grinding my ass down in his lap, feeling his cock stretching me from the inside out, renewed pleasure spreading through me painfully fast.

"That's my good slut," he says, kissing around my jaw and neck and face. "Milk the fucking cum from my cock with your tight ass."

I shout as he thrusts up into me, then Vinny and Beckham are running their hands over my skin too, through my hair and down my back and ass. I cry out again, loving the feeling of all three of them touching and treasuring my body, and I feel an orgasm so intense burning in my core that my eyes water.

Kai's hand goes between us, two fingers sliding inside my pussy while his thumb presses my clit. "Are you going to come again for me, baby?"

Nodding lazily, I put my head back and it falls against

Vinny's chest, and then my body is shaking and twitching and trembling through an orgasm that makes me scream, tears trailing down my cheeks at the strength.

"There it is, princess," Vinny whispers into my ear, and Beckham kisses my lips to swallow down my cries.

Kaiden's cock swells then, pulsing in my ass and making me press my nails into his shoulders as he fills me with cum.

"So fucking good," Kaiden moans, his hands grabbing my tits and squeezing. "You're so fucking good."

"I love you," I moan, my legs tightening around Kai's waist.

"Us too, baby," Kaiden growls. "Always."

PART FOUR

HALLOWS EVER AFTER

CHAPTER 45

SAGE

"Do I look fat in this?"

I spin around and look at Kaiden, who's sitting on my bed watching me get dressed for school.

"I don't know how to answer that," he says carefully, and I narrow my eyes in warning.

Laughing, he stands up, takes the three steps to reach me, then brushes his hand over the front of my dress, curling his palm around my stomach. "Baby, you're pregnant."

I growl in the back of my throat. "Yeah, but I'm also still a high school senior."

"You aren't the first girl in this town to forget to use birth control, I promise," he says, grinning down at me.

Slapping his hand away from my stomach, I wave him away. "Let me get ready. Go to school, and I'll meet you there."

He sits back down on the bed, leaning backwards on his elbow to continue watching me, a chuckle passing through him. "If you think I'm leaving you alone, you're insane."

"You need to make sure Beckham and Vinny re-enrolled, *please*," I snap, using the excuse that the other two boys who own my heart need assistance.

Kaiden stares at me, his face neutral. "Keep giving me attitude and see what I do."

I groan, ripping my dress over my head and throwing it back into the closet, letting it land on the pile of rejected articles of clothing I've tried on today.

I'm only now realizing that my stomach has swelled, as I'm trying on something that isn't sweatpants or leggings, because none of my clothes fit right. It's frustrating, and all I want to do is put sweats back on, crawl into bed, and scream into the pillows.

After another ten minutes of trying stuff on, I settle on a pair of leggings and an oversized sweater that hangs to my thighs. Sitting down at my vanity, I stare at my exhausted features and pale skin, trying to remember the last time I needed to get myself dolled up to go somewhere.

Everything is so different now—things that used to matter haven't mattered for a really long time.

Kaiden sits silently on the bed while I do my hair and makeup, and once I'm done, I stand up and walk over to him.

His hands curl around the backs of my thighs and he pulls my body closer to his so he can rest his face against my stomach. "You look beautiful."

Threading my fingers through his hair, I exhale a long breath while we savor the feeling of each other.

After a moment, I pull away. "Let's get this over with, then."

He stands, following me out of the bedroom. "Everything will be fine."

Turning, I look at him over my shoulder. "I know."

His hands tighten around my hips as we take the stairs. "I'll always protect you."

"So, when Rachel and the cheer squad call me fat today, you'll take care of them?" I grin, leading him into the kitchen to get some coffee.

"I'll fucking kill them if you want." He kisses my hand, then leans against the counter as I step up to the coffeemaker. "What are you doing?"

"I'm just going to make some coffee, then we can go. One minute, tops."

He snorts, grabbing my arm. "Coffee? You know you're pregnant, right?"

"Coffee is fine to drink while you're pregnant, in moderation." I roll my eyes at him, trying to shake off his grip.

Grabbing my waist with his other hand, he pulls me against his body. "We'll just ask the doctor next week."

I stare into his dark eyes for a breath, then I kiss his mouth softly before pulling away. "You're being overbearing, Kaiden Thorne."

He smiles, showing me his teeth. "Stop testing me, then."

My gaze catches on the necklace hanging around his neck, the one I gave him for Christmas, and a small smile pulls up my lips as I reach forward and grab it. Running my thumb over the designs on the silver, I hum between my lips in satisfaction. "I love this."

"Me, too," Kai breathes, sliding his hands into my hair and pulling my gaze to his. His eyes are shining with gold from the reflection of the light behind me, and his teeth are pressing into his bottom lip.

"I wish I still had the necklace you gave me." I frown. "My uncle must have thrown it away."

Kaiden grins, then removes his hand from my hair and goes into his back pocket. Pulling his wallet out, he opens the billfold and slides a finger into one of the slots that's meant for credit cards. My heart stops when he pulls out the silver chain he got me for Christmas, the pendant with his initial still intact, only a little bent at one edge.

"Oh my god." I press my fingers to my lips. "Where did you find that?"

Kai clicks his tongue, using a finger to signal me to turn around so he can put the necklace around my neck. "Your uncle sent it to us. One of the many gifts we got when you were in that fucking house."

I feel sad as I think about what they must have thought when they started to get mystery packages from my uncle. We haven't directly talked about everything the three of them went through when I was gone; I only heard their story when they were telling the police.

When the necklace is fastened around my neck, I turn back around to face Kai. "You didn't give the necklace to the police?"

He shakes his head. "Didn't see the point—we had already given them everything else, and I wanted you to have it back one day."

Humming, I grin up at him as he cups my face again. We stare at each other for a moment, like everything else has suddenly frozen around us, and my stomach fills with butterflies.

"I love it when you get all sweet."

He chuckles, leaning forward to bite my lip. "Don't get used to it."

———

SURPRISINGLY, EVERYONE AT SCHOOL IS SOMEWHAT WELCOMING.

I go the whole first half of the day without trouble, only getting some sideways looks that I guess are warranted since I came back from the dead last week.

Thankfully, Beckham and Vinny are able to re-enroll without issue. News and gossip spreads quickly in Blackmore, so even the principal of Blackmore High is aware of everything that's happened to the four of us this year.

That also means that everyone and their mama know I'm pregnant.

However, I didn't expect the administration to be so flexible when Kaiden, Vinny, and Beckham *requested* that their schedules were changed to mimic mine. I don't know what kind of strings they pulled, or what threats they made, but now I have every class period with three sets of very protective eyes on me.

When me and my three bodyguards get to lunch, I'm happy to see that our usual table is vacant, like the student body left it empty on purpose.

"You want salad?" Becks asks me, and I roll my eyes.

"I can get my own lunch," I protest, and Vinny laughs.

"First day back, princess," Vinny says, eyebrow quirked. "Might as well let us do everything for you."

Sighing, I look at Beckham again. "Salad is fine, thanks."

Becks and Kaiden head for the lunch line to get all four of us food, and Vinny walks me to the table, my backpack thrown over his shoulder.

When we've found our seats, Vinny sits sideways in his seat so he can face me. "You okay, princess?"

"Fine," I say, finding his worried gaze. "Are you okay?"

He shuffles closer, putting his hands around my waist. "I'm perfect."

Vinny slides one hand around my belly, then he leans into my neck to breathe in my skin. "I love you, princess. I can't wait to worship your body tonight; we can play pretend that I'm filling you with another baby."

My skin heats, and he chuckles as I grab his forearm. *"Vinny."*

"You know the baby's mine, right?" He speaks against the skin of my neck, his mouth warm and wet.

I smack his chest, making him pull from my neck and laugh. "It's *all* of ours."

He smiles like a shit, his hand rubbing my stomach. "Alright, princess."

"Vinny?" A voice yanks me from the secure bubble we've made around us, and Vinny scoots closer when we both look to where Rachel is standing at the other side of the table. "Can we talk?"

"No," he says without a thought, and I feel a little bad.

"It's fine, V," I say, and he looks at me like I'm crazy. Before a small laugh can rumble through me, I look up at Rachel. "What is it?"

"Vinny?" she says, ignoring me altogether. "Can we talk, just you and me, please?"

I start to get a little pissed then, because I have hormones taking over my body, and *this bitch did not just ignore me when I was fucking nice to her!*

"Hello?" I snap my fingers to pull her attention. "Talk, or go away."

Rachel looks at me, and even as sadness glitters in her gaze, there's still malice behind the next set of words she spits at me. "*So*, who's the dad?"

Vinny shoots up out of his seat, and I grab his hips to hold him in place. "Excuse me?!"

"Sit down, Vinny," I say, and he looks at me as he slowly moves back down into his seat. Looking at Rachel, I sigh. "What do you want, Rachel? Because if you just came over here to be a bitch, then you can walk away."

She chews on the inside of her cheek for a moment, then she clears her throat. "I just want to know if Vinny is the dad."

"He is," I tell her without missing a beat. "Even if it's not through blood. And I don't owe you any more explanation than that. Your time with Vinny is over. It's time to move on."

Rachel's eyes flutter as she rolls them, and she walks away without another word. Even as my heart pounds in my chest, I feel satisfied that she'll leave us alone. There's only so much you can do when the dude you like is having a baby with someone else.

Beckham and Kaiden appear then, dropping our food down on the table. Beckham gives me a concerned look as he finds his seat. "What did she want?"

"Vinny." I roll my eyes, and he laughs.

Kaiden hands me my salad, and I give him a smile in thanks, then we all find a comfortable silence as we dig into our food, letting the drama and trauma and pain simmer away around us as we enjoy this simple, high school moment like normal students for once.

CHAPTER 46

SAGE
FOUR MONTHS LATER

I never spent much time thinking about my high school graduation. I wanted to get through senior year, stack my transcripts with as many academics and extracurriculars as possible, then head off to an Ivy League University and start a life that was all mine.

That is… until I moved to Blackmore.

With the changing environment, my goals changed too.

Looking back at the girl I once was makes me sad now, because all I cared about was being the *it girl*—the valedictorian, the most popular girl in school, the rich girl who got *everything she wanted*.

But why did I want any of it? At the end of the day, I was so fucking lonely that I don't think any of it would have mattered in the end. I would have continued the fake life my parents had created, living a lie laced with diamonds.

I got lucky, even though my parents had to die to get me here, because I was able to see the things in life that are actually important. I got to know my grandmother, and she taught me in the small time we were together that there is more to life than being the best of the best.

I came to Blackmore, and I found family and love, and I can see a future that's so much more beautiful than anything I would have had as Sage Lindman. I have Beckham and Kaiden and Vinny and our shared love and our baby that we all made together.

My future may not include Harvard fucking University, but it includes love and peace and safety and happiness.

And that's all I need as Sage Blackmore.

I have my town, and my guys, and our family.

That's all I fucking need.

————

THE DAY OF OUR HIGH SCHOOL GRADUATION, I'M WOKEN UP with someone's head between my legs.

I'm too consumed by the mix of sleep and pleasure, that it isn't until an orgasm has rocked through me that I lift the blanket to see who it is.

My knees are shaking beside Vinny's smiling face, and I reach down to thread my fingers through his silky hair. "Good morning."

He wipes the side of his mouth with his thumb and crawls upwards, until his face is resting over my swollen stomach. He circles the baby bump with his hands and presses kisses there, mumbling against my skin as his mouth touches every inch. "Good morning, princess."

I slide my fingers through his hair lovingly. "Where is everyone else?"

"Downstairs." He continues to crawl up my body until he's out from under the blanket and he sits back between my knees to look down at me. "I told them I would wake you up. Beckham's making pancakes."

He's shirtless, only a pair of tight boxers on his lower half, so I reach forward and skim my fingers over his abs. His cock is hard under the fabric of his boxers, and I reach under the material to rub him softly.

Groaning, his head drops back. "Princess… *Fuck.*"

My pussy is a dripping mess, and the waves of desire coursing through my body have me stroking Vinny's dick faster, jerking him until he's leaking precum in my hand on every swipe. His gaze seeks mine out, and I lick my lips. "Do you want me, Vinny?"

He nods, his mouth dropping open and his tongue coming out to lick his bottom lip. "Always."

I spread my legs farther and he positions himself at the apex of my thighs, then we're both rolling our hips so he can slide inside me with a powerful thrust. He keeps my gaze as he fucks me, his hips pounding hard and fast.

After a few minutes, it's his eye contact that has me screaming and writhing against the sheets, the moment feeling so intimate that I want to pull him inside me and never let him go.

I grip the sheets between my fingers, watching as Vinny's mouth drops open and he begins to pant. Moaning, I arch my back, and my stomach brushes against his. He fucks me harder, faster, making me shout and cry out his name.

"God, you're so fucking sexy, princess." He runs his palm over my stomach, around my hips, over my thighs. "I can't get enough of you."

The door opens on the other side of the room, and we both turn to look at who it is. Beckham laughs as he crosses his arms over his chest. "I told you to wake her up. The food is getting cold!"

I reach for Vinny's throat, pulling his face back to mine, and I kiss him hard enough that I forget about breathing altogether. He moans, and I pull back an inch. "Come, baby. I'm hungry."

He laughs, sitting back on his knees and jack-hammering his hips as one of his hands goes to my clit and the other holds my hips in place.

"*Jesus,*" I hear Beckham say from where he's leaning against the door frame, but I keep my gaze on Vinny's as my orgasm burns and throbs in my center, finally exploding when his cock pulses inside of me.

"Take it, princess," Vinny says, leaning his head back as he fucks me through our shared releases. "Fucking *take it, take it, take it.*"

I cry through my climax, grabbing the sheets while Vinny's release spreads inside of me, then we're both stilling, our chests heaving as bliss takes over our bodies.

Vinny leans down and kisses me, breathing through his nose. "I love you."

Curling my hand around his jaw, I smile. "And I love you, V."

"Let's *goooooo!*" Beckham says from the doorway. "Now I'm hungry *and* horny!"

Laughing, I push Vinny's sweaty chest to get him up, then I swing my legs over the side of the bed. "Patience, B. Patience."

He steps toward me, wrapping his hands around my naked body. "I made you pancakes, beautiful."

"I heard," I hum between my lips, then I catch the panties Vinny throws me from the dresser. Slipping my legs into them, I stretch my arms over my head, groaning. "My back hurts."

"Why?" Beckham asks, grabbing me again as worry passes through his features.

I push him off with a playful look and take the shirt Vinny is holding out to me. "Because there's a baby living in my ribs."

"God, that sounds like something from a sci-fi movie," Vinny groans, pulling up a pair of sweatpants.

"You're telling me," I say, rolling my eyes as I slip the shirt on.

Vinny leads the way downstairs to the kitchen, where Kai is still at the table on his laptop. Sliding my hand through the back of Kaiden's hair when I reach him, I smile as he looks up at me. "Morning."

"About time. Beckham wouldn't let me eat until you got down here." Kai stands up and kisses me on the mouth, then he sits back down and goes back to whatever he's doing on his computer.

Laughing, I circle the table and sit down between Vinny and Kaiden, watching as Beckham starts putting stuff down on the table.

Syrup, butter, a big plate of pancakes, and a plate of bacon are placed in the center of the table, and then he hands out empty plates to all of us before he gets a pitcher of juice from the fridge and fills four glasses.

Once Beckham has sat down, I smile at him. "Looks great, B."

"Our little chef." Vinny pinches Beckham's cheek playfully, and Beckham swats him away.

"Shut up and eat," Beckham groans, and I laugh, reaching forward to get some pancakes.

Kaiden stares at his computer while he eats, even as the rest of us fall into conversation. After my plate is clean, I tap my fingers on the table next to the laptop, and Kai looks up at me.

"What are you doing?" I ask, raising a brow.

"Trying to find us somewhere to live next year," Kaiden growls. "Since they don't offer dorm rooms with a *nursery* at the University of Georgia."

"We have months to figure that out, Kaiden," I say, trying to ease his mind, and he shrugs.

Even though we missed so much school, we all got accepted to the University of Georgia next year. It was Kaiden's dad's idea for all of us to apply, since it was always his dream for Kaiden to go there after graduation.

He's been more accepting than anyone else of our *situation*—and he's really excited to be a grandfather. He even talks about what holidays will be like with all of us. I think after so many years of missing Kai's mom, he finally has a shot at a happy family again, and he wants to soak in that feeling no matter what.

I decided I would take online classes, so I can stay home with the baby after it's born, and even though Vinny offered to do the same, I told him he needed to get the whole *college* experience with Kaiden and Beckham—maybe even get his ass back into football.

It'll be hard, but it'll be worth it.

We'll all get a degree, then we'll come back to Blackmore and live our life.

Maybe I'll revive the Blackmore name, run for mayor or something. Who knows? All I know right now is that the future is ours, and we can have anything we want.

Vinny clears his throat. "I can sell my house."

"No," Kaiden says, shaking his head. "It isn't necessary."

"Why not? It's not like we're ever going to live in it again. And when we come back to Blackmore, we have *this* house." He waves around the room.

"I have that savings account my parents made for me, too," Beckham says, stuffing a pancake in his mouth.

"That's for your tuition," I remind him before I look at Kaiden again. "Relax, please. I have my parents' money, the insurance, gran's money, and my uncle's... we are going to be fine, king."

Kaiden sighs, putting a hand on my chin. "I just don't want you to worry about anything."

"I know." I smile, standing up. Kai's hand immediately goes to my stomach, and I step closer to him. "How about we worry about graduating high school before anything else?"

He looks up at me, circling my belly with his palm. His face splits into a smile. "The baby is kicking me."

"It's always kicking when you're near." I grin, and he puts his other palm on my stomach as well.

"Maybe the baby already knows you're the mean daddy," Beckham says, and I laugh a little harder than I should.

Kaiden narrows his eyes at Beckham. "Maybe *you* should remember that I'm the mean daddy too."

Vinny chokes on his juice. "That sounded kinky."

Shaking my head, I step around the table to grab my phone to check the time, then I turn to look back at my guys. "Can you guys be ready in the next hour? I have something to show you before we head for graduation."

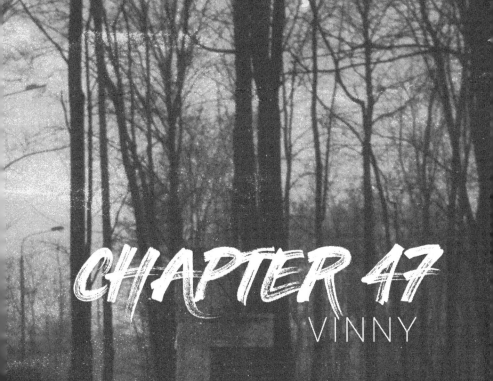

CHAPTER 47

VINNY

WHEN WE'RE ALL READY FOR GRADUATION, OUR CAPS AND GOWNS folded nicely in the back of Sage's car so we can slip them on before the ceremony starts, we head out to whatever surprise Sage has planned.

She's extremely thoughtful, carefully planning every gift she gives or gesture she makes, so when she pulls onto the side of the road next to Blackmore Cemetery, butterflies attack my chest and stomach.

"What are we doing here, baby?" Kai asks, leaning forward on the center console to look at Sage as she puts the car into park.

"C'mon," she says, her face spreading into a smile.

We all get out of the car, and Beckham grabs Sage's hand as they walk in front of me and Kai. Stepping into the graveyard, I take a deep breath in, savoring the smell of the freshly cut grass. Summer is upon us, and the birds are singing in the trees above the headstones, the sun beaming through the leaves and branches.

"So," Sage says, stepping carefully through the headstones as she leads us farther into the cemetery. "For a while, after things went back to normal… after I *came back from the dead* …" She says that part with a roll fluttering through her eyes, a small snort following the words.

"I felt like we never really had the chance to say *goodbye* to everyone who was lost this year…" She pauses, pressing her lips together and looking directly at me. "V, you lost your dad, and we never even said a word for him. It feels wrong."

"Princess." I reach for her delicate hand. "He was a prick, why would we?"

Sage's eyes glisten with tears, so I reach for her and put a thumb under her eye.

She waves me off. "I don't know if it's the hormones or what, but I feel like we need to do this to close the book and end this chapter. We need this so we can move on and celebrate the new life coming." She puts a hand to her round belly, and I smile.

Kai grabs her hand. "Show us what you want to show us, Sage."

She turns back around, and Beckham slides his arm through hers when she keeps walking through the cemetery.

After a minute, we're nearing an area of the cemetery that looks brand new, the grass green and the trees fresh. We can't see the road anymore, instead only headstones are behind us, and in front of us is a newly constructed crypt, the word *BLACKMORE* carved above the door.

"You built a crypt?" I ask, feeling confused yet awed.

She turns about ten feet from the white stone structure and faces the three of us. "This is where we found each other, this is where we made our daughter, and I'm not ready to let go of the moments we shared here."

"*Daughter?!*" Kaiden yells before it even clicks in my head, but there's no anger in his tone.

Until now, Sage has kept the sex of our baby a secret, insisting she would tell us when the time was right.

"It's a girl?!" Beckham asks, taking a step toward her.

Sage's face splits into a smile that rivals the most beautiful sunsets and the most breathtaking sights in the world—because there's pure joy in her expression, her entire body radiating warmth and maternal love.

"Princess?" I ask, my lips curved. "It's a girl?"

"It's a girl. We're having a girl."

Kaiden, Beckham, and I all move as one, getting as close to Sage as possible without smothering her, the unfiltered happiness bringing moisture to all our eyes.

We're all a symphony of *I love yous* and praise as we get our individual moments with Sage, then she clears her throat, putting a finger to the tear sneaking out of the corner of her eye.

"Now we need to say goodbye to everyone who's left this year, okay?" Sage says, and a boulder settles in my gut.

"How?" I ask, and she gives me a smile that's a mixture of sadness and pride.

"C'mon." She holds a hand out for me, and I thread my fingers through hers before she leads me around the edge of the crypt.

On the other side of the stone structure, there are a few headstones standing out of the fresh earth. I feel a little nauseous as she leads me to the first one, then she kneels, pulling me down with her.

VINCENT PATRICK DONAHUE, SR.
FATHER AND HUSBAND
1981-2020

My stomach burns, even as Becks' hands thread into my hair and his warm body presses against my back. I look at Sage, unable to find any words to say, and I clear my throat a few times.

She reads on my face that I can't get the thoughts together, and she reaches for my hand. "He was mean, and he was angry, and he was heartbroken, but he was your dad, and maybe we need to mourn what could have been if he got his shit together. If he didn't go down the path he did when your mom died. Maybe instead of mourning his death, we say goodbye to the pain he brought when he was here."

Nodding, I feel a tear slide down my face, and I wipe it away with the back of my hand. "Yeah, princess. That's perfect."

She's crying now, brushing the tears from under her eyes with her fingertips. "I want so badly to go back in time and rescue the tiny little Vinny who was in so much pain."

"Hey, hey, hey." I grab her jaw, making her look into my eyes. "It's okay. I had these two protecting me."

Smiling, I nod backwards to Kai and Beckham, and Sage smiles as she sniffles.

"I think we need to say goodbye to that pain too… the pain that came when he died." Sage looks up at Becks. "The pain you feel every day for taking his life."

Beckham's chin falls onto my shoulder, and he sniffles. "Yeah."

She looks at Kaiden then. "And the pain you feel for not doing it sooner."

I hear Kai before I see him, then he's crouching down in

front of me and putting a hand on my shoulder silently, his dark eyes swirling with anger and sadness and grief.

"We can all say goodbye to this chapter," Sage says, being our strength. "No more pain, or guilt, or anger for him, okay?"

I look at Sage, this girl who has every reason to be broken and shattered, who is still standing and thriving, healing three broken boys who dragged her into the darkness with them, and giving them the salvation they never thought they deserved.

Memorizing the way my girl looks right now, I smile softly and reach forward to stroke a thumb over her wet cheek. "I love you, princess."

She smiles at me, her decadent eyes filled with life that gives me hope. "I love you too."

I kiss her softly, then I move away and brush my fingers over my father's name carved into the headstone. Whispering, I feel a lump form in my throat again. "Bye, Dad."

Beckham puts his arms around me, kisses my neck and breathes deeply. "I'm sorry."

Nodding, I turn to look at him. "I forgive you, Becks. It was never a question. I love you."

He kisses my neck once more. "I love you, V."

Kaiden stands up first, holding his hands out for Sage to grab onto so she can stand up too, then he brushes her hair over her ear. "Who's next?"

She smiles, clearing her throat as she takes the two steps to the left and puts a hand on the next headstone. "Juliet."

JULIET MCINTOSH
FRIEND AND DAUGHTER
2003-2020

Becks, Kai, and I stand behind her silently, letting her think over what she wants to say for a minute before she finally turns to look at us.

"Juliet was my cousin, and she just wanted to feel good enough for her dad," she says solemnly, and then she shakes her head. "It wasn't fair she was forced to be this person."

"Someone who stalked you and wanted to kill you?" Kai says gruffly, and I want to smack him.

"Yes," Sage says, frowning. "She was the product of her environment, the result of everything her dad left her to learn by herself here in Blackmore."

Silence washes over us and sweat starts to bead on my lower back as the sun hits me. After a minute, Sage sighs. "I forgive you, Juliet. Rest easy."

Sage moves to the next headstone, and as I read over it, I move closer to her—we all do, like we need to protect her from the emotions that are about to hit her.

JOYCE GRACE SPENCER
LOVING GRANDMOTHER
1956-2021

"I'm sorry I couldn't save her," Kaiden says, and my heart sinks.

Sage looks at him, and she crosses the few feet that separate them, puts her hand on his face and smiles. "My fucking king, it wasn't your job to save her. You weren't saddled with that responsibility, so stop blaming yourself for what happened to her. You don't have to save everyone all the time, Kaiden. Let the rest of us take some of the burden from you sometimes."

He shakes his head, wrapping his hands around her face as well. "I will always fucking protect you. I will *always* save you and our family."

"I know." Sage smiles up at him. "My mean boy who loves so hard that it shakes the world, but let us save you back, okay?"

He kisses her, his hands tightening on her jaw, like he can't help it. Becks slides an arm around my center, and we watch as our best friend and brother finally gets everything he wants—his heart so full that he can't stop himself from feeling it anymore.

CHAPTER 48

SAGE

As Kai kisses me, I feel the baby kick inside my belly, and it brings a smile to my lips. Pulling away, he brushes the hair from my face. "Say goodbye to your grandmother, baby."

Feeling moisture lick at the backs of my eyes, I drop my hands from Kai's face and turn around to face the headstone for my grandmother. I read over her name in my head a few times before it starts to feel real, then I slowly lower myself to the grass to sit in front of the stone.

Putting my hands against the headstone, I feel a sob roll through my body, one I can't even attempt to contain.

My guys are there then, each of them offering comfort to get me through my grief, and I'm thankful I have such selfless and loving partners with me through this.

"She didn't deserve what happened," I whisper. "But I know she isn't angry—it wasn't in her soul to be angry. She was always so understanding."

"What do you mean, Savage?" Beckham asks, putting his

face against the back of my neck. "You think she understood why your uncle did it?"

"Yeah," I whisper. "I know she did. That's just who she was."

Silence falls over us again, and I take the chance to sit and stare at my grandmother's headstone, wondering if she can see me now. Is she watching us from above? I wonder what she would say to me about Kaiden, Beckham, and Vinny... Would she approve of the life we've started, the baby we're going to raise together?

Kai's fingers thread into my hair and he kisses my ear. "We need to get going, baby. We're going to be late for graduation."

I nod, feeling tears still streaming down my face as my hand smooths over the top of the headstone. My voice hurts as it comes out, a small whisper that breaks my heart and pieces it back together all at once. "Bye, Gran. Thanks for everything."

Kai, Vinny, and Beckham walk behind me through the cemetery, and my hands rest on top of my swollen stomach as I admire the headstones I've grown to recognize, wondering how I got so lucky to end up in this town with these boys. I must have done something right in a past life to deserve so much love in this one, because even through everything, the trauma only brought us closer together.

EPILOGUE

"ALRIGHT, PEYTON GRACE, THIS IS THE LAST HOUSE, THEN we're going home, alright?"

My five-year-old looks up at me, her blue eyes filling with sadness. "*Mommy, please,* a few more! I haven't gotten enough candy yet!"

She's dressed as a football player—and not in a jokey way. No, my beautiful little girl wanted to dress like one of her daddies in one of the old pictures we have in the house for Halloween. He even dug out one of his old jerseys with his name and number on it—*Donahue, #9*—and ordered her a little helmet online.

And—courtesy of another one of her daddies—she has black makeup on her cheeks, right under her eyes, like a real football player. All my costume suggestions were rejected—*princess, fairy, unicorn, witch*—and my crazy daughter idolizes her dads, so I don't know why I was surprised when she came running out in full padding this evening, Vinny laughing behind her.

"Yeah, Mommy, a few more houses," Beckham whines from my other side, his hand curling around my waist.

Peyton jumps a few times as she laughs, her hand squeezing mine. "See, Mommy, Daddy wants to get more candy too!"

I laugh as we approach the next driveway, the lawn covered in blow-up decorations and the house twinkling with white and orange lights. Looking at Beckham, I narrow my eyes. "Daddy knows the babysitter will be showing up soon, and Little Miss Peyton needs to get ready for bed so we can go out."

Becks grins at me, secrets dancing in his eyes.

Peyton huffs, dropping my hand as Beckham leads her up the driveway and to the front door. I stay behind, watching them from the sidewalk as he lifts her up to reach the doorbell.

I never had a paternity test done because, no matter what, Peyton is all four of ours, but her blue eyes, black curly hair, and warm soul give away whose DNA runs through her. We don't talk about it, any of us, but I know deep down Vinny and Kai know she's Becks' flesh and blood. It doesn't change their bond with her, though, because Beckham is just as much their family as me and Peyton.

The front door opens, an older couple smiling behind it, and Peyton screams as loud as she can, too excited to get the words out at a normal volume. *"TRICK OR TREAT!!"*

She holds out her black-cat-shaped bucket, and the woman smiles at her as she picks out a few pieces of candy and drops them in. I smile as my daughter says *thank you*, then she and Beckham turn around to walk back over to me.

I smile at Peyton as I slide my fingers through Beckham's. "What did you get, beautiful?"

She digs around in her bucket, pulling out a few mini candy bars. "Twix and Snickers!"

I raise my brows. "Wow! You are getting all the good stuff tonight!"

As we walk down the sidewalk back toward our house, Peyton talks to me, going on about all the candy she's gotten, and she tattles on Beckham for eating one of the Kit-Kats she got a few houses down. I click my tongue and shake my head. "You'll have to hide the rest of your candy when you get home so your daddies don't eat it!"

"I already know where I'm going to put it," she says, matter of fact, and I laugh.

We reach our home, the large Victorian-style house I once shared with my grandmother, and walk up onto the dark porch. All the lights are off inside, since Kai and Vinny are already gone for the evening, and I spot Ms. Potter across the street, stepping out into her lawn to head over and sit with Peyton for a few hours. As Beckham unlocks the front door, I wave to the old woman heading our way.

"Alright, Pey, time to get ready for bed, okay?" I lift off the helmet, then run a thumb over her cheek, smudging the makeup. "You need to take a bath and get all of this off."

We follow Beckham inside, and Peyton pouts at me. "Can I eat some candy first, mommy?"

"One piece now, and one more after your bath. Then brush your teeth," I say, and her eyes light up as she starts digging around in the bucket.

Beckham looks into the bucket too, humming between his lips playfully. "I think I want something sour this time…"

He reaches for the bucket, and Peyton screams, then takes off, her little legs sending her flying over the wood floor and toward the staircase. If she didn't have so much padding on, I'd probably worry she was going to get hurt.

I look at Becks and shake my head, laughing. "She's going to kill you."

He barks out a laugh, coming closer and grabbing me by the hips to pull me against him. His face falls into my neck, and he kisses my skin. "I'm excited for tonight, *Little Rabbit.*"

My core lights up, and I lean my head back without meaning to, giving him more room to assault my neck. "Me, too."

The doorbell rings, and I find Ms. Potter's smiling face behind the glass when I stand up straight.

Growling in the back of his throat, Beckham kisses my skin one more time. "Go get Pey ready for bed. We'll leave for the cemetery in twenty minutes, okay?"

———

EVEN THOUGH IT'S CHILLY OUTSIDE, I PUT ON A SHORT BLACK dress and stockings, leaving my arms bare, a pair of black boots covering my feet. Once I've said goodnight to Peyton, and thanked Ms. Potter for babysitting, I meet Beckham at the entryway.

He's dressed in a black hoodie and black pants that hug the muscles in his thighs, and I take a moment to look him up and down a few times before he clicks his tongue at me. "Sage Blackmore, are you checking me out?"

Nodding, I smirk, feeling turned on and excited about what's to come tonight in the cemetery. Since moving back from four years at the University of Georgia, we haven't spent much time in Blackmore cemetery, simply getting acclimated to being back in town. With Peyton, too, it's hard to take time for ourselves since she's the center of our universe.

I think we've all come out here a few times separately, to visit the headstones that remind us of our past, or to reminisce about the games, but we've never all come together. We've certainly never spent a night in the crypt or recreated the night Peyton was conceived.

Putting my hand on Beckham's chest, I push him toward the door. "Let's go, B."

His hand slides around my waist, and he pulls the front door open, leading me outside. "You ready for this, Savage?"

My arms prickle with goosebumps from the cold breeze, especially now that the sun has completely set from the sky, leaving everything to exist in shadows and darkness. As Beckham's fingers squeeze my waist, I smile up at him. "So fucking ready."

"Good," he says, looking forward as we walk down the road. There aren't any cars on the road, and a part of me hopes that none of the high school students are partying in the cemetery tonight. But if I know anything about my guys, I'm sure they made it so we have the graveyard to ourselves.

The walk takes five minutes, and a small weight I didn't know was there lifts off my chest as I take in the cemetery for the first night in a really long time. It still feels like coming home —being here in the dark—and my entire body buzzes and burns with desire and happiness.

Humming, I step onto the grass, loving the way it crunches under my boots. The trees are overgrown this close to the road, and the headstones are littered with fallen leaves and branches.

"God, I fucking missed this place," Beckham says, and I turn to look at him.

His dark blue eyes are filled with joy, and it makes butterflies attack my stomach. Grabbing his arm, I pull him after me when I start walking. "Let's go."

He moves with me, deeper into the cemetery, letting the light disappear behind us as the road gets farther and farther away. After a minute, Beckham stops, making me turn to look at him. "What's wrong?"

He grins, stepping toward me, close enough that his lips brush mine when he speaks. "Do you wanna play, Little Rabbit?"

My body lights up, my lips tingling as he traces them with his tongue. When he pulls away from me, my mouth drops open so I can breathe through my lips.

Beckham smirks at me, something playful but devious behind the expression, then he reaches into the back pocket of his pants and pulls out a black mask. Slipping it over his head, my stomach drops when I'm reminded of the first night I saw this particular mask—the one with hearts sewn around the eye sockets.

My mouth waters, and Beckham stares at me for a silent moment before he blinks and steps closer. *"Do you wanna play, Little Rabbit?"*

Two large shadows appear behind him, then I'm staring at all three of them—my Hallows Boys—Kaiden in his mask with X's on the eyes, and Vinny's with circles, and my entire soul vibrates with desire at the memories.

"What's the game?" I ask, hunger in my breathy tone.

Kaiden pushes up the sleeves on his hoodie, showing me the dark black ink that covers his skin, and takes a step forward. Vinny chuckles, stepping next to his brothers, his green eyes flaring with heat through the holes in his mask.

"Run, princess," Vinny says. "Whoever catches you gets to use you first."

Beckham rubs his hands together. "We'll even give you a head start."

My pulse races, adrenaline hitting my bloodstream when Kai takes another small step toward me, starts cracking his knuckles, and whispers, *"Go."*

I squeal with excitement as I spin around and take off running through the cemetery, my boots thudding against the earth. My heart thrashes around in my chest, and my panties dampen as I think about all the things my three guys are going to do to me when they catch me. I just hope I make it to the crypt before I'm caught, not wanting to get dirt and grass on my clothes and skin.

After half a minute, I hear steps approaching behind me, making me push my legs harder. Dodging headstones, trees, and broken branches, I keep my eyes wide as I try to see through the darkening cemetery. It's as if the light is being sucked away from me the farther I get, and before I know it, I can barely see a foot in front of me.

My chest heaves as I wrap myself behind a large tree trunk, the moon sneaking through the leaves above my head as I try to catch my breath.

"*Liiiiiiittle Raaaabbittttt…*" Vinny sings. "*I can hear yooouuu.*"

I plaster my hand over my mouth and nose, trying to silence my heavy breathing as I search my surroundings.

A cloud moves across the moon, making darkness swallow me whole, and my stomach throbs with welcome anxiety.

"*Little Raaaabbit…* I can smell you!" Beckham shouts, and I hear leaves crunching behind me, next to me, in front of me, then a hand is wrapping around my throat, pulling a scream from deep in my lungs.

Kaiden laughs, his breath coming out hot against my cheek, telling me he's taken his mask off already. "I guess I'm better at hide and seek than them."

His free hand grabs the hem of my dress, and he pulls it up and over my hips, the cold air kissing my thighs. Then he runs his fingers over the front of my stockings. "Why would you wear these, baby? You know I'm just going to rip them."

I smirk. "Maybe I like it."

He drops down in front of me. "I know you do, *fucking slut.*"

Grabbing my stockings at the hem in the center, he uses

both hands to rip a giant hole in them, then he's leaning forward and kissing over my bare pussy. "And no panties? You really are a slut, huh, Sage?"

Moaning, I slide my fingers in the thick hair on the back of his head. "For you, king? Always. Now do what you do best and make me come."

I lift my thigh and attempt to push his face into my dripping cunt, but he laughs and stands up before I have a chance to, his hand circling my jaw. He speaks between teeth that are gritting hard. "This isn't your game, so stop trying to be in control."

My head rolls back, a small laugh rippling through me as I slide my hands under the front of his hoodie and scrape them down his solid stomach. He hisses between his teeth and grabs my wrists, squeezing them.

"*Sage,*" he says in warning, and I melt into a million pieces, knowing how much I'm pushing his buttons.

I smirk as I decide to push a few more. "Fuck me, or I'll go find someone else to do it."

He laughs, an evil, maniacal laugh that has my blood burning hot. One at a time, he takes my arms and wraps them around the tree, then, before I can protest, he's tying something around my wrists to hold me in place. Growling, I tug on the restraint, my skin digging into the sharp bark of the tree. "Kai!"

Laughing again, he undoes his pants quickly, grabs me by the hips, and lifts me up, wrapping my legs around his waist.

"Is this what my desperate girl needs?" he taunts, holding me under the ass with one hand as he grabs his cock with the other and rolls it through the wetness between my legs.

"*Uhhuh,*" I moan, nodding, my hair brushing against the tree trunk at my back. "Fuck me, king, fuck me so hard I can feel your big cock in my dreams tonight."

"Jesus Christ," he breathes, still running the head of his cock between my slit, ghosting over my clit and entrance over and over, turning me to a mess of moans. "Beg me, baby. Fucking beg for it."

"Please, Kai, *please,*" I plead, flexing my hips to roll against him the best I can while I'm suspended in the air without the use of my arms. "I *need you* so bad, *please.*"

A long moan claws its way from my throat as he slides into me, and then his mouth comes crashing down on mine in a kiss so harsh that my teeth rattle. Kai's tongue glides against mine, his hips flexing between my legs rough and fast, his cock impaling me again and again.

Both his hands move under my ass to hold me in place as he fucks into me harder, and a scream has me pulling my lips from his as my back arches against the tree.

"Keep screaming and my brothers will find us and make you take their cocks too," Kai taunts, pounding into me. "That's probably what you want, though, huh? My gorgeous, dirty little fucking slut loves all her holes filled at the same time, doesn't she?"

"*Yes, king, I love it so much,*" I moan, then I lean forward and bite onto his neck, making his fingers squeeze the flesh of my ass in retaliation.

"*Sage,*" he growls, and my cunt throbs as he fucks me faster. "Get your fucking teeth out of my neck."

I shake my head and bite down harder, knowing he loves it, and he groans long and loud.

"You're going to make me come already, baby. Is that what you want?"

Nodding, I suck on the skin between my teeth, and flex every muscle in my pussy to send Kai catapulting over the edge of his climax. As he thrusts into me through his orgasm, he growls and groans and pants between his teeth.

"Always so fucking desperate for my cum, baby. Will you still feel that way when I tell you I swapped your birth control out, and I'm fucking a baby into you right now?"

His thumb presses against my clit before I can respond, and my orgasm takes over my body, my teeth releasing his skin as my head goes back and my legs squeeze around his waist. "*Kai!*"

"Take my cum, baby." He fucks me so hard against the tree that I worry the scratching from the bark may make me bleed. The hand he had between my legs slides up onto my stomach. "You're going to be so fucking beautiful with another baby inside you."

I cry out, pulling my arms against the restraint as I shake through my climax, then I'm falling lax against the tree while Kai slowly thrusts between my legs.

"Fuck," he breathes, dropping his face into my neck and kissing my sweaty skin. "I fucking love you."

Sighing in pleasure, I let him kiss my body until he's gotten his fill, then he carefully puts me down on my feet and undoes the tie around my wrists. Pushing my dress back into place, I put my hands against his chest and lift onto my tiptoes to kiss him softly.

After a moment, he pulls away. "C'mon, Little Rabbit, Becks and Vin are waiting for us at the crypt."

"You guys planned *you* finding me first?" I laugh, running my fingers through his hair.

"I *suggested* that they let me catch you." He grins, kissing the tip of my nose.

I laugh. "You're spoiled fucking rotten."

Kai slides his hands down my arms, threads his fingers between mine, and starts to lead me to the crypt. "I know."

After a moment, I feel his cum drip onto my thighs between my legs, and I stop to look at him. "You were kidding about the birth control thing, right?"

He laughs, grabbing my chin between his thumb and

forefinger. "Am I the funny one now? Does that sound like something I would joke about?"

"Kai!" I shout, slapping his chest. "This is something we should have talked about!"

"Peyton wants a little brother!" he shouts back. "And I want to see my fucking baby in your stomach. Why do you think I've been coming inside you so much?"

"Because you know I like the way it feels!" I yell, and he laughs, brushing my hair aside and tucking it behind my ear.

"*Baby.*"

"You're so fucking annoying, Kaiden Thorne," I growl, not feeling angry, just aggravated I wasn't brought into the loop.

"Oh, yeah?" he says, lifting a brow. "Keep fucking yelling at me, Sage. I'll take my belt to your ass once we get to the crypt."

"No, you won't. You wouldn't do that if I could be pregnant." I smile like a shit, remembering the months I had Peyton in my stomach and how all three of my guys acted like I was made of glass, destined to break if they touched me wrong.

Kaiden steps toward me, a cocky smirk curling his lips as he grabs me by the hips and lifts me, wrapping my legs around his waist before he starts running through the cemetery in the direction of the crypt.

———

BECKS AND VINNY ARE INSIDE THE CRYPT WHEN WE PUSH through the stone door, both of them sitting on a small couch at the edge of the room with their masks off.

I didn't do much to the crypt after having it built. I thought maybe it would end up being somewhere we did something like this, but we moved away to university shortly after Peyton was born, and we never talked about it after that.

Thankfully, though, the three men I've chosen to spend my

life with had similar ideas, because the crypt has been set up in preparation. As well as the couch, there's a dresser, a pair of armchairs, and a bed covered in a fluffy white comforter.

I take my time admiring the room, even as Kai shuts the stone door behind us and sits down on the couch with his brothers. After a few silent minutes, I make my way to the bed and lean against the edge to stare at all three of my men.

They all love me so differently. There isn't one single thing missing from our relationship, because they are all completely different humans.

Kaiden, who needs to be in control, who I crave games and degradation with.

Beckham, who makes love to me and brings me to passionate tears under the sheets.

And Vincent, who drinks me down in starving gulps that make me feel worshipped, like I'm the only woman on earth.

Slowly, I reach behind my back and tug down the zipper on my dress, letting the fabric grow loose enough that when I let go, it slides down my body and lands on the floor in a pile. With nothing but a pair of ripped tights on, I sit down on the bed and shuffle back on my ass, keeping my gaze straight forward.

There's an unspoken command in my position as I lay myself out on the bed, nothing covering the places the three men before me own in every way, and as I move back far enough that my back hits the pillows, I spread my legs open.

Between my knees, I stare at the three sets of eyes glued on me, then I slide my hand over my stomach and down between my thighs. Spreading myself open, I curl my fingers into my opening to drench them with Kai and I's mixed release, then I glide it upwards onto my clit.

I moan, curling my back as my fingers rub the perfect spot between my legs. "*Fuck.*"

Licking my lips, I continue to play between my legs as I zero in on Vinny's burning gaze. "Vinny…"

He stares at me, answering me by pressing his teeth into his bottom lip as he stands up.

I make circles on my clit, my whole body shaking. "Come here, V."

He walks slowly, lifting off his hoodie as he crosses the room, leaving his chest bare. When he reaches the end of the bed, he undoes his pants and takes them off, but leaves his boxers on.

Lifting a knee onto the bed, he climbs onto the plush mattress and slowly crawls between my legs, his eyes on mine. "Yes?"

I moan softly, whimpering as my fingers speed up between my legs. *"I want you."*

"What do you want, princess? My fingers?" He presses a finger on top of mine, and adds some force behind it, making me moan. Hovering on top of me, he kisses my bare breasts. "Or my mouth?"

"Your mouth," I moan desperately, feeling my orgasm blossoming in my core.

Vinny smirks at me, then rolls over to my side, onto his back. "Come sit on your throne then, princess."

In a hungry panic, I climb on him, straddling him and moving upwards until I'm hovering over his face.

"C'mon, don't be scared. Give me your cunt." He grabs my hips, yanking my pussy down flush onto his puffy lips, his tongue sliding into me.

Putting my hands flat on the wall, I grind my hips against his face, his tongue curling inside of me before he licks to my clit, the wet muscle turning rigid as he feasts. Shouting my pleasure, I feel my orgasm slam into me within minutes, then I'm shaking and riding Vinny's tongue through my climax.

"Christ, princess," Vinny gasps underneath me, his fingers

digging into my hips to hold me up as my body sags in relief. "You taste so fucking good."

My legs shake as I lift and flip over to sit against the pillows next to Vinny, my face splitting into a lazy grin. Vinny's hands wrap around my waist as he sits up, then he kisses me on the mouth for a moment before he pulls away. "Don't move."

"Okay," I breathe, watching as he stands up and goes over to the dresser next to the couch, opens a drawer, and pulls something out.

When he comes back to me, he slips a blindfold over my eyes, then puts handcuffs around my wrists and attaches the other ends to the bedposts.

I don't resist when he walks around the bed and grabs my legs, cuffs my ankles, and attaches those to the bedposts at the other end.

Once I'm spread out like a starfish, I wait for what's next.

After a minute, I feel someone press a knee to the mattress between my legs.

"V?" I ask softly, but no one answers me.

I feel his body dip the mattress, then something cold touches the skin of my thigh and makes me jump.

Vinny laughs from my left, telling me it's someone else on the bed with me. "Relax, Little Rabbit."

Whatever the cold object is slides over my skin, up my thigh and around my hip, my stomach, between my breasts, then around the column of my throat.

"You trust me?" Vinny asks, close enough now that I can feel his breath against my face.

"Always," I say without a thought, and a second later, someone is pushing inside me, stretching me and making me purr. "Oh, God."

I know it's Beckham simply from the feel of him. I've been

with the three of them enough times; I would know their touch, no matter what.

"Becks…" I moan, doing my best to spread my legs wider.

He doesn't respond, just rolls his hips to stroke me deeply with his cock, and a whimper passes through my lips. He does it a few more times, pleasing me with deep, slow, thoughtful strokes that have me dripping and shaking in no time.

"Now," Beckham says, and the cold object that's now above my breasts digs into my skin, slicing me with a shocking pain that makes me scream.

"Fuck!" I scream again, the knife slicing down my chest for about two inches before I start to shake and writhe against the bed, my orgasm slamming into me hard and fast.

"That's it," Vinny says, moving the knife to the other side of my breastbone and cutting a matching line down that side, the pain intensifying my orgasm into something so powerful that Beckham can barely move inside of me.

Yanking on the handcuffs on my wrists, I feel tears slide down my cheeks in mindless pleasure as my orgasm rocks through me in chaotic waves.

A hand threads into my hair, then the blindfold is yanked from my eyes, giving me the chance to see what's happening. Beckham is between my legs, thrusting through my orgasm as he grips my hips to hold me in place.

Vinny leans forward from my side, his mouth sucking my skin before his tongue slides over one of the small slices above my breast, making me hiss and moan and arch my back.

My body releases all the tension as my orgasm dissipates, and Beckham pulls out, leaving me feeling empty.

When Vinny lifts from my chest to look at me, his thick lips are red with my blood, and the sight makes me burn.

He licks his lips, then kisses me hard, making butterflies rage through my stomach. When he pulls away, I yank on the handcuffs again. "Undo these so I can touch you."

I hear someone click their tongue, and I turn to look to the side in time to see Kai shaking his head at me. "How many times do I need to tell you, Little Rabbit—*you aren't in charge here.*"

He laughs as he reaches me, his hand threading into my hair to turn my head, then his cock is sliding between my lips and deep into my throat without warning. Moaning around him, I suction my mouth and let him use me, his hips thrusting against me.

Vinny slides down my body while Kaiden fucks my mouth, and he undoes the cuffs around my ankles so he's able to lift and bend my legs up. Someone pours lube between my legs, then fingers are pressing into my ass to stretch me out.

Kai's fingers stroke my hair, his eyes staring into mine. "We know how much you like being gang-banged, baby, so just lie there while we fuck all your holes, okay?"

I nod, looking up at him through my watering eyes, and he smiles at me while he thrusts his hips harder. "Good girl."

My ass is stretched in the next few minutes, then my legs are held in the air while someone's cock slides inside, making me yank on the handcuffs again, whimpering around Kai's length.

"Ready, princess?" Vinny asks as he climbs over me and slides his cock into my pussy. "Goddamn, you're fucking tight."

While Beckham and Vinny thrust in tandem, Kai slides farther down my throat, making me choke and shake as I gag around him. "Holy shit, you're fucking swallowing me whole, Sage."

I gasp as Kai starts to come in my throat, the thick fluid going down as I swallow through my gag relax. He groans, yanking on my hair so hard that my eyes water painfully, and then he's pulling from my mouth with a relieved sigh.

Kai slides his hand around my face, caressing my cheek. "So

fucking perfect."

While Vinny and Beckham fuck my ass and pussy, Kai removes the restraints from my wrists, then he lies down next to me and kisses around my throat. "Does it feel good, baby?"

Nodding and moaning, my core burns and tingles with another orgasm as Vinny and Beckham torture me in the best way from the inside out. When I meet Vinny's gaze, I reach out to put a hand on his thigh to deepen our connection. He leans forward, sliding a finger through the slice mark on my chest that's still wet with blood, and I cry out.

"I love you," Vinny says, and I know he's close because his abs turn solid and stiff as he thrusts his hips. Kaiden knows too, because he reaches between my legs and rubs my clit softly to get me to the finish line with his brothers.

Beckham is kissing around Vinny's neck, his hands holding my legs in place while he fucks my ass punishingly.

As my orgasm slams into me, my pussy gushing fluid around Vinny's cock, I feel my guys start to come as well, one in my ass and the other in my cunt, and my body shakes in a chaotic bliss that has my vision going black.

We're all a mess of moans and groans and shouts and slaps until we're falling into a pile of limbs and heaving chests.

Looking around the crypt that looks so similar to the one that started all of this so many years ago, a smile makes my lips twitch as I revel in the post-sex bliss with the three men who complete my world.

Maybe this place brought pain and suffering for a long time, but we turned it into somewhere that birthed so much happiness and joy. This cemetery, and the crypt that this one represents, started our love story—our family, our whole life—and I will always be thankful for that.

THE END

ACKNOWLEDGMENTS

Tiffany – without you, there is no book. For all the nights you stayed on facetime with me, the endless voice messages, texts, memes, and everything else… you are the reason this book was written. Maybe I'm the author, but you're my emotional support best friend and my endless pool of inspiration. I've never met someone so selfless, so dedicated, with her hand in everyone's bags to make sure we are *all* successful…. It's so fucking beautiful, and so fucking inspiring. You took my characters and you made sure they were okay, that I was pure with them, that I followed my heart with them, and you dragged me by the hair out of so many writers blocks that I'm surprised I have any left. I love you, pretty girl.

Vanessa – what can I say that I haven't said for the last 6 books? You know how I feel. *Nadean* – you're endlessly amazing. *Kenz* – the best editor in the industry. *Taylor* – who does all my promo… without you, this would still be half written. *Brit Benson* – who always answers the most chaotic text messages & shares everything inside her brain. You're my favorite.

My readers, my favorite girls, who blast my books across the internet. Without you, there's no me.

Leonidas. My heart and soul. The reason I breathe.

ABOUT
ROSIE ALICE

Rosie Alice is an author, graphic designer, virgo, pop-punk princess, bengals fan, chaotic bisexual and dreamer.

She believes in coloring outside the lines and wants to experience everything in this lifetime.

She writes sweet and forbidden, dark and spicy, emotional and playful, and wants to taste every other inch of the romance genre as well.

If you're looking for her, you can find her hunched over her computer, looking for alligators or binge-watching sitcoms.

Born in the UK, she currently lives in Florida—where sweet tea & sandy nights are a religion—with her 14lb cat, Leonidas.

Find her here: https://linktr.ee/rosiealice

ALSO BY ROSIE ALICE

The Sinful Series (Forbidden Romance)

The Star - *Logan & Carson*

Paradise - *A Sinful Novella*

The Wicked - *Hayden & Penelope*

The Lover - *Levi & Serena* - **coming soon**

V—-- *A Sinful Novella* - **coming soon**

The Dark Duet (Reverse Harem)

The Hallows Boys - *Book One*

The Hallows Queen - *Book Two*

The Fate Series (Dark, Emotional Romance)

Nightmare—*Olivia & Travis* (**re-releasing soon**)

Made in the USA
Columbia, SC
16 April 2025

56717855R00233